Gangrene

ALY RENWICK
Gangrene

GREEN PRINT

First published in 2017 by
Green Print, an imprint of The Merlin Press
Central Books Building
Freshwater Road
London
RM8 1RX

www.merlinpress.co.uk

ISBN 978-1-85425-118-3

A CIP record of this book is available from the British Library

Printed in the UK on behalf of Stanton Book Services

For Elsie

Squaddie: a regular private soldier (can also be squaddy).

Andy Capp's Commandos: squaddie speak for the Army Catering Corps.

Benny: squaddie speak for an inhabitant of the Falkland Islands. The name is taken from a slow-witted rural character in the TV series Crossroads.

Bootnecks: squaddie speak for Royal Marines.

Duffing up: colonial police and squaddie speak for extreme physical violence dished out to natives. The name comes from Douglas Duff, who was the British police chief in Jerusalem in the late 1920s – after serving in Ireland with the RIC as a Black and Tan.

Dickers: squaddie speak for locals, usually youths, who act as lookouts for, and/or give warnings of army/police activity to, the IRA – or other similar organisations.

Fuckwits: squaddie speak for government ministers, or members of parliament.

Full screw: squaddie speak for a corporal.

Green Slime: squaddie speak for members of the Intelligence Corps.

Hockey: squaddie speak for a Heckler and Koch assault rifle.

Krautland: squaddie speak for West Germany.

Lance jack: squaddie speak for a lance corporal.

Lumpy Jumper: male squaddie speak for a female soldier.

Oppo: squaddie speak for a close friend or colleague.

Osnatraz: squaddie speak for Osnabruck, a British base area in West Germany.

Razz Man: squaddie speak for a Regimental Sergeant Major (RSM).

Redcaps: squaddie speak for members of the Royal Military Police.

Rupert: squaddie speak for a new junior officer.

Shreddies: squaddie speak for underpants.

Spammed: squaddie speak for being unwillingly, or unwittingly, volunteered.

Willy Wonka: squaddie speak for a Chinook helicopter.

GLOSSARY

CESA: Catholic Ex-Servicemen's Association.

EOKA: *Ethniki Organosis Kyprion Agoniston* (National Organisation of Cypriot Fighters).

Green Team: name used by intelligence and undercover Special Forces for uniformed soldiers and regular regiments of the British Army.

Hush Puppy: a silenced pistol used for assassinations in Vietnam by US forces. Its nickname came from the authorities claim that its intended use was to kill guard dogs.

Int: military acronym for the Intelligence Corps.

INLA: Irish National Liberation Army.

K-M squad: a covert military unit, called after keeni-meeni, a Swahili word from Kenya that describes the slithering movement of a snake.

PIRA: Provisional Irish Republican Army.

Nutting-squad: colloquial name for the PIRA's Internal Security Unit.

RA: colloquial name for PIRA members, or units.

PTSD: post-traumatic stress disorder – combat related PTSD can be severe.

Psy-ops: psychological operations – carried out covertly by military personnel.

Q cars: locally sourced civilian vehicles, which were bought, borrowed or stolen by the military and then modified and used for undercover operations in hostile areas.

Q squad: name given to a group of soldiers, who masquerade as locals to carry out undercover operations in hostile areas.

SIG 229: a compact hand-gun made by SIG Sauer.

Widowmaker: colloquial name for the IRA used Armalite AR-18 assault rifle.

Bilderberg Group: annual invitation-only meeting of high-ranking people from the US and Europe.

CFR: the US Council on Foreign Relations pursues the interests of the American establishment.

Chicago boys: a group of Chilean students who studied under Milton Friedman at the University of Chicago. They advocated 'shock treatment' to secure free market objectives.

Pinay Circle: the French founded Pinay Cercle is an international grouping of top people, who have links to the deep state and intelligence services in many countries.

Shield: a secret committee organised in the UK in the 1970s by intelligence officers and right-wing activists. Their aims were to combat subversion and make Margaret Thatcher PM.

TC: the Trilateral Commission is a US founded group that brings together global power brokers.

Gangrene:

1 – Localized death of body tissue, accompanied by putrefaction and usually caused by obstructed circulation.

2 – **Moral corruption.**

Shorter Oxford English Dictionary

The Gangrene of that Heresy began
to spread it self into this Island
Thomas Fuller (1608-61)
English historian

Ireland is the only excuse of the English Government for maintaining a
big standing army, which in case of need they send against the English
workers, as has happened after the army became turned into praetorians
in Ireland …
Karl Marx (1818-1883)

For a period, Blidworth resembled not a mining village in the heart of Notts, but the blooded, oppressive and fearful streets of Belfast …
The Miner, **June 1984**

LOG 1: MUGSFIELD GENERAL – *June 1994*

A flashback sometimes zooms across my brain – a vivid blaze of light, followed by a vast wall of sound. Then oblivion. But, in that fraction of a second before the explosion hit me, I swear I'd clocked on to what was happening.

'A mercury-tilt bomb? The bastards have gotten me!'

It's an instilled reaction in a trained bloke, like the green team boys, who are taught and drilled nonstop for the riots and all the other aggro. They talk about going 'on auto' when it all kicks off and we are the same, but in Intelligence we need to know as well as to act. So, with us, insight and clarification is high on our agenda.

I'd been in a hurry and gunned the car engine as I set out. I remember starting up a steep hill and then the flash, bang and wallop. Connected by magnets, the bomb had been placed underneath the vehicle – but a bit behind my driving seat. This saved my legs and probably my life, but the Semtex, exploding up through the back of the seat, sent fragments blasting through my lower back and around my spinal column.

I was out for about three weeks and then came to, with tubes and wires sticking into and onto me. At first, I was bewildered – and Elsie's was the first face I saw. Afterwards, she told me that my right eye had started twitching and later slowly opened. That's when they thought I had a chance of making it.

When I started to stir, though, a feeling of dread overcame me. I clocked Elsie's olive skin, dark hair, brown eyes the perky nose – and it all screamed mick to me. So, just for a second or two, I thought she'd come to whack me. But I wasn't in a fit state to react, thank God, and straight after realised she was a nurse and doing her best to help me.

I then got into a panic thinking I'd lost my legs.

'I can't feel the fuckers,' I screamed.

At that point Elsie gently cupped a hand around the side of my head and reassured me.

'You'll soon be better dear,' she whispered in my ear, 'your legs are okay. It's just that, for the time being, you're paralysed from the waist down. But, that'll be sorted soon, and you'll be up and running again in no time.'

Later, the darkie nurse, Gwendolyn, told me that my stay in Mugsfield General was causing a fair amount of consternation. Apparently, I'd constant protection, with two Ministry of Defence policemen on guard outside my room 24/7.

'Armed to the teeth,' Gwendolyn said.

When the door was open one day, a MoD plod had glanced into my room and I'd taken a quick dekko at his squat-barrelled hockey and the holstered Sig 229.

'Thank fuck the Major's looking after me,' I thought, 'in case the micks come back and try to finish the job.'

To start with, I couldn't move and my mind was fucked-up for a while. But, I suppose I gradually recognised that after my big kaboom I was lucky to still be alive. So I became calmer and, perhaps, a little fatalistic.

Now, although still immobile in my hospital bed, I've time to consider the action that had so nearly caused me to cash in my chips. I'd cleaned the car interior just before my last trip and had moved the driver's seat back. The bomb had been set for that position and would have killed me, if I hadn't moved the seat forward again to drive.

While thinking about the explosion, an article in a local paper had endorsed my initial thought, which had whooshed across my brain just before the bomb's impact.

'Probably had a mercury-tilt switch,' the journalist speculated, 'as the victim's car had climbed the hill, the angle of the vehicle would have set the liquid metal flowing.'

'To join the connections and booom,' my mind ruefully added.

This all took place just after the helicopter crash; the Chinook that got spattered all over a hill on the Mull of Kintyre. We lost a lot of our top brass there, along with those of the RUC and MI5. Then Geordie's end had come too, so death had seemed to be all around.

I travelled back to the mainland to go to Geordie's funeral. That he'd died in a car crash surprised me, as he'd always been a safe driver – even after a drink or two. Perhaps that sort of thing would catch up with you in the end, though. It certainly had with Geordie – and now, just after his demise, I'd nearly ended up a stiff too.

After munching a sandwich and sipping a beer at the reception following Geordie's cremation, I took my chance to have a quiet word with his wife. I remembered him saying 'my Enid this and my Enid that.' He'd clearly been very fond of her, but this was the first time we'd met, as he'd always kept her and his army life far apart.

'She probably was quite pretty once,' I thought, 'around Geordie's age, with sharp, almost bird-like, features.'

Though now her black outfit and minimal make-up inhibited her looks, which were brightened only by the flash of ruby on her lips.

'He was a great man,' I said, after offering my condolences.

Her mournful face turned into a sombre smile.

'You worked wi' him?' she murmured back.

'Yea, he taught me all I know,' I said.

'Well, ah hope you divvint start seeing the faces,' she replied.

'The faces, what faces?' I asked, taken aback.

'They came in the night,' she quickly replied, after seeming to clock my alarm.

She'd caught me off guard and realisation must now have flooded my face.

'He was having night ... nightmares?' I stuttered back.

'Aye,' she said, 'the faces then the voices an' screams.'

Turning away, she shot me a final earnest gaze and fleetingly gripped my arm.

'Think on canny lad,' she whispered in my ear, 'make sure they divvint come for you too.'

Later at home, I finished off a bottle of whiskey as I tried to put the thought of Geordie's torment behind me. His stories of Kenya and Cyprus then came to mind.

'Harsh methods for tough times,' he'd often said.

'Perhaps, that's where his anguish had come from?' I thought. Although he appeared to have no bother vindicating all that while he was serving, maybe those subjected to his treatments had come back to haunt him in Civvy Street?

In truth, some things to do with the job were doing my head in too. I understood what we had to do in Ulster, even if it did get a bit out of hand at times. I then discovered that the Major was fighting a somewhat different battle, one that kept drawing us into something that seemed more about Blighty – than the micks.

It wasn't until the aggro with the miners, though, that questions really started flashing up in my mind. Especially after he'd sent me home to act as a mole. I still couldn't make any sense of it all, but it was around that time that I'd first thought about divulging my story.

This went against every instinct I had; we have this sacred code: 'what happens at the sharp-end stays at the sharp-end.' You would only talk about it with your oppos. But, the idea persisted and I sort of thought, if I told my account, then perhaps someone with better brains than me might come up with some answers – and maybe even vindicate my part in it?

Clandestinely, I'd been half-inching bits of gen from HQ for some time, but that was all squirreled away at home. In my hospital bed, I've just the stuff in my battered and confused mind. Nevertheless, I feel I am now adapting to my circumstances fairly well and my stay here is providing me with an ideal opportunity to start.

I knew I'd need an ally to help, though, as the Major and the plods had to be kept in the dark. To that end, therefore, I was already grooming someone, just as I did when running informers in Ulster. But here, it has to be a much more gentle process than my usual one in Belfast.

I still feel bad about doing it, because it has to be a nurse. But Elsie had already got me money from my card at the cash machine – and offered me further help. Anyroads, by now the process is ingrained in me just like a habit, so, when she next checked the wires and tubes, I put a finger to my lips and whispered to her to get enough out and buy a small recording machine, which I could keep hidden under my pillow.

Elsie was doing a sheet change a few days later, when she gave me a knowing wink and produced the small device, with a couple of blank cassettes.

'When you speak it comes on,' she whispered, 'then switches itself off if there's no sound for a while.'

It's a Jap make, a real neat machine, simple to operate and it works even when hidden under my pillow.

'Just the job,' I murmured, flashing her a big smile. 'I'll start on it tomorrow.'

So, here I am – working on my first dispatch. I'm cursing myself for telling tales out of school, though, because doubts about undertaking this still fill my mind.

'No names! No pack drill!' I find myself muttering – as I gabble out this first log.

COAL-LAND

The first casualty when war comes
is the truth.
Hiram Johnson, US Senator, 1917

In the heart of England the headlines in the local papers boomed with the buzzwords of a conflict, which had now come across the water. 'IRA Car Bomb Atrocity,' 'Soldier Victim Hero' and 'Local Man Survives Terror Blast,' the titles raged. One paper speculated that an IRA cell was in the area. Another said an IRA active-service-unit had visited from Ireland, done the dastardly deed, and then fled back like the cowards they were.

The next Sunday, a vicar in Bloodworth reflected on the incident.

'The Troubles in Northern Ireland once looked so distant,' he mused, 'but nowadays they regularly seem to stretch out and affect us in England too – even ourselves here.'

Set in Sherwood Forest, this was a tiny village, until they decided to mine the coal that lay nearly half-a-mile below. Rows of terraced houses were then built for the miners, and the population more than doubled. The town of Mugsfield, five miles to the northwest, provided many of Bloodworth's essential amenities; like the hospital, where this newest drama to the area bubbled away.

Mugsfield General had not seen such excitement since the miners' strike, when B ward had filled with both injured cops and pickets. The MoD police, outside the wounded soldier's

17

room, had their rifles and pistols on full view – and Alec, one of the porters, jerked his thumb in their direction.

'Fookin Nora,' he said, 'it's like something out of The Professionals.'

'Aye, but I hope it wasn't Bodie or Doyle who's gotten blown up,' Kate, one of the nurses, replied.

The day after the bombing, a number of doctors, nurses and support staff were summoned to a meeting. A senior administrator outlined how the injured soldier would remain in their hospital until he was judged okay to be moved.

'We'll be in charge of looking after the medical needs of the bomb victim,' he continued, 'but the army said to me, 'We want to ensure the safety of our man,' and have insisted that they be in sole charge of all security matters. We must respect that and give them any help they need.'

The military also required that the hospital team involved were not to be changed in any way. They could do other hospital work of course, but no other staff would be allowed to work with, or come near, the bomb victim. The porter Alec and the nurses, Kate, Elsie and Gwendolyn, had been selected, along with several others. Those chosen, however, were not told about the background checks that the security services quickly carried out on them.

Elsie was on shift in A&E as the victim had arrived, and she knew how close to death the soldier had been. She was also tending him when his eyes first fluttered open, suggesting he might yet make it and recover.

'It's sad but perhaps understandable,' she said to Gwendolyn, 'that our soldiers have to deal with violence in places like Belfast or Derry – but why are the bombings and shootings now following them home?'

'I haven't a clue,' Gwendolyn replied, 'but I know it's not

my fault. After that Falkland thing, the army seemed to be all about guns and emblems. The flag here has the colours of England, Scotland and Ireland – but there ain't no black in the Union Jack, so leave me out of it.'

A few days after the injured soldier regained consciousness, Elsie saw the MoD policemen talking animatedly to two locals, who said they were friends of the bomb victim from Bloodworth. The police, however, refused them entry and told them not to return. Elsie felt sorry for the two, when she saw how upset they were.

Eddie and Amy were dismayed at not being allowed to visit their old friend, but they felt they had no other option than leave.

'Why have they turned us away?' Amy said dejectedly, as they made their way home.

'Security,' Eddie stated. 'I'm as pissed off as you are, but they're probably right. We don't know what work he was doing, but the IRA – or somebody, tried to kill him. So, I suppose, as far as the army's concerned, they need to protect him.'

'But we're his friends,' Amy muttered.

'Aye,' Eddie agreed, 'but how would the military know that?'

Eddie and the injured soldier had joined the army together as boyhood friends. Eddie, however, had grown disillusioned by his experiences and left the forces, while his friend stayed on. When back in Civvy Street, Eddie experienced rehabilitation difficulties – and he and Amy had embarked on a journey to uncover the roots of his alienation.

For a while the couple had been members of the local history group, helping to dig out information about Bloodworth's past. Then the struggle around the pit had traumatised the village and they'd supported the strike. But the full force of the state had been deployed to crush the miners.

Now, almost a decade later, they'd joined a small group of former strikers and their allies attempting to organise a little local commemoration of the protest.

'We'll make the display panels,' Amy had said at the first meeting. Volunteering both herself and Eddie for the task to make about ten or so information boards, to remind the local people of the strike and how it had affected their village. The boards were to be displayed at the Miner's Welfare and anywhere else that would agree to take them.

'I told you, after the army I don't volunteer for anything,' Eddie had muttered, when they arrived back home after that meeting.

Amy realised that this was a typical show of mock petulance from Eddie. He'd once confessed to her that the only thing he now missed from his army life was the banter between soldiers. When he described it to her, however, it sounded more like hard line nastiness than joshing.

So, although knowing he was really just taking the piss, she still gave a placating reply.

'Come on, we'll both enjoy this. It'll give us something interesting to do.'

The commemoration group wanted their display to promote discussion and reflection – not just about the strike, but also the wider issues around it. And Eddie and Amy were soon building up a collection of photos, other images and cuttings from the papers. Their intention was to combine these with an explanatory text and produce, one by one, the required number of panels.

After returning from the hospital, Amy and Eddie settled down to attempt to compose the text for their first panel, which they'd already been working on for some time. This was to be about coal itself, the valuable mineral that still lay in vast quantities below their former pit village.

'We can make use of some of the things we discovered, while doing all that history stuff,' Amy said.

Eddie nodded in agreement.

'Aye, anything helps – and we have to make this work,' he said.

Amy smiled, because she could see he was now as enthusiastic as her about their task. But, it wasn't till the end of the week that she at last typed out their final words, on their little office typewriter:

During the evolution of Homo sapiens, the people of this world sought to extract from the earth its treasures. Gold, diamonds and valuable metals may firstly come to mind. The real prize, however, was a carbon-based mineral that was utilised to provide power.

Coal was used to fuel the furnaces and steam engines of the Industrial Revolution, thrusting Britain into a dominant world position and ultimately enabling the conquest of the largest empire the world had yet seen.

Over three million years previously, well before the dinosaurs, the earth had been covered by foliage. In time, this included gigantic ferns and mighty trees, like the tall Lepidodendron and the tubby Sigillaria. They needed large amounts of water – and as they grew they hoarded energy from the sun and carbon from the air.

The world was still experiencing earth-shattering changes and the demise for carboniferous period plants often came when they were submerged in seas or engulfed by soil and mud. Before humans first trod the earth, the now trapped energy and carbon in this vegetation had gradually turned it -first into peat, then a hard black mineral, waiting to be ignited. Coal, created by Mother Nature, now slowly poisons her. The history of its extraction has also often embodied many of the contradictions inherent in our own human social conditions: Enterprise and Exploitation; Toil and Subjugation; Struggle and Solidarity.

During their earlier history research, Amy and Eddie had also discovered that the origins of their local woodlands dated back to at least the last Ice Age. In prehistoric days hunter-gatherers had lived in the area, using flint tools to eke out a living in the forest. Many centuries later, the Romans had built their villas and barracks and discovered uses for the nuggets of the hard black mineral they'd found, fashioning the coal into small pieces of jewellery and also burning it in their fires.

In the medieval period, Sherwood was subject to the Forest Laws of the monarch, and the poor could be blinded, have a hand chopped off, or even hanged, for taking a deer. Robin Hood was reputed to have fought the Norman overlords from Sherwood, which was then regarded as the core of old England. It was claimed that Will Scarlet, one of Robin's outlaw band, was buried in the grounds of Bloodworth's Saint Mary's Church.

Within living memory, towards the end of the 1920s, the Oldstead Colliery Company, which owned other local mines, started to buy up land for a new pit in Bloodworth and build homes for the miners. They also commenced the difficult task of sinking a shaft to the seam of hard bituminous coal that lay over 700 yards below.

Some of these excavators were locals, but others from Ireland were also recruited to do this hard and dangerous work. On completion, most of the Irish had moved on to other projects, or back home across the sea. A few remained, however, and Elsie the nurse occasionally mentioned her grandfather.

'He was the first to strike the hard black seam – then he stayed on to dig it out,' she'd say.

Her father had followed on, working down the pit from 16 years of age to provide the railways, the steel industry and the power stations with the black mineral that had fired their engines, furnaces and turbines. Sean, Elsie's brother, continued the tradition, working the deep-level seams with his father till the threat of pit closure led to strike action.

LOG 2: KRAUTLAND – 1966

I was born a few years after the end of the Second World War and brought up in Bloodworth, a small mining village in Nottinghamshire. Dad worked down the pit and we lived at first in one of the terraces built for miners. He didn't piss all his wages away like some, and later managed to buy a little cottage, on the edge of the village – near to the Druid Stone.

I was an only child and Mam often criticising me for speaking the 'gutter language' used by all the other kids. She also kept on to me about making a better living than mining.

'Your dad is pit through and through,' she often said, 'but you will be different.'

I think she meant better, although she never said it openly. She insisted that I 'spoke proper' and tried to further my education, but my school reports usually disappointed her.

My two best mates were Eddie and Amy – I kept it quiet, but I had a bit of a crush on her. They both lived in the terraces, but they stood by me when some of the other kids had laughed at me for talking like a 'posh ponce'. Coming up for sixteen Eddie and I decided to join the army; it was either that or digging coal, which we considered to be boring and hard work.

We saw those army adverts, the ones that promised 'Sport, Adventure and Travel' – and we reckoned we'd be well up for that. Dad didn't say much, but I knew he was glad I'd found an alternative to mining. But, Mam was not best pleased; although she'd wanted to get me away from the pit, I believe it was something a lot grander than the army she'd had in mind.

I was thinking, though, that at least this would get me away from the village, mining and her. So, we went ahead and were taken on, initially in boys' service – and then as foot soldiers with our local regiment. It felt good to get away and basically, to start with, we'd just been a couple of hairy-arsed young squaddies, putting ourselves about a bit.

Eddie loved it and, just as a hand fits a glove, fitted into being a cog in the machine. I lagged a bit behind; maybe I wasn't as keen. We both did well, though, and found ourselves as lance jacks, in different squads, but with the same unit, at Osnatraz in Krautland. I then heard that Eddie had been put forward for a second stripe.

'You jammy cunt,' I said to him with a grin, knowing that two stripes at that age could mean you were heading for the top.

I think my only reluctance with the army, was about being away from Amy. As kids, she used to knock around with Eddie and me. We went to the same school and I'd always been keen on her, but I had never been sure if she felt the same way about me.

Mam had always been a bit off with her, probably because, like Eddie, Amy came from the terraces. That didn't help and me being away for long periods was also a turn-off. Then when Eddie came back from leave and didn't make any move to contact me, I wondered what was up.

A letter from Mam, a few days later, put me in the frame.

'I feel I must tell you this,' she wrote, 'your dad said he has seen Amy and your mate Eddie going about together.'

When I finally managed to confront Eddie a few days later, he confirmed my worst fears. Not only had they been out together, but were also now – according to him anyroads –

'engaged.'

'I'm sorry,' he whispered, but then claimed that Amy had said that her and me had never been an item.

I didn't take it well and I called him and her a few words I shouldn't have. There wasn't much I could do, though. And a bit after that, when I was out on the piss one night, some other mates dragged me off to a Kraut knocking-shop.

From then on, whenever I had the urge, I'd use prostitutes. Sometimes, I'd think of Amy and anger would well up. I'd then fuck the dirty whores with urgency and no little contempt, which some gave me back in spades.

Otherwise, I just kept my head down and concentrated on soldiering. At that time we faced the 'commie menace' and massed Russian tanks, which threated us from across the border in East Germany. Our main task was the big NATO exercises aimed at preparing us to 'halt the Ruskies.'

It was on one of those that I met up with Geordie. We had to find and capture a few 'red agents,' which were actually other soldiers playing the role. This type of exercise happened fairly often and the prisoners were usually given an interrogation – and sometimes bashed around a bit.

This time, though, I was ordered by the Lieutenant to hand over the soldiers we captured to a unit I hadn't seen before. It consisted of four corporals, with Geordie, then a sergeant, in charge. He was a little shorter than me, but with a burly frame and short cropped hair and he looked like he was late twenties, or early thirties, while I was still in my late teens.

As I passed the prisoners over, we chatted, and Geordie seemed to take a shine to me, mainly I think because we were both Manchester United fans. Anyroads, we'd nattered on about Bobby Charlton – who'd come from the northeast like him – and Nobby Styles, because those two had just played a key part in England's great victory, when we'd beaten the Krauts to win the World Cup.

As we moved on to other Man U players, like Dennis Law and Georgie Best, Geordie suddenly burst into a bit of a commentary.

'Nobby crunches inter a tackle, wins the ball an' knocks it out ter Besty, who sweeps down the wing beating three defenders an' nears the goal line. Besty looks up an' sees the Lawman darting ter the near-post, but two defenders are on him, so, instead, he knocks it back ter Charlton, who's running towards the box. Wor Bobby hits it first time – a daisy cutter, so hard the goalie didn't even have time ter dive – an' the net's bulging a split second later. Yee canna beat them man!'

After that burst of enthusiasm for the Reds, Geordie asked if I wanted to stay and view their interrogations. As a fellow Man U man, I felt I couldn't refuse and I was also curious about what was going to happen. Usually, this sort of thing was rough, crude and sometimes violent, but I'd seen right away that these men were professionals – and been fascinated about how they would go about their work.

Most of the prisoners told all they knew fairly quickly, but two of them were especially stubborn. Geordie then thrust hessian sacks over their heads and ordered them to be stripped naked. The men's bound hands were raised over their heads and tied to a rafter, so they were stretched upright.

'I'd gotten our crowd to knock this up for us,' Geordie said to me, producing a small box.

As he handed it to one of the corporals, I clocked the protruding dials and knobs. Wires from the box were then attached to the captives' goolies and ears, with what looked like crocodile clips.

'It emits electrical impulses of variable voltages,' he

whispered to me, as he plugged the contraption into the mains.

Geordie then moved to one of the prisoners.

'Wild Thing, I'll make your balls go zing,' he snarled his version of the Troggs' hit into the captive's ear.

He then grinned at me as he set the voltage pointer and pressed the red button, causing the prisoners to scream and jump about. The voltage was then gradually increased for ten minutes, or so, causing increasing distress to the captives.

'Talk you cunts, or your bollocks will be scorched off an' sent ter the cat food factory,' Geordie shrieked into their ears.

All their bravado was now gone and they quickly spouted out all they knew. After which they were cut down.

I was both fascinated and a little perplexed by what I'd witnessed.

'If they can do this to our lads,' I thought, 'what the fuck will they do to an enemy?'

Later, Geordie told me he'd welcome another Man U man into his unit. And if I was interested in their work to let him know, because the Int Corps recruited within the army – the same as the SAS. By then I'd grown distant from Eddie, and anyroads he, with half of the regiment, were ordered off to Aden in a bit of a rush.

My squad stayed behind in Krautland and I started to feel that our routine was becoming a bit boring. So, a little later, after deciding to put aside any apprehensions, I contacted Geordie and he put the wheels in motion for my transfer. First, though, I knew I'd have to complete and pass a course at the Intelligence Training Centre back in England.

Perhaps, because of this, I felt my doubts rise again.

'I need a new challenge,' I reassured myself, 'and anyway the change will do me good.'

HOMELAND

Men make their own history,
but they do not make it as they please;
they do not make it under self-selected circumstances,
but under circumstances existing already,
given and transmitted from the past.
Karl Marx (1818-1883)
18th Brumaire of Louis Bonaparte

In Mugsworth General the excitement about the injured soldier soon abated, as he and his armed guards slipped into the routine of the hospital. Elsie, Kate and Gwendolyn split their time between their main tasks on A&E and looking after the bomb victim. Their patient was now able to chat and he revealed that his name was 'Ginge.'

'Please call me that, it's the name all my mates use.' he said, with a grin, before inclining his noggin and shaking his ginger tresses.

The nurses could see where his nickname had come from. They were surprised, however, that Ginge not only looked somewhat timeworn, but also that his hair was so long and untidy. To them, his raggedy ginger locks, together with the freckles and green eyes, suggested a somewhat dishevelled hippy from the 60s – rather than the usual youthful skinheaded-style squaddie.

'He's nothing like as glamorous as Bodie or Doyle,' Kate said, with more than a hint of disappointment. 'Looks like he's been around the block a few times too.'

Gwendolyn chuckled.

'He's no spring chicken,' she agreed, 'so you'll have to continue the hunt for your dream man elsewhere.'

Elsie smiled, but remained silent. She was curious – and not only about the soldier's unusual appearance.

'What do our troops chuffing do in places like Belfast and Derry?' she thought.

Later at home, as they ate their evening meal, Elsie mentioned the wounded soldier and asked her Dad the same question.

'The questions you should really be asking are: Why is Ireland in two pieces? And why has Britain still got one of them?' he replied. 'Look, its unfinished business between the peoples of the two islands. Partition never solved any problems – anywhere in the world – always created trouble. And now your soldier is paying the price – as well as the people of Derry and Belfast.'

Elsie couldn't really put her finger on anything definite, but she knew something needed to be sorted out – just like her Dad said. And because that hadn't happened, the Troubles had come to England and her hospital.

As a nurse, Elsie knew she was required to care for Ginge and she did this gladly. That was her job after all and, anyway, she now regarded him as a friend. She also felt sure that the ordinary soldiers were not at the root of the problem; although the big shots who deployed them – and the orders they were given by their top brass – might be a part of it.

So she resolved to find out what she could from Ginge and hoped he wouldn't think her too nosey. To Elsie it did seem that he was glad she was friendly and had proved helpful to him. At the same time there was still a distance between them, which he appeared intent on keeping. In her opinion, this only increased the sense of mystery about him and the hush-hush messages that he'd started to record began to intrigue her.

When the papers had been full of the bombing incident, Elsie recollected that they had said the victim was a local man. But given little detail, beyond the fact that he was a soldier. In the hospital, some suggested that he might have been involved in undercover work.

'A bit of a spook?' she'd heard whispered.

That evening Elsie asked her family if they knew anything about her patient.

'They say the wounded soldier comes from Bloodworth, but nobody seems to remember him – or anything much about him,' she said, with a questioning look.

'There's somebody I know, a bloke called Eddie,' her brother Sean piped up, 'who was a mate of the soldier. I think they joined the army together, but they had a falling out – over a woman.'

Sean then looked around and laughed.

'Amy she was called, or it were something like that,' he continued.

'Perhaps it wasn't the IRA then?' her Dad said.

'That blew him up,' he added, seeing their puzzled faces. 'Perhaps Eddie was just getting his own back?'

'No! The wounded soldier thought the woman was his girl,' Sean said, 'but she was taken off him by Eddie. He's still around, he bought himself out of the services around the end of the '60s and worked for a bank for a while.'

'I hope this isn't Sean playing silly buggers again,' Elsie wondered, thinking of the tricks he sometimes played. But it all appeared to be on the button, so she resolved to find this Eddie.

'If he's still around?'

And see if she could piece together a bit more of Ginge's story.

'God knows,' Elsie reasoned, 'it's certainly hard work trying to get anything out of Ginge. He can talk the hind legs off a donkey at times, but when I run our conversation over in my noggin afterwards, there's no information – nothing of substance anyway.'

'No names, no pack drill,' Elsie had heard him mutter to himself.

'Perhaps, in his own mind, he's still in the war-zone,' she thought. 'Maybe in Ireland, if you don't know who is a friend, or who's the enemy – that's how soldiers operate.'

In Mugsfield General there were plenty of other things to be concerned about. The hospital seemed to be going from bad to worse and most of the staff thought that they urgently needed more doctors and nurses. All they seemed to get, however, were more administrators, who were making everyone else's lives more complicated, drowning them in forms, reports, targets to meet and meetings to attend.

Some staff thought there was also a hidden impetus towards the privatisation of various services, which could lead to the breakup and perhaps the sale of all the NHS.

'It's all getting on me tits,' Alec the porter claimed, and he said he would join the fight-back against it.

Alec had been born with a clubfoot, which, even though it had been corrected by medical treatment, still left him with an uneven walk. When he joined the hospital unit, Kate commented on his limp, specs, lank brown hair and nerdish appearance.

'We should call him Specky Herbert,' she said, grinning.

'Your tongue is like a sharp knife, it kills without drawing blood,' Gwendolyn muttered distastefully, while Elsie screwed up her face.

'Not all blokes look like James Bond,' she said.

But now, Kate couldn't resist saying something cutting concerning Alec's comment about opposing the changes. Although she decided to somewhat modify her nickname for him.

'I bet the big bad bosses are fair cowering,' she said, 'now the milkybar kid is against them.'

The others, however, ignored her remark.

Elsie felt she agreed with a lot of Alec's criticisms, but was cautious about saying so openly. Her Dad and Sean were both on the dole and had been since the strike. And she knew her Mam relied on the little bit of brass she passed on every week. Therefore, at work, she tended to keep her head down, as she didn't want to get into any trouble that might lead to the loss of her job.

Alec, however, became increasingly belligerent and often took exception to anyone who he thought was kowtowing to the new managers.

'Stop submitting,' he would say, 'if you lie down with dogs you'll get fleas.'

Although many didn't like what was happening, most hospital staff felt the same as Elsie.

'The miners took a stand and look what happened to them,' some said.

Over ten years ago, just before the strike in '84, Arthur Scargill, the leader of the National Union of Mineworkers, had visited Bloodworth to warn about a plot he'd uncovered to close nearly all of the British Coal mines. 'King Arthur' had then led the battle to save the pits, but the state had been well organised this time and unleashed all its forces against the strike.

When the pit was closed five years after the miners' defeat, to many it felt like the village's heart had been ripped out. While most people struggled to understand, a feeling was rising that something new was threatening their lives. That the shiny bank towers, springing up in the city of London and Canary Wharf, were increasingly dominating the lives of those now scraping a living in the rest of a wasteland Britain.

LOG 3: PC AND THE RUSKIE – 1967

On my way back to England for the Intelligence course, my head was full of contradictory thoughts.

'Was I making a mistake? Was this really the right path for me?'

Still, I was cheered-up by the thought of the two stripes newly sewn on the arm of my uniform.

'Me, a full screw – chuffed to bits,' I remember feeling.

I knew if I passed the course I'd get to keep them and would be a Field Intelligence NCO.

The Joint Services Intelligence Training Centre is near Ashford in Kent, and there was high security on the gate as I entered. Both my car and myself were examined thoroughly and, as I made my way to my allocated billet, I noticed the infrared beams of the high-tech alarm system protecting the grounds. That evening, doubts still simmered in my mind, and I went to the NAAFI for a couple of beers and a bag of pork scratchings.

The next morning, as we waited for the Colonel who was due to give the introductory lecture, my fellow trainees and I introduced ourselves to each other. Out of ten of us, six, including me, were NCOs. The rest were officers; one was an old boy, probably waiting out his time, but the other three were 'Ruperts' – our nickname for fresh young officers – who were eager to win their spurs.

The Colonel emphasised the secret nature of our work and warned us not to speak about it to anyone outside. He spent most of his lecture telling us about his own experiences taking on the commies in West Germany. Tales of moves and counter moves, of hiding places for secret messages and of tracking Soviet troop movements and monitoring their communications.

It all sounded exciting, but we were there to absorb the rudiments of this intelligence work. So, firstly, they made sure we could handle the basic tools of out trade – our guns. Weapons training continued throughout the course, till we were totally familiar with our own firearms and those of our expectant enemy. And we had to be up to marksman standard with all of them.

We also learned how to take photographs and develop the film. On any of the exercises, we carried different types of cameras and had to produce pictures of anything, or anybody, of interest.

'It's funny,' I thought, 'how taking photos covertly can give you a feeling of power and superiority.'

On these and other tasks, I often found myself teamed up with Seth – one of the other NCOs. He, like me, had been recruited internally. We had a good few piss-ups in the NAAFI together and gone out to Ashford a couple of times, where we took on some of the locals at darts. We came from similar areas and backgrounds and had become good friends by the end of the course.

You might not expect soldiers to become expert burglars, but we were taught to pick the locks of any door, or safe, and how to blow the latter – if it could not be opened in any other way. To do this and other tasks we learned how to use plastic explosives; you can mould it like plasticine and we travelled to a tank firing range one day, to blow bits off the redundant vehicles used for targets. We were even shown how to make and use Molotov cocktails for unspecified clandestine purposes.

A lot of our time was spent playing at undercover agents, mainly in Ashford, but also out in the countryside. We dressed in civvies, carrying clothing changes and were dropped off at odd locations, with tasks to complete. We were told to be relaxed, to slip into the background, and to make a change in clothing and appearance if we thought we'd been spotted. I found this was easier said than done, but it made me realise that you would really have to work at it, if you were ever required to do it for real.

The most interesting part of the course though, was about the art of interrogation – and the different ways it can be applied. Sometimes a prisoner is deemed surplus to requirements, or there are reasons to want them dead. Perhaps, a confession will be required to justify this, or, as they're living on borrowed time anyroads, extreme and often lethal methods will be used.

A more subtle form of treatment, though, should always be applied to extract information. While physical actions can be threatened, psychological routines are actually used – basically you fuck with the prisoner's mind. The most sophisticated method was a series of sensory deprivation techniques, during which you make your captives uncomfortable: by removing their clothes; by subjecting them to loud noise; by forcing them to adopt muscle-aching positions; by ensuring a lack of sleep.

Our instructor laid this on a bit thick, so we knew he wanted us to get it.

'The art of interrogation is to break the prisoner, getting them to speak and spill their secrets,' he said. 'Sometimes, force and intimidation in various forms can be applied, but you have to question any information you might get by violence.

You have to ask yourself all the time: is it true? Is it accurate?'

He stopped speaking for a minute or so and glanced at us in turn, as if assessing if we'd been taking it all in.

'If you are required to ensure that the information obtained is correct,' he continued, 'you should use mental, but non-violent techniques, like the hostile cop, sympathetic cop, routine. With the prisoner being softened up beforehand – with a bit of slap and tickle, our style.'

We giggled at his last words, but we knew that this was all serious stuff.

There was a special area of camp where we were called upon to put these techniques into action. At first, we were sitting in a room with a large one-way glass window, through which we observed our instructors carrying out the interrogations of various tough looking foreign types. They were not spared and things appeared to get quite rough at times.

Then we were told it was our turn and the instructors picked one of the 'Ruperts' to be our first interrogator. Now he was a new, young, toffee-nosed, know-it-all type, who'd clearly been getting on the instructors' wicks. Seth nudged me and grinningly mouthed 'PC.' This was our little joke, as we'd taken to giving the others nicknames and this Rupert's was 'Poncy Cunt'.

The officer went in all sure of himself to interrogate a big bloke who spoke with a heavy Ruskie accent. The man did not cooperate and acted aggressively when PC attempted to put any type of pressure on him. Frustrated at getting nowhere, the young officer suddenly reached out and slapped the prisoner across his chops.

Like lightening, the big man's left hand flashed forward and grabbed PC's shirtfront in a vice like grip. At the same time his right hand had moved under his jacket and reappeared holding a luger pistol, which he pushed against the officer's noggin. We were watching heart in mouth – and jumped back startled at the flash and bang, as the Ruskie pulled the trigger.

'That's your first lesson,' our instructor said, 'always make sure yourself that any suspect has been properly searched before you do anything with them. You will be doing a dangerous job and you have a duty to ensure your own safety.'

After we got over our surprise, Seth and me were laughing our cocks off – and I think all the instructors were pissing themselves too. Especially, when it became clear that PC had lost control of his bodily functions after the blank was fired. And he had to go back to his billet to change his shreddies.

At the end of the course we were told that three officers and four NCOs had passed, and I was happy to find out that Seth and I were among them. I felt a little sad that I'd now be moving from my home regiment, where I'd been a part of the front line cutting edge. But Geordie had introduced me to a more selective and secret corps, one that promised to be a good deal more interesting and exciting.

I also found out that somehow, true to his word, he'd fixed it for me to be posted to his unit – back in Krautland.

AWAYLAND

I think it would be a good idea.
Mahatma Gandhi (1869 – 1948)
On being asked for his view of Western civilization.

It was a few weeks before Elsie found time to have a look for Eddie. She'd no luck to start with and began to suspect that the whole thing was indeed one of Sean's wind-ups. Elsie was just about to give up, when she popped her head around the door of one of the shops at the far side of the village – and asked the shopkeeper if he knew anyone called Eddie.

He shook his head, but as she turned away he called her back.

'I think he might be Amy's husband,' he said, 'I think he had that name.'

The shopkeeper said he thought they lived in the end house, or the next one in, at the end of the street to the left, but on the other side.

Elsie glanced at her watch and thought she'd just have time to make contact, before her shift's start time. So, she crossed over the street and hurried towards the end of it. Elsie stopped at the house one in and rang the bell, and a woman came to the door and gazed inquiringly.

'I'm looking for Eddie,' Elsie said.

'He's not in at the moment,' the woman replied, 'he's down in London looking for old records. I'm Amy his wife, can I help?'

Elsie recognised Amy as the woman who, with a man who must have been Eddie, had been turned away by the cops and stopped from visiting Ginge. Elsie did not, however, let on. Instead she explained about being a nurse and looking after the soldier blown up in the bombing. She said she'd been told that Eddie was an old mate of his and that they'd joined the army together.

Amy immediately looked concerned and somewhat distraught.

'How is he now, is he getting any better?' she asked anxiously, before quickly adding, 'look, do come in, I'll put the kettle on.'

'Thanks, I'm due on shift soon,' Elsie replied, glancing at her watch again, 'but I've time for a quick cuppa.'

'Sorry the place is in a bit of a mess, we're doing the boards for the strike commemoration – ten years on,' Amy said, indicating the clutter of layout boards and boxes of files in a corner, as she led the way to the kitchen.

'So this is Amy,' Elsie thought, 'she seems a bit homely, but with a dash of chic too. She might have caused a rift between the two men, but she doesn't look as if she's a femme fatale? Well, not like Kate at work, anyway.'

Over tea and chocky bickies, Elsie told Amy about Ginge's condition. Amy looked concerned, but she smiled at the nickname.

'Aye, they called him that in the army,' she said. 'We tried to visit him you know, after we heard about the bombing, but the police wouldn't let us in to see him.'

Elsie nodded sympathetically and then indicated she had to rush away to make the start of her shift. Before she left, arrangements were made for another visit, when Eddie would also be there. Amy said to leave it for a couple of weeks after Eddie got back, because they needed to get on with the display

41

they were doing for the strike group.

'I suppose if they're doing these boards,' Elsie thought, 'they must've supported the strike.'

On the journey to the hospital, Elsie considered how nice Amy had seemed: 'Down to earth, but with a touch of elegance – accentuated by the silk scarf tied French style around her throat.'

But such thoughts soon vanished as Elsie became caught up in the hurly-burly of the perpetually busy A&E.

When Eddie had returned from London it was clear that he'd spent his time productively, scouring the government's records depository at Kew and the similar one for newspapers at Colindale, for anything on the miners' strike. After taking copies of whatever he'd found interesting, he returned to Bloodworth and then with Amy gathered together their photos, notes and cuttings and settled down to plan their next layout board.

Every fortnight they'd meet up with the others who'd supported the pit strike, and who were now organising the tenth anniversary event. And during these meetings Eddie and Amy would seek ideas, advice and guidance.

'Perhaps, we should write some more stuff about our area?' Amy suggested at their next meeting, 'some said our first effort on coal was interesting.'

'I'd agree on that,' Jed, an old miner, said 'but we need the political bits in too.'

'Follow the brass,' Doris, a miner's wife, said loudly, 'because that's percolating up to the rich and not down to the poor – and it's doing it at both local and national level.'

Eddie nudged Amy.

'We should make some notes,' he whispered.

They both knew that Jed had been one of the main strike organisers and Doris had been a stalwart of the local support committee, which had provided back up and organised a soup kitchen.

Eddie was determined to prolong their conversation.

'Did you think you'd win, when the strike started?' he asked.

'Well, we had that Heath and Wilson before,' Jed said, shaking his head. 'We hated the bastards – Heath more than Wilson obviously – but we bested them, or at least scored a few draws wi' them. Thatcher and the new lot – we thought it'd be the same. But it weren't, her crowd were much, much worse.'

'That's because the first two were the old school of capitalism,' Doris said, 'Keynesian, I think they called it. They believed in the welfare state and all that, but Thatcher's crowd don't, her lot are zealots – free market – or something like that. Anyhow, it means extreme predatory capitalism – red in tooth and claw – they hate the welfare state, public bodies and the unions. When the strike happened, they came for us and they haven't stopped since – even now they're at it!'

'Doris is right,' Jed said. 'Did you ever see a stoat kill a rabbit? I've seen it a few times in't woods. The stoat weaves and dances around, as if it's demented, but all the time it's getting nearer and nearer to the rabbit – then suddenly it goes in for the kill. We thought Thatcher's lot would be like the Heath and Wilson ones, so we were mesmerised, just like the rabbit. They went for our throats, before we realised the difference – but then it was too late.'

As they walked home, Eddie and Amy talked about the discussion at the meeting. The words from Jed and Doris inspired their thoughts and sent ideas pinging about in their brains.

'Rescue the poor and helpless from the grasp of evil men,'

Amy muttered, 'that comes from Psalm 82, I think. The hidden threads of understanding.'

Eddie grinned.

'Yea, but Jed and Doris want it political,' he said, 'so don't let's turn this into a God slot thing. We need to draw it all together and work out how to explain it.'

'But can we do it – sort it out?' Amy questioned. 'If we can, it could be the text for our second board.'

'Politics, finance and history were all crucial,' they thought, as they got down to work. And they felt compelled to try to understand how all these threads knitted together. They also knew that for this project their writings would have to be short, sharp and concise.

After several weeks' research and discussion, their final draft for the next board was slowly typed out:

After the First World War, there had been a widespread feeling in Britain that the nation had failed its returning veterans. Two-and-a-half decades later in 1945, Labour, swept to power by a huge ex-forces vote, set about building a land fit for heroes – for those who had just defeated the Nazis. There was a temperate version of the ruling free enterprise system then in vogue. Keynesian capitalism favoured manufacturing and state participation, which proved to be compatible with Labour's new welfare state.
Indeed, private enterprise could – and did – mould Labour raft of new measures to its own profitable uses. On the other hand, the labour movements interaction with industry helped to soften commerce's hard edges and make big business friendlier to the needs of society.
As some crumbs from the rich man's table fell to the workers, trade unions blossomed and a professional middle class grew,

along with the expectations of all working people.
Taking root on the fiscal right, however, a new vision of
extreme monetary capitalism was germinating. It advocated a
global free-market, the removal of regulations from companies
and banks – and the rolling back of the welfare state.

Ever since the miners' strike Eddie and Amy had become increasingly interested in the political and economic situation – both in the past and in the present. His experiences as a soldier, them both having to leave the bank and what they'd witnessed during the period of the strike, left them thirsting for some form of understanding.

'Keeping us ignorant, helps the bosses more than anything else,' Jed had said at the first meeting of the strike anniversary event.

From their recent research, Amy and Eddie knew that the welfare state, which was built at the end of the Second World War, had engendered a huge sense of hope in many people. They came to realise, however, that Thatcher and the Tories were intent on destroying not just the coal industry and the National Union of Mineworkers – but the welfare state too.

'After 1945, where did all that that hope go to?' Amy asked despairingly, during one of their writing sessions.

'I don't know,' Eddie replied, 'we knew about the pits, but now everything else seems to be under threat too.'

'Aye,' Amy agreed, 'this lot in charge now, they're doing the exact opposite of the post-war crowd. Like Jed and Doris say, they'll go for our throats as soon as look at us.'

LOG 4: THE EMPIRE GUARD – 1968

The location of my new Int outfit was somewhere in West Germany, but even now it's supposed to be top secret, so I can't say exactly where. Our main job was to obtain knowledge of Russian troop movements and intentions. This was the time of the Iron Curtain and the Cold War and, in Berlin, the commies built a huge wall to separate their forces from ours.

Luckily, Geordie took me under his wing and I quickly settled in. After getting me up to speed, he then tried to teach me some additional skills, which he said were required for my new job. Lip reading was something he recommended and gradually he taught me how to do it. It's especially useful for surveillance, or dealing with prisoner, especially if there are crowds of them. I even find it helpful here in hospital, because I can usually tell what the doctors are saying, even in their little asides to the other staff.

Geordie also emphasised how important it was to remember, 'in volume and detail,' information obtained during interrogations. He gave me some tips about mental exercises that would enable me to do so. Recalling the stuff for these logs isn't a doddle, but what I can recollect is mostly due to these drills. They're brilliant and I still do them, even now, when I'm all fucked-up in this hospital bed.

A bit after I joined the Int mob, Geordie told me he'd managed to get two tickets for the Man U European Cup final at Wembley – where the Reds would face Benfica.

'Would you like one?' he asked.

'Silly question!' I thought. So I nearly knocked his hand off and we travelled over to Blighty and stayed at the Union Jack Club.

After the match, which the Reds won four one, we were full of good cheer and went on a piss-up in central London to celebrate. Half-cut and jubilant, we ended up in Carnaby Street, where Geordie suddenly burst into song:

'Aal the lads and lasses,

Wi smiles upon their faces,

Gannin along the Warwick Road,

Ter see Matt Busby's aces!'

'Trust Geordie to combine the Blaydon Races with Man U,' I was thinking. But I joined in enthusiastically, as we belted it out with some gusto.

The street was full of longhaired Nancy-boys talking about freedom and free love with girls, whose mini-skirts barely covered their fannies. They seemed so unrestricted, enlightened and full of life. As I looked at them, though, I felt a flush of anger – and perhaps in retrospect, a little bit of envy.

We were well pissed by then, but I could tell Geordie's thoughts were similar, because he was staring at the flower-power lot with distaste.

'If them hippie cunts were starving,' he muttered, 'it wouldn't be free-love and liberty they'd be spouting about.'

'They don't have a fookin' clue,' I slurred in agreement, 'their freedom comes from the good living in our nation.'

'Did they ever ask what price was paid for that?' Geordie cut in, 'there's not much left of the Empire an' it's us army bods who're its an' the nation's guard.'

My alienation with the hippies had intensified.

'You civvy cunts had better believe you need us, or be

prepared to take the consequences,' I squawked in their direction.

Geordie then flicked his thumb towards the nearest flower-power group.

'The whole shebang is aal ganin tits-up,' he murmured. 'An' being as most people in Britain are weak, cowardly an' easily led, in order for the nation ter succeed an' not get bested, it requires real men, like us, who'll get in the ditch with our country's enemies an' fight them hand ter hand.'

The wars Geordie was talking about were not fought according to any rules, but took place in faraway places like Malaya, Kenya, Cyprus and Aden – and were often brutal and deadly affairs.

'Our fuckwit politicians are complicit in this job,' Geordie had continued, 'an' their task is ter provide cover for our deeds.'

Back in Krautland from time to time, usually over a bottle of whisky, Geordie and the Major used to bang on about their previous experiences in some of those conflicts. The Major was knocking on a bit and his dark hair was now tinged with grey, although this tended to enhance his refined Stewart Granger type looks. He'd joined Army Intelligence in the last year of the Second World War and decided to stay on after its end.

The Major had been in the Far East and, at the time of the Japanese surrender, ended up in Vietnam. He often told us how Britain had decided to hold this area for France, till their forces could get back to run it.

'Goodness me, it did feel a bit beastly,' he said. 'We'd just been fighting the Japs and Ho Chi Minh had helped us against them. But afterwards, we just turned on him and his chappies – the Viet-Minh. I suppose we had to do it, because they were all bolshies. We gave them a right duffing up in the end, then the French returned and we handed the country back to them.'

Geordie, who especially liked a tipple, would top up our glasses and sometimes he'd give me a sly wink, as the Major jawed on.

'As well as a few of our own fellows from Blighty, we mainly used our local troops against the commies. But when we also re-armed the Japs and got them to fight alongside us too – the Indian Divisions got a bit uppish. They didn't like the slant-eyed blighters, but noblesse oblige and all that – we needed the numbers.'

The Major ended with a warning.

'Whatever we do, we mustn't mention this to the Yanks though. Vietnam is bleeding them dry just now, so we shouldn't be reminding them that we started it all.'

There had also been trouble in various parts of our own empire. Like Malaya where, working with the local police, the Major had helped to track down Chin Peng's commies, who'd threatened our rubber and tin trades. The most dangerous were dispatched with a bullet in the head; others tortured and locked away in special camps.

Geordie joined the army later in the early 1950s, after spending much of his young life in boy's homes in the northeast. He'd fought in Cyprus against Greek terrorists, and Kenya, where they sought to convert Mau Mau rebels into loyalists by extracting confessions and then forcing them to take an oath of loyalty. Those that resisted were often beaten to death and some were mutilated with castration or other lifelong injuries. Rebel bitches were made to bare their arses and forced to sit on red-hot stoves, others had bottles stuffed up their cunts, or were gang raped by their loyalist warders.

'Being as them Mau Mau were aal peasants,' Geordie told us, 'that's why the ones who didn't cooperate – we cut off their goolies. It was the worst thing we could do – then they couldn't have any bairns ter pass land onto, or anything else. It made the fuckers less than men an' even their own rejected them.'

'Isn't that fookin' cruelty?' I was thinking uneasily, the first time I heard it – and the Major must have clocked the look on my face.

'We mustn't get torture and retribution mixed up,' he said to me. 'Once the foreign Johnnies step out of line they must be punished, all great empires, the Romans, the Normans, did this. Look, if they kowtow, then okay, but when they rebel it's a bloody good duffing up.'

Geordie said there had been some unthinking sadism from the ordinary soldiers in Kenya, but was adamant that what was done in the prison camps was thought out and had good objectives in mind. He taught me that actions, used in that way, could become a means to an end.

'Last but not least,' he said, 'they can be used not only ter break prisoners, but also ter intimidate aal those who might think like them. It has ter be severe enough ter deter anyone wanting ter follow in any rebel's footsteps. If used extensively, it can break and mould a whole population.'

The Major then pointed out that a number of places in our Empire had become independent, but remained friendly to British interests.

'This benefits both them and us,' he said. 'In essence, we prepared those chappies in bongo bongo land for independence, so their rulers would be pro-British and free from reds and agitators.'

To tell the truth, to start with I was a bit horrified by some of the things they mentioned and thought there must be conventions and laws against the methods cited. But I remembered my own interrogation training and soon realised that all armies must be able to deliver retribution by extreme means; most even have special units with experts in these techniques. The British army is no exception and now I'd argue that such methods are integral to our success and reputation.

There was one story that seemed stuck in Geordie's mind and he recounted it to me quite a few times. It concerned Cyprus, where he and the Major had first met up. They'd been fighting against Colonel Grivas and his EOKA gunmen and a young Greek Cypriot had been arrested and handed over to Geordie for interrogation.

After weeks of alternating beatings and kindness, the prisoner had at last admitted his involvement with EOKA. Appearing broken, he'd then indicated that Grivas's hideout was in a certain area of the Troodos Mountains. Many green team soldiers were dispatched to this location and Geordie was ordered to go with them.

He said it was very hot and once in place the sweating squaddies prepared to commence searching. Suddenly, fires were lit below the troops, to the bushes and trees that covered the lower part of the mountains. Some soldiers were caught in the flames and perished – others were badly burnt.

Geordie said he'd realised straight away that it had all been a set-up. So, he hurried back to deal with the prisoner, only to find he'd been spirited away from a local jail during an EOKA raid. After determinedly, but unsuccessfully, trying to re-capture the escaped prisoner, Geordie and his mates found out months later, from an informer, that the young Greek Cypriot had flown the island.

Later, they established that their target was now at large somewhere in the western Mediterranean. The Major then put out feelers. He had contacts with the Franco police in Spain and with the authorities in France, whom he'd helped during their little bit of bother in Algeria.

In the end it was the Frogs who'd come up with the goods. In Provence they'd been keeping an eye on a team of young men, called raseteurs, who played a game with bulls. This crew contained a couple of Algerians the Frog plods were interested in – and, from the photo provided by the Major, they'd clocked that the young Greek Cypriot was also in the group.

Geordie sorted out his civvies and travelled to Nimes and made contact with the French police. The next evening he was taken to a village, on the edge of the Camargue, which had an old Roman arena, featuring 'Sport with Bulls'. The plainclothes police then led the way to their seats on the arena steps – at the back where they could view unnoticed.

Twenty minutes later a team of young men, dressed in tight fitting all white outfits, filed onto one side of the arena floor. Tucked under their arms, a number of the raseteurs carried a rolled up white towel, which they proceeded to tie to the outer railings. At the same time they pointed to girls in the crowd, shouting out for them to help.

'Please keep an eye on it,' they'd pleaded.

'Some boys these raseteurs, there're hoping to fix up a fuck – for after,' a grinning Frog plod had leant over and whispered to Geordie.

Then another policeman indicated a well-tanned youth at the rear of the group and Geordie, recognising him, knew instantly he had got his man. The Frog plods said to just enjoy the game and do nothing while it lasted – and, afterwards, they would arrest the Greek youth and tomorrow hand him over into Geordie's custody.

A sudden roar from the crowd indicated the entrance, from the other side of the arena, of a wild black bull; it had large deadly looking horns, between which a tassel was attached.

The object of the game was to grab the decoration without being gored by the bull, and to achieve this the raseteurs had to work together. Some of the team made passes in front of the bull to distract him, while others tried to find a position close to the bull, from which to make a final speedy dart to snatch the ribbon.

The first raseteur to try a grab had almost succeeded, when the bull detected him at the last second and slashed him across the chest with a sweep of it's horns. Pursued by the increasingly mad bull, the youth, his white tee-shirt now torn and stained red with blood, retreated rapidly. He desperately flung himself over the inner railing, which the bull, just behind him, then crashed into.

It was Geordie's man, the young Greek Cypriot, who made the successful grab. He managed to surprise the bull, with a lightning run from the rear. After snatching the tassel from between the bull's horns as he raced alongside it, he'd sprinted away holding the ribbon aloft in triumph.

Geordie said he smiled at the youth's audacity.

'Let him have his triumph,' he'd thought, 'it will be his last.'

The French plods were as good as their word, arresting the youth later that evening and handing him over to Geordie the next day. The Major then arranged a safe passage and for two MI6 men with a car to help convey Geordie and his prisoner, via Spain, down to Gibraltar. And, a few days later, a Royal Navy Destroyer took them back to Cyprus.

During the journey, and back in Cyprus, Geordie made sure that the youth did not suffer any ill treatment. The prisoner had proved himself to be a brave opponent.

'I liked him,' Geordie said, 'he was one we'd have welcomed into our army – if he'd been born in Britain.'

As an opponent, though, the Greek could not be seen to

have won in any way, shape or form.

The first time I heard the story I asked what had happened to the boy and Geordie just grinned.

'Shot trying ter escape,' he replied. 'A week after we returned ter Cyprus, I'd already gotten aal of the information I could from him mind. So, me marra an' me, we took him ter the Troodos Mountains an' let him look over the scene of the fire – the area of his triumph. Then I put my revolver ter the back of his head an' blew his fucking brains out.'

'The Empire Guard, that's us,' the Major muttered, after Geordie had finished his tale.

I heard Geordie's story every now and then, usually after a few drinks. I think he was making the point that what we do is not personal; we might even have a bit of admiration for our opponents, but we will do our duty in the end – come what may. We do it for ourselves; we do it for our oppos; we do it for our regiment; we do it for our Queen and country!

PIGGYLAND

My way of joking is to tell the truth.
It's the funniest joke in the world.
George Bernard Shaw (1856 – 1950)
John Bull's Other Island

A few years after the National Health Service was born in 1948, Aneurin Bevan, the Labour Health Secretary, had opened the new hospital in Mugsfield.

'You will pay into it according to your means,' he'd said, 'but good healthcare will come to all.'

Forty-six years later new managers now abounded, with NHS hospitals becoming bearpits between these harbingers of market forces and those who championed the old caring ethos of tending the sick. The nurses, Elsie, Kate and Gwendolyn, were glad to take care of Ginge, mainly because they'd grown fond of their patient – but also for the reason that the high security around the injured soldier meant that they were left alone to get on with this work. On the A&E wards, however, they were always short of staff and continuously felt under pressure.

Everyone was also desperately trying to find time to fill in all the paperwork and meet the latest set of targets. This turn towards the market had been forced on the NHS four years previously, after which local health authorities managed their own budgets. The following year trusts were established to buy healthcare, both within and outside of the NHS.

'Teambuilding' was a buzzword from the start. With most staff, including Alec, Elsie, Kate and Gwendolyn, forced to attend courses that included puerile exercises and lectures, which endorsed 'private enterprise' and a 'free market'.

'You mark my words, it's a slippery slope,' Alec said. 'Teambuilding is really about manufacturing obedience for the new regime. The bastards will reward those who favour the new path and punish those who don't.'

Kate flashed him a look of scorn.

'Well, I enjoyed my day out at that,' she said. 'Anyway, if you're punished, you can always get yourself a soapbox at speakers corner in Hyde Park.'

A few weeks later, Elsie spotted a crowd of nurses around Alec and his trolley, so she went over to see what the fuss was all about.

'He's had his final warning,' Kate said, when she saw Elsie's questioning look.

'I don't give a continental fuck, what them bastards think of me,' Alec said, but then wailed in mock despair: 'They keep threatening to sack me and send me home.'

He glancing around at the nurses, then stretched out his arm and put a hand on Kate's shoulder.

'This little piggeh went to market,' he said, before jerked his thumb towards himself, 'while this little piggeh stayed at home.'

Alec next moved his hand to Elsie's shoulder.

'This little piggeh had roast beef,' he said, before patting his own tummy, 'while this little piggeh had none.'

Crossing his arms he put both his hands on his own shoulders.

'And this little piggeh,' he cried out, 'went 'wee wee wee' all the way home.'

In Mugsfield General, neglecting a patient would probably just be swept under the carpet now, but telling one of the new managers to 'go fuck yourself' was considered a serious crime. And Alec had got himself into a lot of trouble for committing this offence. Facing dismissal, he apologised and asked for clemency.

'Me words were just a turn of phrase,' Alec pleaded, 'and anyroads, I was being asked to do something unreasonable.'

With the help of the union he kept his job, but only just – and from then on he was working under duress.

The rest of the staff gave each other knowing glances and 'told you so' was muttered. Nurses felt that not only were they worked off their feet, but also most of their freedoms were being lost too. It was becoming clearer that opposition to the new regime would not be tolerated and the staff started to feel that they were now living under a tyranny.

When Elsie told Ginge about Alec and the new set-up in the hospital, however, he just laughed.

'Yes sir, no sir, three bags full sir,' he said, 'the army's full of cunts like your bosses, but we just have to get on with it.'

The next time Elsie went to check on Ginge there was a man sitting on the seat opposite the bed, talking to her patient. He turned to glance at her and she saw he was smartly dressed in an officer's uniform.

'Ah, you've come to look after my chap,' he said, 'I hope he's been behaving himself?'

'Aye, he's the perfect gentleman,' Elsie replied, flashing him a mock salute.

The officer grinned and turned back to Ginge.

'Goodness me!' he said, 'I won't tell them that back in

Belfast, or they'll think you've gone a bit poofterish.'

Ginge laughed back and Elsie got on with her checks.

After the visitor had left, Ginge beckoned to the nurse.

'That's the fookin' Major,' he said, 'don't tell him anything, or he'll cut off my nuts, fry them up – and scoff them in a goolie-burger.'

Elsie smiled, feeling perplexed, not by Ginge's coarse words, but because she'd overheard him ask the Major why he hadn't been transferred to a military hospital. The officer replied that this was because of the soldier's condition and promised him a move as soon as it was safe to do so. Elsie thought this was strange, because she'd heard doctors in the hospital saying that the injured soldier could now be moved 'any time the army wanted'.

Personally, she was glad to have him stay around, but the mystery around the injured soldier seemed to deepen and she felt this was not likely to change anytime soon. Ginge was continuing to record his messages, or logs as he called them. And they both kept this activity a secret from everyone else. At first Elsie bought him tapes that recorded for only half-an-hour, but now the ones she purchased lasted for hours.

Ginge wrote a number on the finished tapes – then adding a title and date. When he said he was worried about storing the completed tapes in his room, Elsie volunteered to take them home and keep them there for him.

'They'll be safe,' she said with a grin. 'I'll put them at the back of my underwear drawer in my bedroom, no one but me looks in there.'

'Great,' he said, smiling back. 'And remember shush,' he added, putting a finger to his lips.

Elsie knew that Ginge was still doing his recording, and that, to avoid detection, he'd often do them late at night, or very early in the morning. She was happy to encourage him in his project and be a part of this secretive activity.

'He's putting down a lot of dialogue,' she thought, 'well, he's demanding a fair amount of tapes, anyway.'

Elsie decided that she wouldn't tell Ginge about her making contact with Amy and Eddie – at least not for a while. Because she didn't know if this would upset him – and if so, might even turn him against her. She also wanted to find out more about the wounded soldier before she let him know about her contacting his old friends.

'It's interesting,' she thought, 'that the MoD police stopped Amy and Eddie from visiting. Of course, Ginge might have told the cops to refuse them entry. On the other hand, could it be that the police are not just Ginge's protectors – but also his jailors?'

As Elsie left her soldier patient, Alec was having a laugh with the cops in the corridor outside.

'Oh! Go on – gizza a go on your gun, there're a few fucks around here that need putting down,' Alec joked.

'Neya,' one of the policeman responded, 'but why don't you run them down wi' your trolley. You're such a bad driver, you could probably get away wi' saying it wor an accident.'

Elsie walked away laughing. But in her mind she was trying to rationalise the situation that Alec and everyone else in the hospital, including her, were in.

'I don't know what can be done about it,' she thought, 'but I do know that this is one little piggy that won't be going to the market.'

LOG 5: AN INTERLUDE IN ULSTER – 1969-70

A couple of years after I started with the green slime, as we in Intelligence are often called by some green team shitheads, word got around that the Major might be retiring soon. The old boy had done 'Donkey's years,' according to himself – and the previous twelve months, 1968, had been a quiet stretch for a change.

'Since 1945, it's the first year in my time that a British soldier hasn't been killed in a conflict somewhere across the world,' I remember him saying.

There had been some mutterings, though, that the micks in Ireland were getting a bit uppity again. But we all thought a little bit of paddy-bashing would soon sort them out. I didn't see any connection at the time, but not long after that our unit moved back to a secret location in 'good old Blighty,' as the Major called it.

The old boy then went in some redundancy programme – by all accounts with a little pot of gold and a good pension. That's when I met the new Major and, at first, I found it difficult to figure him out. Compared to the old boy, the new Major was almost nondescript; a gentlemanly manner, sure enough, but a gaunt figure and he'd something about him that suggested you'd better be careful in his presence.

'Watch out!' Geordie whispered, 'you don't want ter see his fangs.'

The old Major had been as tough as teak, but charmingly

old school. A Queen and Empire man who distrusted all politicians, or 'fuckwits' as we called them. This new one was different – but it took me a while before I realised he was just as political as the 'wets and reds,' he often railed against.

Geordie said he'd heard the new man had been coordinating arrests and interrogations in Aden and probably earned his promotion there.

'He was a captain then, so he's just been made up,' he said, 'the word is he got caught up in a lot of bother out there, after the fuckwits set a date for withdrawal. A lot of our wog police turned against us then – said we'd be deserting them, an' they knew they'd get chopped after.'

I still don't know if that was true or not. To start with, though, we didn't see a lot of him. Geordie claimed the new man was obsessed with the latest version of our Land Operations Manual, which had just come out.

On the occasions we did meet the new Major, we found him quite chatty with us. We soon realised, though, that he could suddenly change, and take on a menacing air in an instant. The social graces would vanish and he'd blast you with both barrels.

'He's a bloke on a mission,' Geordie said to me one day, 'but fuck knows what it is?'

Then Ulster blew up and our troops moved out of their barracks and onto the streets. To us, it seemed mad and chaotic, but we all thought it would soon calm down again. After the green team had put the boot in a bit, anyroads.

When it continued, the Major said a request had been made for us to teach the infantry the rudiments of intelligence work. Seemingly, they'd found the local plods' information was biased, not to mention almost non-existent. So they wanted to start collecting their own and some of the top brass thought we could help.

Geordie told me the Major had seen this as a chance for us to make an 'on the ground assessment' of the situation, with a view to seeing what role we could play. Consequently, they'd arranged for me to join a Jock regiment in Belfast and teach them intelligence techniques. My main job, though, was to report back with as much background information as possible.

So, I arrived from the ferry onto a Belfast dock in March 1970. It was a dank overcast day with pelting rain being driven into my face by a gusty wind. I made contact with the redcaps at the docks and a lance jack offered me a lift in his Land Rover to the Jocks' base, which was situated in an old factory.

As yet the aggro hadn't really affected us, but the micks and the prods were knocking the shit out of each other. According to the redcap lance jack, they'd tried to remain friendly with both, but this was starting to break down.

'It's just like wogland again,' he said, 'here, they're just as bad as the Greeks and Turks in Cyprus.'

My first impression, through the rain-splattered windscreen, was how like back home the layout and buildings of the town were. Little streets of terraces, with scattered shops and pubs – and in the midst was this derelict factory. It had been hastily refurbished and reinforced with wriggly-tin and barbed-wire protection.

The Jocks were taking no chances and it quickly became clear that they did not think they required some 'English bastard' to instruct them in anything.

'Up yours! Fookin' haggis bashers,' I muttered, under my breath.

Now normally I might have taken real offence with the attitude of the sweaty socks but, as my actual job was to report on the situation, I thought I could use this state of affairs to my advantage.

The Major had also suggested that I should try to interest the Jocks in starting an intelligence register of the area they patrolled.

'It will be good practice, anyway,' he told me, 'and if we stay it will be the start of good on the ground information – that can be built up over time.'

To my surprise, I found the Jocks receptive to this idea. But after I returned Geordie explained that, anyroads, this sort of thing was all laid out in great detail in the new Land Operations Manual. In that case, perhaps I was actually doing a bit of pioneering work when I agreed to work with the young officer that the Jocks had appointed to be their intelligence coordinator.

I wanted to assess the basics of what was happening, though, so, while providing a modicum of training in information gathering, I also arranged to get around the area as much as possible. I found that, while appearing to court both sides, it was clear that in the last resort the green team boys would back the Unionist's status quo. This seemed to me, to be the only reasonable thing to do; after all, nobody wants to find themselves fighting both sides in this type of situation.

And the Jocks, indeed, who all seemed to be Rangers' supporters, were already beginning to make their pro-prod allegiances clear. I found it strange, though, that no one seemed interested in the activities of the loyalist armed organisations. Especially, as they'd taken a pro-active role in the bombings and shootings that had happened so far.

There was also an incident that gave me pause to think, when I'd accompanied a Jock patrol in a nationalist area. A little crowd had gathered and there'd been a bit of banter between the Jocks and a few of the local youth.

'We bate yous the last time yous were here,' one lad shouted out, 'an we'll bate yous again.'

The intelligence officer, a fresh-faced lieutenant, politely replied that the boy was mistaken, as this was the Jocks first posting in Belfast. We then moved on, with the Jocks muttering 'stupid feckin' fenians,' and other uncomplimentary things.

Back at the factory base, for some reason this exchange played on my mind. I then asked to see the Jocks' regimental history – a copy of which the unit had. Looking through it, it took me a while to find it, but sure enough, back in 1798, the Jocks had served in that part of Belfast and one of their units had been forced to retreat during a vicious riot.

The local youth who'd spoken out did not strike me as being a history student, and a question then started flashing in my brain.

'Was there a folk memory in these areas that went back hundreds of years?'

If so, the implications might be that the situation was more complicated than we'd first believed – and perhaps we'd find ourselves involved in Ulster for a lot longer than we thought.

Talking to a Jock corporal, a few days later, I asked him about it. But he didn't seem to think there was anything much to be worried about.

'They're aw feckin' fenians sure enough, but ach, dinna fash yersel,' he replied, 'the actual IRA are probably na mair than twa men an' a dug. Na, they hav'na got the guts for a real fight – not with us anyhow.'

DOGMA-LAND

*Propaganda is that branch of the art of lying
which consists in nearly deceiving your friends
without quite deceiving your enemies.*

F. M. Cornford (1886 – 1960)

When Amy said that Eddie was away in London trying to dig up some old records, Elsie first thought he must be a music nut – perhaps an old rocker, trying to find some ancient LPs. As Amy explained afterwards, however, it was government documents and newspaper reports about the miners' strike that Eddie had been seeking.

Amy said to give Eddie and her a week or two after he came back, as they might be busy for a bit – working on their next layout board. Elsie felt sure the couple would be able to fill her in with information about Ginge. So, as soon as that time was up, Elsie, as arranged, was now ringing the bell on their door again.

Eddie answered and greeted her warmly.

'Na then, so you're the one who is looking after Ginge,' he said, ushering her inside.

Elsie found them both anxious for any news about the wounded soldier and she quickly brought them up to date on his progress.

'He's recovering well, but he has to take it slowly – a day at a time,' she said. 'Sadly, he hasn't gotten back any feeling in his legs yet, so it's touch and go if he will ever fully be able to use them again.'

Elsie could see that her words had disturbed them both, so she changed the subject for a time and told them about the problems that were occurring in the hospital. She also mentioned the new administrators, with their market fixations.

'I wouldn't care, but they're not even good managers,' Elsie said.

Amy and Eddie had glanced at each other and nodded their heads as she outlined her tale of woe.

'Surely the folk won't let the NHS go to the dogs,' Amy said sympathetically, when the nurse had finished.

Elsie decided to press on and find out what Eddie and Amy could reveal about her soldier patient. Eddie confirmed that they'd all gone to the same school and that he and Ginge had been good mates then. They'd both wanted to get away from the pit and had joined the army together at sixteen. After a period in boys service they'd moved on to their regiment and subsequently ended up in West Germany.

Elsie was taking all this in, but now she looked keenly at Eddie and Amy.

'Did something happen to spoil your friendship?' she asked.

Amy looked away and Eddie's face took on a pained look.

'Well,' he said, indicating Amy, 'Amy, him and me all went around together – just as mates. I suppose we were both keen on her, but happens he showed it more than me.'

Amy now looked embarrassed.

'I saw him as a friend, I never had strong feelings for him,' she said stridently.

Eddie shot her a comforting glance.

'Anyhow, I came home on leave once and Amy and me were on our own. We got on well and decided to get engaged. I thought he might not like it, but in fact he went apeshit about it. Called us a few names, then he wouldn't talk about it and cut me dead. A bit after, he left our regiment and joined the Int boys.'

'Nobody meant to hurt him,' Amy muttered.

Elsie asked if they'd had any contact with Ginge since then and was surprised when Eddie nodded his head.

'Not for a while,' he said, 'we'd sometimes bump into him, if he were home on leave, or that. But he'd look away, or cross the street to avoid us – if he saw us.'

'It was the same with me,' Amy said. 'Eddie was away working for a bit, and if Ginge was around and saw me, he'd just turn away.'

'So, when did you have contact with him?' Elsie asked.

'During the pit strike,' Eddie replied.

Elsie stared at him in surprise.

'The big one?' she enquired.

'Aye, when I thought about it afterwards, it seemed a bit strange,' Eddie replied. 'He just appeared then and was around for a while. Suddenly, he was friendly again. He even started to nip down to the Miner's Welfare and chatted away to everyone, even us.'

'Some of the lads were a bit suspicious of him,' Amy said.

'Well, he hadn't been near the club for ages,' Eddie added, 'an then, during the strike he appears and starts talking to all the miners?'

Elsie looked keenly at Eddie.

'You thought he was a spy?' she accused.

'It was the intelligence thing,' Eddie said, looked embarrassed. 'He didn't look like no squaddie, not with his long hair and that.'

'Look, have you got a brother called Sean?' He then asked Elsie.

'Yea,' she replied with a nod of her head.

'Thought so,' Eddie resumed, 'I helped him a bit with things during the strike. Well, ask him about that time, there were a lot of bad things happening then – that most people don't know about.'

'After the strike, was Ginge still friendly?' Elsie asked.

'Well, he's kept on the cottage and he still comes from time to time,' Amy said. 'He's spoken to us, but he hasn't appeared as friendly as he was during the strike.'

Amy and Eddie then said they were both 'a bit put out,' that they weren't allowed in to see Ginge after the bomb.

'Was that down to him, or were it just the cops?' Amy asked. Elsie shook her head.

'Don't know,' she said, 'but I'll try to find out.'

Before she left, Elsie had a final query for Eddie.

'Why did you leave the army then?' she asked.

'It's a long story,' Eddie replied, 'I'll tell you about it the next time we meet.'

Elsie then realised it was getting late and took her leave.

'Same time, next week?' she questioned, as she left. And Eddie and Amy nodded their agreement.

Back at home, Elsie thought about the visit, which she'd hoped might clarify a lot about Ginge. Instead, she felt that the mystery surrounding him had deepened.

'Did Ginge play a hidden part in the strike?' she wondered. 'Perhaps the answer lies in the tapes he's recorded?'

Elsie now had a number of them hidden away at home. Although tempted, she still believed that it would be a betrayal of Ginge's trust to attempt to listen to them – without his approval anyway.

Amy and Eddie were delighted with Elsie's visit, knowing that she could now give them a link to Ginge and provide news of his recovery.

'It's also interesting what Elsie was saying about the hospital,' Eddie said.

'Perhaps, it's something we can mention on our boards,' Amy said.

'Yea,' Eddie muttered, 'but everything seems to be going upside down, even keeping track is a problem.'

To them, it appeared that hidden forces, outside the control of ordinary people, were reshaping their lives – and their world. Using their experience of what had happened at the bank as a guide, Amy and Eddie then set out to look into the issue of the new managers at the hospital and other public bodies. And, in due course, they used this as the text for their next display board:

Since the coming of Thatcher, with the introduction of a new economic agenda into Britain, most public organisations, like British Steel, the NHS, the Coal Board and British Rail, were subjected to the introduction of new managers from outside their fields of work.

They immediately went into action, advocating 'private enterprise' and a 'turn to the market'. They harassed and bullied long-term bosses and staff onto the new path; trying to turn public bodies into businesses and those they catered for into customers. In the long term, just as they have destroyed the mining industry, they intend to shut down, or totally privatise, other organisations, including the NHS.

Many longstanding members of staff, in the public bodies, often complain that the new bosses do not understand their work, or ethos – and often say: 'They are not good managers anyway.'

This, however, is to miss the point. These new administrators are not overly concerned about the day to day running of public bodies. They are the carriers of the new economic ideology – effectively political demagogues for a globalised free-market system. What matters to them, and their masters, is how quickly and how far they will prove able to pursue and advance their dogma.

Amy and Eddie had reluctantly left the bank and accepted the redundancy packages, which had paid off their mortgage. Nowadays, from home, they ran their own little financial services business, mainly doing the books for local shops and providing fiscal advice. It did not make a lot, but mostly paid their bills – and kept them rubbing along happily.

It also gave them plenty of time for study and creating the ten display boards for the strike anniversary. When they remembered losing their jobs at the bank, however, they felt they'd been like the miners, steelworkers and many others, who were suffering under the new system.

'I suppose, like most folk, we've just been upset by it all,' Amy said.

'Aye,' Eddie agreed, 'alienated – feeling like victims.'

'But of what?' they both then asked.

They often discussed how they'd become estranged from the bank and supported the miners during the strike. They felt that to do so had been their gut reaction. But now they wanted to fully understand what they had struggled for – and also against.

Turn on the TV news and the screen would fill with stories of doom and gloom from around the world. So, thinking about the troubled times they lived in, they both felt that the cause was now something global – affecting everything and everyone. But to understand and make sense of it all, that was the conundrum?

LOG 6: WAR MOVES AT HOLYWOOD – 1970

After my month with the Jocks in Ulster, I speedily made my way back to the mainland. But the Major, although he seemed elated about the situation, was uninterested in my assessment of it.

'Things have moved on,' he told me.

He then shrugged his shoulders dismissively, when I tried to deliver my report.

'Look, a decision's already been made for us to go in heavy,' he added curtly.

When I saw Geordie he was gleeful, and not just because he'd been promoted up a notch to Warrant Officer.

'Knick-knack, paddywhack,' he said, 'we'll wipe out the IRA before they've even got off the ground. The old man's given the go-ahead for us ter set up a Q squad in Belfast.'

He whispered to me later that the Major had made him study the new edition of the Land Operations Manual.

'It lays out our new way of operating,' the officer had told him.

A few days later, the Major gave us all a pep talk along those lines, and outlined how he wanted us to function in Belfast.

'We've spent decades clearing up abroad, against blacks, yellows and slant eyes,' he said, 'now we're going into action in the UK, after the enemy at home. Our command structure will bypass the usual army ones – we'll report to the top brass only. First we'll sort our intelligence side, then we can grow our work, with additions slotted in later.'

He then added that the new commander for our proposed area in Belfast had a wealth of experience in past colonial wars, like Malaya, Cyprus and Kenya: 'Where he was instrumental in introducing the counter-gang tactic.'

'He intends to implement a tough hard-hitting approach,' the Major continued, 'and will use no-nonsense units, like the Paras, to enforce it. We'll also be working to a plan along those lines, and must be prepared to do everything we can to defeat, or at least make vulnerable, the IRA.'

He also insisted that we'd need to be really genned-up on our area of operations. So the subsequent weeks were hectic, with us processing an increasing pile of info. The Major had used all his contacts to procure the data, with most of the stats coming from scraps of existing intelligence from the green team regiments' area reports and the RUC's Special Branch. But he'd even got some stuff from MI6 and MI5, who'd agents and informants in both Ulster and the South.

So, four months after my first visit, I felt fairly confident and ready and able, as I made my way back to Belfast. But this time I was with my Int unit and we took our own vehicles and equipment. Soon, we'd made our way in convoy from the docks to our allotted area in Palace Barracks – which was situated a little bit east of Belfast at Holywood.

Geordie and the Major had gone in advance, to try and ease our passage into the tangled knot of military and other intelligence organisations setting up, or already operating, in Ulster.

'This is a prime location,' Geordie said, after greeting me, jerking his thumb to indicate the barracks. 'Here we'll be distanced from our enemy, an' therefore unlikely ter be disturbed by them – but they'll be well within our striking range.'

The Unionists had been pushing hard for a tougher line to be taken against the IRA. And the green team boys had responded by setting in motion an operation to search for arms and explosives in the lower Falls area of west Belfast. Soldiers, smashing down doors and ripping houses apart, seriously pissed off the micks and sporadic gun battles broke out.

A few locals were killed, or wounded, and the green teams brought more troops in and declared a curfew over the whole area. This settled things down, but the embarrassing thing was that they then found out it was not legal, at that time anyroads, for us to impose a curfew. The top brass, though, soon sorted it out by getting the fuckwits at Westminster to hold an emergency session in Parliament and pass legislation that allowed the army to impose curfews. And made this retrospective to cover the action in the lower Falls.

The 'Falls Curfew', though, was our crossing of the Rubicon and from then on the battle lines were increasingly drawn. In Nationalist areas, the green team boys had gone from chats and cups of tea to being seen as an occupying army. Most of us felt a bit apprehensive, but the Major appeared to be pleased.

'It's all brewing up nicely chaps!' he said.

We'd been given an isolated part of Palace Barracks, where we could carry out our activities away from prying eyes. Our instructions were to organise a covert network, mainly to gather information on, and hit back against, IRA members and their supporters. But at the same time to establish contact with others, like some loyalist groups we were interested in.

To start with, we constructed a tribal map of the city; nominally the prods and micks, marking out Nationalist and Unionist areas – and the hard-core republicans and loyalists.

We had to know where our indigenous enemy lurked, so we'd be able to hunt them down to their rat holes. We knew, though, it would be some time before we'd be able to carry this out.

So, for a while, we did little else than try to marry our existing information to the circumstances in our areas of interest. We then started to remove the tell-tale signs that signified us as 'Brits' to all and sundry. On active service, we wore civvy clothes and our hair became longer.

Gradually, we acclimatised ourselves into our zone of operations. This wasn't our territory, so we knew, if we wanted to dominate it – to be the hunters not the hunted – we'd need to have an edge. Information would help to give us that, but we also accepted it would need to be combined with ruthless actions and fierce determination.

To acquaint ourselves with the hard-line mick areas, which we called Indian country, we began to drive through them. At the start in our army uniforms and using our military vehicles, then, increasingly, we wore civvies and used Q cars. These were local motors we acquired by buying or stealing, which were then tarted-up and re-sprayed in our army workshops.

We'd use them with false number plates and they were ideal for clandestine activities.

'I've often used them in the past,' Geordie said, 'for surveillance, assassinations an' other special ops. It all worked then an' it'll work again now.'

With our long hair, civvies and Q cars, we were all sorted to blend in locally. Now, able to pass as natives, we started to assemble a list of possible informers. We knew the best targets were the vulnerable, or those with a weakness – so we dug deep, to ascertain if any on our lists were compromised in any way.

Were they involved in crime? Were they in debt? Were they addicted to gambling, drugs or booze? Were they married, but having a bit on the side? Were they shirt-lifters? – We all knew you could squeeze queers till the pips squeaked.

After deciding on a mark, we then became the fishers of men and dangled some bait. With the first hook we'd arrange a chance to bump into them, in a place that was quiet and discreet. We'd then politely introduce ourselves and ask them to come back to us with a bit of information that was small and known to everyone.

Most would refuse and we'd then reveal what we knew about them.

'Do you want your friends to know?' We asked.

Some would then comply, thinking that the information we'd requested did not matter much, anyroads.

With the second hook, we'd ask for more and better information.

'What do you think I am – a feckin' tout?' Most would angrily reply.

'Yes!' we'd say, 'we know you to be an informer and what is more, we've a recording of you giving us information. Do you want your friends to hear it? Look, just comply and we'll give you a bit of bunce as well. Come on, you know it makes sense.'

If they agreed, they were now well and truly on the hook and we made sure they could not get off it.

To obtain really good information, though, the target had to be in a position to get it. We could get hoods and fookin' druggies easy enough as we could take our pick from the RUC files. But they often proved unreliable, and anyroads anything they gave us was liable to be piss-poor.

We knew that what we really needed were informers linked to, and especially agents within, the IRA, and other organisations.

'Then we can do some serious damage,' the Major said.

DIVIDE&RULE-LAND

'History,' Stephen said, *'is a nightmare
from which I am trying to awake.'*
James Joyce (1882 – 1941)
Ulysses

It was on Elsie's next visit to her new friends that Eddie told
her about his time in the army – and why he'd quit. After the
bust-up with Ginge, Eddie had continued soldiering on in
West Germany and was soon a corporal. He was doing well
and it had been suggested that he was on his way to making
sergeant.

'Then I made an honest women of her,' Eddie said, jerking
a thumb in the direction of Amy, who fluttered her eyes, made
a face and stuck out her tongue.

'After we'd got married,' he continued, 'I tried to persuade
her to join me over there. But she's a home girl and weren't
keen.'

Eddie stopped for a moment and rubbed his eyes.

'And then,' he resumed, 'I were posted off to Aden in a
hurry – 'to suppress a revolt,' we were told. Our orders were to
'pacify the town,' – it were hectic, with all sorts of stuff going
on. It wasn't just us, our undercover troops were operating
in civvies, in K-M squads, as if they were Arabs – and were
doing god knows what to those hostile to us. On at least two
occasions our lot shot a couple of them, because we thought
they were armed a-rabs.'

'Bloody hell, shooting your own blokes,' Elsie said, 'but what they were doing seems a bit sneaky. And a K-M squad, what is that, when it's at home?'

'Our lot named them after a Swahili word from Kenya, keeni-meeni – it's the slithering movement of a snake,' he replied. 'Anyroads, after we'd been there about two months, a local dock union called a strike to stop our supplies being unloaded and I was given a list of addresses to raid. We were ordered to arrest any trade unionists found there. I found they were all really poor people, but we were told: 'They're all commies. Paid with Moscow gold.' Well, this little runt we picked up hadn't gotten any of it, he was living in a right hovel.'

Eddie then stopped talking for a bit and Elsie thought she could see a tear glinting in the corner of one of his eyes.

Amy looked anxious, clutching her hands together.

'It affects him, he sometimes has nightmares,' she whispered.

'We have these two wrens in our back garden,' Eddie said quietly. 'We usually don't see them, except for now and again – then we get a little glimpse. Anyroads, one day I was in the kitchen, when I heard a squeaking coming from the cupboard on the wall, where the boiler is. I thought it were a mouse, or worse a rat. But when I opened the little door it were this tiny bird, which fluttered down to the floor. 'How'd it get in the cupboard?' I wondered. Thinking it was just a fledgling, I went to get a box to put it in – to get it outside and let it go. But it wasn't going in no box. It drew itself up to its full height and started to cheep away at me in an angry tone – gave me a right dressing down. That's when I realised it were a full-grown bird and must be a wren. So, I put the box away and went and opened the kitchen window, then moved back to the door. The wren had turned and watched me all the way. I think it could feel the fresh air, because it suddenly flew to the top of the sink unit, beside the window. It then turned to look at me again, as if to say: 'that's better, now you're helping me,' before flying out the window. It settled on a bush at the bottom of the garden and another wren suddenly appeared, and flew around and around the freed bird chirping noisily away. "Where the hell have you been, you dirty stop out," it seemed to be saying to its mate.'

Throughout the tale Eddie's head was dropping, till he was looking at the floor. Now he straightened and stared directly at Elsie.

'That's how this little runt in Aden acted,' he said, 'when we smashed our way into his hovel. His wife and kids were screaming their heads off and, like the wren, he drew himself up to his full height, and gave us a right mouthful in his lingo. But one of my men just lumped him behind the ear with his rifle-butt, and two others grabbed a leg each and dragged him outside, banging his noggin on the doorstep and the ground. He soon shut-up then! We took him to the confinement and interrogation unit at Al Mansura Prison and handed him over. The Intelligence Captain told us it was a vital job: 'well done,' he said. But with the heat, we were sweating our cods off, so we went and found some shade and got some tea and buns off the char wallah, to celebrate.'

Eddie hacked up a cough to clear his throat and had a sip of tea.

'The next day, just as it was getting dark, we were told to report to that unit again – and the Int Captain now said we'd to get rid of a number of bodies. 'Take them to the bridge over the inlet and throw them over – into the water,' he ordered. Some of the bodies were from that batch of prisoners we'd collected up the day before. Although most had been beaten to a pulp, I suddenly recognised the little runt. I quickly felt for a pulse and shouted out 'I think this one is still alive.' But the Captain explained that the ones still alive had been given an injection to keep them quiet, and should be thrown into the water with the others who were already dead. 'Look, it's just a bit of housekeeping,' he said. 'Most will end up out at sea and disappear anyway. And any bodies that are found, will act as a deterrent to the rest of these chappies – not to try and fuck us about again'.'

'My God!' Elsie thought, 'but at least he appears glad to be getting this off his chest.'

'We done as we were told and, at the time, we were all up for it,' Eddie continued, 'laughing and joking as we threw the rag-heads over the parapet and into the water. It was a bit later, when a little voice in the back of my noggin started to ask questions: 'Was that a nice thing to do? Was that a good thing to do? Was that the right thing to do?' It were like our orders and my conscience were going at it hammer and tongs – and I found it difficult to sleep. Then, one night I had this thought: 'What if a foreign army had invaded Blighty and treated us the way we'd treated them in Aden?' The next day I went to the Padre and told him about the conflictions in my mind. But he just said: 'We are here to bring a little light to these poor afflicted heathens – and God is on the side of those who bring light – so cast out the darkness and doubt and just remember the light.' I got angry and told him: You're about as much use to me as a chocolate teapot would be to the char wallah.'

Eddie rubbed his hand across his face; these were memories he'd tried to suppress, but now he was determined to persevere in telling Elsie about them.

'When I got back to Krautland,' he resumed, 'Ginge had gone off to the green slime boys. And I found I still couldn't shake off the questions and the voice in my head got louder. I didn't want to listen to it, but in my heart I knew it were right. So, in the end I bought myself out of the army and returned home to Amy.'

When he was back in Civvy Street, Eddie said he'd tried hard to push the memories of Aden from his mind. But then the conflict in Northern Ireland, which began soon after, had started to revive them.

'It happens with a few of the lads,' Eddie explained, 'it's in your head and you think you've got it all under control, then, something else kicks off, and suddenly it all comes back again.'

'It were the same for the Yanks, with Vietnam,' Amy said, 'loads of them had PTSD and that. Some of their vets sent us a load of information about it, after I wrote to them.'

'That's what helped to save me,' Eddie said. 'Well that and Amy, anyroads.'

LOG 7: DUFFING UP THE MICKS – 1971-2

After six months at Palace Barracks we were getting used to being in Ulster. By then, we'd gotten our Q squad up and running and we'd also built up a significant level of information, from both informants and surveillance. After another few months, the Major told us that it was time to bring in 'some muscle'.

By this he meant a new section, which he referred to as a 'reaction force'.

'They'll take the war to the enemy,' he said briskly.

There were about eight of them to start with, although this had almost doubled by the end of the year. They were led by a tough looking action-man who held you in his steely gaze as he spoke to you. It was like looking into two shards of flint, and I secretly nicknamed him Stone Eyes.

The new men quickly acquired their own fleet of Q cars, which were modified with armoured panels and all sorts of other innovations in our vehicle workshops. Like us, they grew their hair long and wore civvies most of the time. They were also well tooled up, with their armoury holding not only a wide range of our weapons, but also a selection of guns used by the micks. They seemed to be proficient in all of them, including the Thompson sub-machine gun that was favoured by the IRA.

Stone Eyes was a sergeant and therefore was outranked by Geordie. The Major, though, constantly seemed to give the new man precedence and I could see this was pissing off Geordie big-time. It even seemed to put him on a short fuse at times.

One day, after a new green team regiment had arrived in the barracks, Geordie, along with a bunch of us who were about to leave in our Q cars, bumped into their regimental sergeant major and one of their young officers. The Rupert spluttered that we'd 'refused to salute him' and the RSM looked distastefully at our long hair and civvy attire.

'You're more like fucking gypos than the Queen's soldiers,' he screamed.

The thing is with undercover work, you can't be playing soldier one minute and civvy the next. Like actors, we need to keep in character. Otherwise, we might inadvertently reveal ourselves – and with us, that could get you killed.

All that could have been explained diplomatically, though, but Geordie quickly lost the plot.

'Stop acting like cunts!' he screamed back at the green team's Razz Man and the Rupert.

Thankfully, the Major was quickly on hand to intervene – to keep the peace and calm things down.

At that time, everything in Belfast appeared to be settling down and, as far as I could see, running smoothly. But then the whole situation went haywire again. This time, the fuckwits decided to bring in internment and all the army, including us, were ordered to get involved.

A special area was constructed for us at an old Second World War airfield called Ballykelly, close to Londonderry. The Major, Geordie and I went there a bit before internment took place, to organise ourselves for the busy time ahead. Once there, I was delighted to see my old mate Seth, from my Int training days, once again.

Our orders were to carry out interrogations on a number of

designated prisoners. Using an in-depth variant of the sensory deprivation techniques that we'd been developing for some time. We'd just been teaching the rudiments of this type of interrogation work to some of the local plods – and we knew they'd be joining us to put it into action.

Our selected interrogations, which we called 'Operation Calaba,' were to consist of five techniques. The micks were to be: Hooded, so they could not see; stripped and put into loose fitting boiler suits; deprived of sleep, food and toilet facilities; made to stand for extended periods in a fixed position against a wall; and subjected to a loud and constant whining background noise.

They were then to be interrogated at various times by squads, which were made up of our people and RUC teams from across Ulster. So the policemen would now be able to try out the methods we'd taught them.

'When we get these chappies,' the Major said, 'they might need to be taught some manners.'

'If it's a good duffing up, them prod plods look well up for it,' Geordie said, with a wink. 'If we let them off the leash?'

The green team launched Operation Demetrius in the early hours of August 9th and snatched hundreds of micks from the lists provided by the RUC. Only a few were selected to endure our tender treatment and we put everything in place to give them a great welcome. We requested that they should arrive in boiler suits, already hooded and be scared shitless during their journey.

We all had a good laugh as it started, because the prisoners came in by helicopter and the Major had ordered them to be kicked out, just a couple of yards before landing. With the micks not being able to see, and them thinking they were still high above the earth, they'd all been shitting themselves – till they'd hit the ground. So they were already well fucked in the head before we even got to them.

The truth is, we obtained very little new information, but we did fuck up the minds of a few of them. We needed them to know that there was a price to pay, if they were to get involved with organisations that were against us. We did, of course, rough them up a little, and some of the plods were overly enthusiastic.

As far as we'd been concerned, though, we'd handled them with kid gloves. The micks on the outside, though, organised protests that built to such a pitch, you'd have thought we'd murdered all of them. They also created no-go zones across Ulster, which denied entry of plods and soldiers into hard-line Nationalist areas – and many micks also stopped paying their rent and rates.

'If this was Kenya,' Geordie kept saying, 'we'd have chopped off their goolies – an' we still wouldn't have had aal this fuss.'

In Ulster, though, it was becoming apparent that anything we did would come under scrutiny – and many people would be shouting out about it. There was also a build-up of protests and demonstrations in Catholic areas, where the micks were demanding 'civil rights' and mouthing off against 'internment' and 'torture'.

The green team was then ordered to confront and stop these hostile actions. And, at the start of the next year, a Para unit, who'd been based in Belfast under our top man, were ordered to travel to Londonderry and teach the micks a lesson on their next demonstration. This became known, around the world, as 'Bloody Sunday', when the Paras shot dead a pack of the fuckers.

The march had been declared illegal and the Paras had been told to take no prisoners, so what did they expect? Anyroads, the thing blew up in our faces again. Seth told me that one of his agents was in Londonderry the next day and he'd reported that in the Bogside, 'lines of locals, half-a-mile long, were queuing to join the RA at the Sinn Fein office.'

'Well, at least I'd seen Seth again,' I thought, trying to look on the bright side. When we'd met, he'd put a finger to his head, like a pretend gun and grinned.

'Remember that Ruskie – and Poncy Cunt in training shitting himself,' he'd said, and we'd laughed our cock off all over again.

Although he was also serving in Belfast, his patch was in another part of the city. So, Ballykelly was the first time I'd seen Seth since training. Now we'd re-established contact, though, we agreed to meet up when we could.

Back in Palace Barracks, we all knew that our little area – and us – were now organised into something like we should be.

'We'll need to start coming up with the goods, now,' the Major said.

To this end, we were already running a number of agents, both micks and prods, including some from the various paramilitary groups. We called these agents 'Freds', and set up a special compound inside the barracks for them.

Two of the Freds were PIRA men we'd approached secretly – and who'd agreed to work for us. They gave us a lot of information and were happy to come in for briefings and training. It was all running smoothly and we began to think that we'd struck gold.

We were also working closely with the security services on two operations, intended to trawl for information and sniff out potential informers, which they'd set up. The first was the Four Square Laundry that offered its services around mick estates in west Belfast. The laundry van was fitted with a hidden surveillance platform and all the washing was checked for traces of explosives.

The second was the Gemini Health Studios – a massage parlour, come knocking-shop – which was situated on the Antrim Road. We secretly taped and photographed the clients. So any pussy-hounds, prods or micks, were made welcome, while we recorded their conversations and took pictures of their hanky-panky.

Around that time, the Major said that members of the Catholic Ex-Servicemen's Association were manning many of the illegal car checkpoints in nationalist areas.

'They've had military training,' he said, 'and CESA might be even more troublesome to us, if they were to join up with the PIRA.'

So, he suggested that Stone Eyes and his mates 'should dishearten them,' by going out and 'teaching those chappies a lesson.'

At that time, I was quite happy to have had the security that Stone Eyes and his mates represented – but Geordie was still resentful.

'Fucking gung-ho cowboys,' he muttered to me one day, as we watched them disappear in their Q cars.

I had to admit that Geordie did have a point. I knew they'd been involved in many shooting incidents, where a number of micks had been killed – including some of the CESA ones. Most were drive-byes in mick areas, where no warnings were given.

A few months later things started to go wrong and we realised, too late, that our two PIRA agents had been compromised. We were sitting in our office, when word came in that our laundry van had been attacked in west Belfast, and the driver, one of our men, shot dead. At the same time gun attacks had also been carried out on the Antrim Road massage parlour and another of our premises nearby.

We never saw our two agents again; they just seemed to vanish off the face of the earth. But, we quickly realised that they must have been found out and probably had leaked the info about our laundry and the knocking-shop – and god knows what else – to the PIRA. Later, we learned that they had indeed been picked up and interrogated, then shot dead and buried at some secret location.

CITY-LAND

Wars, conflicts, it's all business.
One murder makes a villain. Millions a hero.
Numbers sanctify.
Charlie Chaplin (1889 – 1977)
Monsieur Verdoux

After a nodded greeting to the armed police, Elsie glanced at Ginge as she entered his room. Both laughed after they muttered: 'Eyup Mi duck,' at exactly the same time.

'He's looking much better,' she thought.

'It will be some time,' she then remembered a doctor saying, 'before he's fully recovered.'

As she'd journeyed into work, Elsie had gone over in her mind Eddie's story of his time in the army, which had shocked her.

'He's had a touch of PTSD,' she thought, 'so conceivably, Ginge might have a hint of it too? After all, if civilians could get it after a car or rail crash, surely soldiers might get it during, and especially after, conflicts.'

Elsie was pleased that the wounded soldier was still doing his logs, although the pace of them had slowed down. Every so often, however, he would slip a completed cassette to her and she would take it home to lodge it in the stash. Sometimes Ginge became restless, through having to lie in bed all the time and Elsie, Kate and Gwendolyn would then encourage him to regularly stretch his arms and move his head and neck muscles.

Kate, who had also just come on shift, joined Elsie.

'I see the hospital cleaners are up in arms,' she said.

Seemingly, they'd got wind that the trust running Mugsfield General was intent on bringing in some outside company to do their work. Some cleaners thought that they might be able to work for the new company, but knew they would have to agree to new rules and conditions. Their union reps had tried to discuss the situation with the hospital administration, but were being snubbed.

The union then produced a leaflet and Alec handed some of them out to the nurses.

'One of the reasons this is happening,' it claimed, 'is that the outside companies will only want to employ non-union workers. So any meaningful discussions between staff and management will be a thing of the past, if they come in.'

'Another reason,' the leaflet added, 'is that, although the cost of cleaning will probably be about the same, or might actually go up, those doing the cleaning will be paid a lot less.'

'Mark my words,' Alec raged, 'if we let them get away with things like this, before long we will all be working for private outfits, and the NHS will be as dead as the dodo.'

Back in Bloodworth, Eddie and Amy started work on the text for their next layout board. Ideas for a theme had come to them at the last commemoration meeting, when Jed and Doris had posed a few questions that the strike and its aftermath had thrown up.

'On a picket line a copper told me once to stop mouthing off,' Jed said, 'saying I were a subject and not a citizen. Were he right? And what does it mean for us?'

'They say we live in a democracy,' Doris stated, 'but after what has happened to us, questions keep coming up about that. So, how is the country run? Who really rules us? How are we ruled?'

'We'll do our best to find out about all that,' Amy said, somewhat alarmed, 'but it might be difficult.'

'Aye, it's a tough one,' Eddie agreed, 'but I think Tony Benn has mentioned issues like this. We'll just have to try and get our teeth into it.'

Later, they then set to work and after a couple of weeks had produced the first draft of their deliberations.

'It's a difficult issue to put your finger on it, but we've done our best,' Eddie said.

'It's not directly about the strike, but it might help explain why the miners lost,' Amy added, as she typed it out:

In most democratic countries the people elect all the houses of their parliaments and their own heads of state. In Britain, we get to elect one house of our parliament, while only those appointed, or with hereditary rights, can occupy the Throne and the Lords.

All MPs, peers, judges, bishops and even soldiers and the police have to swear their allegiance, not to parliament or the people, but to the reigning monarch. The decision to go to war is still a 'Royal Prerogative' and Parliament, never mind the people, does not even have to be consulted. The Prime Minister, who makes the actual decision, is not elected by the public, but is given immense and unaccountable political power.

Control then is concentrated among the few at the top and – when all the paraphernalia of state power is laid bare, including The Crown, the Lords and the Honours List – we can see the important place it has in preserving the status quo. The privileges of the powerful are both guaranteed and protected, while the system subtly ensures that we, 'the lower orders', are all kept in our place.

We were going to start this text with greetings to our fellow citizens.

Then we realised that we couldn't do this, because we are all subjects, not citizens. While this remains so, we will probably continue to lose many of our struggles with the powerful.

At home, after her shift, Elsie remembered that during her last meeting with Eddie he'd mentioned her brother. So she asked Sean about Eddie, to see if he could recall anything of interest about him.

'I saw him at the football, now and again – but it was very rare, him being in the forces and all,' Sean said. 'Then he left the army and came home, and his missus got him a job in the bank. To start with, he worked in one at Nottingham, so he was away a lot of the time. Then he came back, to work at the one here. But there was some kind of bust-up and he and his missus left the bank. I think they then started up their own little business.'

Sean then scratched his head, as if trying to awake his memory.

'He helped us during the strike,' he resumed, 'he was very quiet then, didn't say much, but the lads liked him. They called him 'Steady Eddie,' because he'd always do what he said he'd do. He's a lot more gobby now, I remember bumping into him after the strike and he were saying: 'Arthur was right, all the pits are being shut down and Thatcher's got her way.' Then, he started raging on about that coup in Chile and about the Americans and some crowd called the Chicago Boys. I thought they must be gangsters, or something like that. He laughed when I said that. 'They're that all right, but their ideology is even more ruthless and dangerous,' he said. It were something to do with economics and new ways of running the country, he claimed that the friends of this Chicago lot, in this country, would end up kicking all of us into touch – if we let them?'

'What about Ginge,' Elsie asked. 'Did you know him, or his family?'

'Well, his Dad worked down the pit, of course,' Sean replied, 'till he retired. He died well before the big strike; he didn't join in with the lads much – kept himself to himself. Now your Ginge, we didn't see any of him at all. Well, not till the strike anyhow. It's strange, when you think about it; no sign, then during the strike, there he was down the welfare supping pints and chatting away.'

Elsie then remembered what Eddie had said.

'Did anyone think he was a government spy?' she asked.

Sean raised his eyebrows and looked at her inquiringly.

'Why, have you heard sommat?' he asked.

But Elsie just shook her head.

'Well, we now know there was a lot of that going on,' Sean continued, 'but at the time, he seemed fairly sympathetic to us. We just took that on trust. I think some of the lads had second thoughts afterwards, though.'

His face then took on a pained look.

'It were do or die then,' he muttered, 'to Thatcher and her minions anyway. They knew they'd have to beat us, so they were flinging everything at us. Eddie was right, the bastards got what they wanted in the end.'

LOG 8: GEORDIE THROWS A WOBBLY
– spring 1973

For a while I'd been extremely busy with my workload of recruiting and running informers, while Geordie had been doing other work. So, when I bumped into him early one morning at HQ, I suddenly realised I hadn't talked to him for some time. I could tell, though, that there was something bothering Geordie.

'What's up? – Can I help?' I asked.

But his eyes had zoomed around the office, like a meerkat on lookout duty.

'We canna talk here,' was all he said.

This increased my concern and I mentioned that I'd arranged a meet with an informer in a couple of hour's time.

'I'm about to organise a motor and some back-up,' I said.

I knew Geordie sometimes went out on such operations, so I suggested that this time he could ride shotgun for me – to which he assented.

It had been pretty dismal weather; clammy with an overcast sky and drizzly rain gusting through. 'Dreich,' I remember one of the sweaty socks describing Belfast in weather like this. To cap it all, the radio had said that 'patches of mist were rolling in, around the Lagan,' and I knew this might hinder our vision.

'I've gotten this from the armoury,' Geordie said, holding out a MAC-10 submachine gun, as we met up at the Q car.

I gave the compact weapon a quick once-over.

'You've blagged that from Stone Eyes' arsenal,' I accused, knowing it was made by Ingram in the US and we didn't have one of those in ours.

But Geordie just grinned.

The meet was in a remote run-down area near the docks, which I regarded as neutral and safe. Geordie drove and dropped me off at the rendezvous point, before continuing up the road for about a hundred yards. He then turned around to face me and parked the car in against the pavement – and waited.

About ten minutes later, my informant arrived in his old jalopy and parked opposite me. We'd sorted him out with the motor, to use as a taxi. We'd told him to make connections with local micks, who were suspected of being players – and we'd hoped they'd then start to use him and his car to move men and arms around.

I remember shivering after a cold gust of wind had hit me, as I moved away from the wall I'd been leaning against. I then crossed over the road and walked around the rear of the tout's vehicle, just to make sure that everything looked hunky-dory. As I casually glanced in the back, I noticed a couple of crumpled tissues and what looked like a used johnny, jumbled-up in the opposite corner of the rear seat.

After settling into the passenger front seat, an aroma of stale sweat and after-sex pervaded the air, which reminded me of a back street knocking-shop I'd once frequented in Krautland.

'We get this mick cunt some wheels and he uses it as a shagging-waggon,' I thought, a bit aggrieved.

At the same time, though, I made a mental note to find out who my tout was fucking? Just in case it might prove useful.

He said he'd made progress on the player front, but that he had to be careful. Seemingly, he 'liked his kneecaps the way they were.' I still felt a little resentful, though, about him using the motor for an active love life.

'You'd better come up with something of interest soon,' I snapped, to put a bit of pressure on.

Then, noticing the mist sweeping about us, I glanced up the road and spotted Geordie edging our Q car closer.

'A fookin' peasouper,' I thought, 'that's all we need.'

About half-an-hour later, we'd concluded our business and I'd sent my informer off with a flea in his ear.

After the tout drove away, Geordie steered up a couple of minutes later. He moved the MAC-10 from the front passenger seat so I could jump in. As he repositioned the Ingram on the right-hand edge of his seat, I clocked the machine pistol's suppressor had been fitted.

'Let's drive up the road a bit,' I said, 'and then we can have a natter.'

I'd known Geordie had become somewhat disillusioned, after the Major had brought the heavies in. He seemed to have an aversion to Stone Eyes, which was compounded by the Major increasingly using his new man, rather than Geordie, as his confidant.

'Is that still bothering him?' I pondered.

After we'd parked up a little side road, the mist surged even closer around us and Geordie sat silent for a few minutes. He appeared to be struggling with his thoughts.

'Yee know,' he said, at last, 'I've never said a word against our work here before.'

'Of course, everyone knows that,' I replied, looked him in the eye and nodding.

This seemed to reassure him.

'I just want ter talk to someone I can trust,' Geordie continued, 'I divvent know what's wrong, but I've come across something that looks like complete fucking bollocks.'

He then explained that recently he'd mainly been dealing with issues to do with loyalists, including informers, agents and information gathering. By then, we'd all regarded the prods and ourselves to be on the same side – with the common enemy defined as the micks in general, and the PIRA in particular.

Geordie screwed up his face.

'It's aal very confusing, from as early as the mid-60s there's been loads of loyalist groups, gangs an' individuals an' that!'

He then pulled a bit of paper from a pocket, unfolded it and handed it to me.

It contained a list of proddie groups: 'Ulster Volunteer Force, TARA, Ulster Protestant Volunteers, Ulster Vanguard, Ulster Protestant Action, Shankill Defence Association, Ulster Defence Association, Woodvale Defence Association, Tartan Gangs, Red Hand Commando, Ulster Constitution Defence Committee and Ulster Freedom Fighters.'

He'd made handwritten notes against each name on the list.

Taking the paper back, Geordie then indicated that there were also the Unionist politicians, the Protestant churches and the Orange Order – and all the rest. As a result he was having difficulty trying to follow their various entanglements across the city. Some were intertwined and linked, or merged; others were divided and sometimes bitter enemies.

Geordie had arranged to meet as many of the Unionists and loyalists as he could, because he hoped they might help him build up a clearer picture of them and their movements.

'They aal seemed a bit cautious,' he said, but in the end a few had indicated that they were happy to talk to him.

Geordie said his work had been going well, until two different loyalists drew his attention to a situation that was upsetting them. Both came from east Belfast and claimed that rumours were rife there, that certain of those in charge of the Kincora Boys Home were buggering some of the young lads taken into care. The loyalists had taken their concerns to the RUC, who told them, 'nothing can be done, because the Brits are running that as an operation'.

So, they then requested Geordie's help.

'As we're helping you,' they said, 'can you in return help us to put a stop to this abuse.'

Geordie's first thoughts were that wires must have got crossed somewhere, and that the issue would be easy to sort out. So, he'd contacted some friends in the RUC, but they'd looked at him in astonishment when he'd mentioned it.

'We've been warned off all that, it's your lot who are running Kincora,' they said.

'Who're your lot?' Geordie asked, and was flabbergasted when he was told 'MI5.'

He also was perturbed, knowing it would be difficult to even question the security services.

After thinking about the issue, Geordie then decided to raise Kincora with the Major – in the hope that he might show concern and help to put things right. A couple of days after Geordie had broached the matter, he was called urgently to a meeting at an office in the far corner of the barracks. The Major had opened the door at his knock and, as he entered, Geordie said he'd noticed there was a man in a smart suit, standing in the corner watching him.

The Major then indicated the stranger and introduced him as 'Mr Smith from MI5.'

'He wants to put your mind at rest,' the Major said, 'over that issue you raised.'

The MI5 man then stepped forward and looked intently

into Geordie's eyes.

'We're on a mission here, an orange mission and it's been running like clockwork,' the man said, then turned around and winked at the Major.

After twisting back again, the MI5 man had looked Geordie up and down disdainfully and then jerked a thumb towards the Major.

'Look, your boss said you'd served in Kenya and Cyprus,' he continued, 'so you know how it goes. We need some of the natives on our side – counter-gangs and all that. Well here, Kincora is a key area of interest for us – and we've been running an operation there for quite some time. In our view, it's imperative to our objectives in Ulster that this operation continues and is not impeded in any way, shape or form. Do I make myself clear?'

'Yes sir,' Geordie replied, then waited a few seconds before adding, 'it's just, I didn't realise authorising orphans ter get fucked up the arse is a part of our job?'

Geordie said the MI5 man had glared at him.

'If that is happening and I'm not saying it is, then our mission is far more important than that,' the man said angrily. 'The boys are just flotsam and jetsam off the streets, trash really, and we can't have concerns for them jeopardising our objectives.'

The MI5 man then glanced at the Major.

'You've now heard it from the horse's mouth, so to speak,' the Major said firmly, backing-up Mr Smith. 'We don't want to rile the powers that be. Do we? So, we'll drop our interest in this issue immediately – and that is a direct order!'

Geordie said he'd jumped to attention and saluted.

'Yes sir,' he'd said out loud, and then – 'no sir, three bags full sir' – under his breath, before marching out.

Geordie was now very angry.

'Mr Smith? Operation? – What fucking operation?' he'd thought.

I remembered Geordie's background; of him being brought up in care homes and I could imagine how the MI5 man's words about the boys being 'trash' must have hurt him. He'd known, though, that now there was little chance that he'd be able to do anything about the issue.

I'd been listening intently to Geordie's revelations and was shocked when a man suddenly emerged from the mist that was now surrounding our car. Vision was down to about ten yards, but strangely the man, who'd appeared ahead of us, was moving backwards – and so far, had not seen us. He'd something gripped in his right hand and seemed to be conversing loudly with someone, or something, still hidden in the mist.

In unison, we both clicked our door locks and I eased my Browning out of its shoulder holster as Geordie shifted the Ingram onto his lap. The man then half turned, as if he sensed our presence.

'Dog walker?' Geordie asked softly, his left hand still gripping the MAC-10's suppressor and his right lingering over the trigger. In that same instant I clocked that the object in the man's hand was a scrunched up dog lead.

We saw him stiffen, as he glanced at our motor. He was probably thinking: 'A strange car, with two men in it – paramilitaries? criminals? Or even Brits?' – To him all bad news.

I remember feeling relieved, as a frisky Alsatian quickly emerged from the mist and ran up to the man. He quickly connected the lead to the dog's collar. Then, after rapidly making their way past us, they both disappeared into the fog behind.

We viewed their departure in our wing mirrors and exchanged glances, before I holstered my pistol and Geordie replaced the Ingram at the side of his seat. But we both knew that, although the man was probably just an innocent passer-by, we'd been spotted. Without speaking, Geordie switched on the engine and turned the car around and, after moving onto the main road, travelled a couple of miles.

Parked safely again on another side road, he then turned to me and continued his disclosures. Geordie said that, despite the fact that he knew that he wouldn't now be able to do anything about Kincora, he'd wanted, nonetheless, to put his mind at rest.

'I wanted ter find out what was really happening,' he said.

So, he contacted what he regarded as his best source in the RUC. Geordie explained that this bloke was English and been stationed here as a British soldier.

'He married a local girl an' came back after his stint in the green team an' joined the RUC,' he said.

Geordie's mood now seemed to lighten for a minute.

'It was love,' he said grinning, 'because I know what you're thinking – why would any cunt in his right mind want ter come back ter this shithole?'

'But the girl wouldn't leave,' he continued, 'so he came here ter her.'

'Ah, nice,' I said, and launched into a bit of Elvis, 'love me tender, love me true, and never let me go.'

But Geordie's mood had darkened again.

'Yea, yea, something like that,' he said tetchily.

Geordie said he'd been fairly sure the source could be trusted and when asked about Kincora, he'd immediately replied that the issue was 'off limits, because it was being run by 5.'

'Yea, I know that,' Geordie replied, 'but I'd like ter know

what they are doing, an' why?'

The source had looked uncomfortable and shrugged his shoulders.

'Nobody really knows,' he'd said.

'But there are rumours, aren't there?' Geordie asked, 'I bet a few of your people have ideas about what is happening?'

Geordie said the source had then looked at him for some time, before replying.

'Whatever happens, you didn't get this from me,' he'd then said.

He told Geordie that when the troubles had started, the Ulster Volunteer Force had been one of the first proddie armed organisations to be formed in Belfast, in the early to mid-60s. The operatives were hardline loyalists, but their founders and controllers were high-up Unionists. It was claimed that the objective of the organisation was to 'fight the IRA,' but all its early actions had been aimed at 'bringing down Captain Terence O'Neill,' – a Unionist and then the Northern Ireland PM, who many alleged 'took a soft line on the Fenians.'

About the same time as the UVF emerged, another loyalist organisation, called TARA, was formed in east Belfast. Its main organiser, one of the abusers of the Kincora boys – and therefore open to blackmail – was thought to be a long-term agent of MI5. Besides the main man, there were also others with connections to Kincora, who were doing much the same thing.

TARA itself was continually putting out tracts that outlined ideological reasons for loyalist pre-emptive mobilisations. It also advocated armed actions against the micks. And attacked any hint of compromises, or backsliding, on these issues.

Geordie said the source had then smiled grimly.

'If you put the two things together, anybody would think

that 5 and the high-up Unionists were in cahoots – that they both wanted conflict here,' he'd muttered.

'But why the fuck would they do that?' Geordie had asked.

'Well the answer for loyalists and Unionists is very simple – they're fuck'n paranoid,' the source said. 'They think they have been fighting for their survival ever since Partition; that they are just hanging on; that someone is just about to sell them out; that every situation is doomsday.'

Geordie told me this had reminded him of Kenya: 'A lot of the whites out there were over the edge too,' he'd said.

'But the security services?' The source had then questioned, shaking his head. 'That's harder to answer. But I'm sure our lot wanted a fight here too. It probably started off with that counter-gang stuff; like the top Unionists, they wanted the loyalist groups that emerged to be their creatures. Like Victor Frankenstein, however, they're finding out it's difficult to control a monster.'

Geordie said that he'd been trying hard to take all this in, so he'd remained silent and after a time the source had resumed.

'But it's not just 5 and you Int boys – it's also the ordinary squaddies. Before the Falls Curfew we estimated that there were about 60 men active in PIRA, six months later there were about 800. Some of that was down to them, but mostly it was down to what the army did.'

The source spluttered and then coughed loudly.

'As if his throat was drying up,' Geordie told me.

'And that went on and on,' the source had croaked, 'after Internment, Bloody Sunday and Operation Motorman the conflict intensified and PIRA just grew and grew. Why did our lot do it? Search me, but I know that if anyone asked me who built the PIRA? I'd say the micks did, but their recruiting sergeant was the British Army.'

Geordie said the RUC man had clearly been angry about what had happened, and thought it was so unnecessary. The source had then glanced around nervously.

'There are rumours about the Brits playing the Orange card again,' he'd whispered, 'its supposed to be very hush-hush, something about activate and clockwork – and it might have something to do with this.'

Geordie said his mind had immediately clicked back to the first words the MI5 man had said to him, and angrily wondered if 'Mr Smith' had been playing games with him.

The source then went on to tell Geordie that he admitted there would have been conflict in Northern Ireland anyway, because of the 'civil rights thing' and that 'PIRA were definitely up for a fight' too. He'd claimed, though, that it could have been little more than a bigger rerun of the border campaign of a decade before. Then the IRA had fought, but the Security Forces had contained it by low-key actions.

Most Nationalists had therefore kept out of it, so the conflict had been confined to the IRA hard-core. Subsequently, it'd remained small scale and then fizzled out.

'But why, this time around, is the army acting so provocatively?' The source queried. 'By sending our lot into the Nationalist areas to do it, they were asking for a fight – and then they got it.'

I could see that Geordie was still angry with these issues. Although, he admitted he had difficulty getting his head around some of the stuff that his source had talked about. But the abuse of the boys at Kincora was something that was clearly getting on his wick, especially the fact that it was being allowed to continue to fulfil some secret agenda.

After our morning, with all that had happened, we were both feeling a bit shagged-out. So, in need of refreshment,

Geordie drove us to the KAI Arms, a prod pub in east Belfast, which he reckoned was safe for us to use.

'I used it during my sessions with the loyalists,' he said. 'They have strippers on Friday nights,' he added, grinning.

We each ordered a pint and a big Ulster Fry, which we scoffed in a discreet side bar. We had another pint for afters and it was then that Geordie told me something that left me gobsmacked.

'I might well pack it aal in,' he said, 'I've done my stretch and now an' again I find the memories come crowding up.'

When I tried to placate him, he started to tell me about a time in the boys homes in the northeast, when 'kiddy-fiddlers' had been around.

'I'd stolen a knife from the kitchen,' he whispered, 'so they didn't bother me – well not after I stuck one of the bastards anyhow. After that they couldn't get rid of me fast enough, that's how I got into the army very young.'

Geordie then clammed up about all that.

Instead, he started to tell me about a time in Kenya, when he and a few others had been systematically interrogating Mau Mau detainees in one of the prison camps. They'd been trying to get the prisoners to confess that they'd taken the Mau Mau oath – and then to repudiate it and their allegiance to the movement.

'Some were so stubborn we'd spend all day beating the shit out of them,' Geordie said. 'Sometimes, we went ter our pits at night after spending hours washing the blood out of our clothes an' bathing our bruised hands. Anyhow, one day we were giving this coon a right good duffing up, when one of my mates said that at least the prisoner was better looking than me. Another mate then asked: 'Was that before, or after, we'd smashed his pan in?' We aal burst out laughing, except for the one who'd been battering him the hardest. He just stopped hitting him; started crying, an' then shouted out 'stop, stop, just stop'.'

Geordie then looked at me and shrugged his shoulders.

'Others dragged him away an' later on I went ter see him, with a bottle of whiskey, thinking we might get rid of his tensions with a piss-up,' he said. 'But the thing was, he'd still been like a spare prick at a wedding. He wasn't able ter carry on, the doubts had entered his mind an' he couldn't get rid of them. He told me: 'The Mau Mau are better men than we are – they believe in a cause an' we don't'.'

Geordie rolled his eyes and then was silent for a bit.

'Silly cunt, we sent him home,' he then muttered, 'he wasn't any fucking use ter us anymore. He was gone by the time I got back ter Blighty, they probable fucked the cunt off ter the Andy Capp's Commandos – or something.'

Geordie then glanced at me and I'm sure he saw the concern on my face.

'Don't worry, I'm not going to break down,' he said, 'but now I've some doubts, I divvent want ter be the one throwing a wobbly in the future. So, it's probably time I was put out ter grass in Civvy Street.'

POWER-LAND

Government, even in its best state,
is but a necessary evil;
in its worst state, an intolerable one.
Thomas Paine (1737 – 1809)
Common Sense

Set into the wall of an alcove, in a passageway near to the staff entrance of Mugsfield General, were situated the pigeonholes that contained the instructions and messages for the personnel. These now included a new magazine, which managers said was required reading for the entire workforce. So, for months now Kate, Elsie, Gwendolyn and Alec had been receiving copies of the *Health Service Beat*.

Dotted around the news of NHS changes, the publication carried articles exhorting free enterprise and acclaiming the market. All the staff were urged to meet their snowballing lists of targets and also specified were the rising number of rules and regulations. This was all written with an increasing use of management-speak gobbledygook.

True to form, Alec quickly registered his disapproval about the new journal, and especially with the jargon used.

'I can't understand it – it's written in a foreign language,' he said to puzzled looks.

'Which one?' Kate asked, scathingly.

'Bollocks,' he replied.

Most nurses were more circumspect, but on its day of issue

the litter bin, just along the passageway from the pigeonholes, quickly filled with unread copies of the publication. Anyone aspiring to higher positions, however, found it expedient to read the journal and parrot the key words of the new ideology. While this pleased the managers, Alec called these wannabes 'bloodeh arse-lickers,' behind their backs.

The bomb victim was still a cause of great concern and the nurses kept encouraging Ginge to adopt a regular set of exercises for his arms and upper body. Sometimes the soldier was receptive to the idea, at other times he wasn't.

'Fuck off, I can't be bothered,' he'd sometimes snap.

On the days when the soldier's pessimism spilled over, Elsie tried to encourage him to shake it off.

'If you exercise, it could help the feelings return to your legs,' she told him. 'It will also make it easier to bring them back into use.'

'It might also help to stave off negative feelings, and perhaps depression,' she thought.

When they were on their own, Elsie also encouraged Ginge to continue with his logs, because she knew that mental stimulation was just as important as physical exercise.

'I'm also still dying to know what is in them,' she confessed to herself.

On her next visit to Amy and Eddie, Elsie found them poring over their photos and other images of the strike.

'That's Jed,' Amy said, pointing to a picture, 'he's been a big help with our layout boards.'

Elsie could see a picket line of strikers, among whom – indicated by Amy's finger – was a tough looking little man, with greyish hair. He was thrusting his face upwards to confront a tall policeman, who was trying to hold back the strikers.

'And that's Doris,' said Eddie, handing over another photo, in which a rather stout women, with short frizzy brown hair, was handing out sandwiches to a picket line.

'She's a handful that one,' Eddie added, 'our little barrel of dynamite.'

'I'd like to see you call her a barrel to her face,' Amy said laughing, 'she'd slaughter you for that one.'

Elsie found the images interesting and they did evoke in her memories of the strike, but she was determined to find out more about the couple's time in the bank.

'How come, after the army, you chose banking for a job?' she asked Eddie.

'Well, Amy was working in the bank, when I left the army,' he replied, 'and, knowing that I didn't want to go down the pit, she asked the bank to take me on.'

'The bank was different then,' Amy chipped in, 'before they were taking over by the big boys. You could talk to the branch manager, and if you'd a reasonable request, he would help you. I'd told him about Eddie and he said he would see what he could do. He got him in, although it were in a branch in Nottingham, to start with.'

Eddie glanced at Amy and smiled.

'Yea, it went well to start with,' he said. 'I'd gone back to college in the evenings and after a couple of years I got my certificates and moved from counter-clerk to advisor. It were good. Of course, you were selling the bank's products, but we were told to advise the punters and to also help them choose the product that most suited their circumstances. We felt we were doing a good job, both for the bank and the customer.'

'Then an adviser's job came up at the bank here,' Amy said, 'that Eddie went for and he got it. We were both then in the same place, and he was home. It was great for a while.'

Eddie sighed and his face took on a troubled look.

'It were a bit before the pit strike, when the bank was taken over by some financial big boys, that everything went arse about face,' he said.

'Why?' Elsie asked, taking in the distressed look on both their faces.

'Well, it started after the takeover, although it went fairly slowly for a bit,' Eddie replied. 'We'd gradually been getting new rules, instructions and directions to go in. Then, before we knew it, we were swamped in them. And it were all couched in gibberish, wrapped up in bullshit – it fair did your head in.'

'Sounds a bit like us, at the NHS,' Elsie said, and Eddie and Amy both nodded.

'Were you forced to leave the bank?' Elsie asked.

'It started when I went on this course,' Eddie replied. 'They were saying we had to sell more products, but I explained that we always looked at our customers background and needs. So we'd have a few meetings with them, before we recommended an account that seemed appropriate for them.'

Eddie shook his head.

'They looked at me as if I was mad,' he continued. 'They then said to me: 'we don't give a shit if it suits them, or not. Just sell them the products, any products – and if you want to treat them as if they're your friends, you're no good to us'.'

Amy, who'd been listening intently, then cut in.

'I went through something similar,' she said, 'so we both were thinking of going then.'

'Especially, when we knew they were gunning for us anyway,' Eddie murmured. 'I learned that Amy and me had been put on a redundancy list, although we never asked for it. The friend who told us said: 'Once you're on their list, they will get rid of you sooner or later'.'

'So we just took their money and ran,' Amy added.

'The funny thing is,' Eddie muttered, 'we thought all of this was just something out of step – an aberration or something. But then we realised it weren't just the bank, it were happening everywhere.'

'Is that why you helped the miners during the strike?' Elsie asked.

'Well, both our dads were out, so we wanted to help anyway,' Amy said.

'It's funny,' Eddie said, 'I left for the army because I didn't want to be a miner. But I still knew we had to support them, when the pits were threatened by closure and they went on strike.'

'We also started to look at where all of this free-market stuff was coming from,' Amy said. 'The thing is – it were always there, but in the background – covered over. Then it just took off and were starting to be imposed everywhere. You'd have to be a mug not to think it weren't planned – and that somebody, or something, weren't pushing it.'

LOG 9: THE HUSH PUPPY – autumn 1973

Throughout this period, we'd been busy passing on our interrogation techniques to the green teams and the plods. From time to time, though, we were still required to give some micks the third degree. Especially if they'd been arrested for serious offences and a confession was needed to put one away for a long time.

I remember harbouring hopes that I'd be able to persuade Geordie to stay on. And feeling happy, therefore, when the Major said that both of us were required to do some work together on a mick prisoner.

'No blood, no marks, but anything else is okay,' the Major said.

'It's jobs like this,' I thought, 'that are helping us to keep our hand in.'

Now, in the past, on a few occasions like this, we'd used a bit of electrics. Nothing drastic, but it'd sometimes caused a bit of a hullabaloo. But this time, when we asked, the Major said that electricity was out.

'In case those do-gooder chappies complain again,' he added.

'What about waterworks?' Geordie queried.

The Major hesitated, before reckoning that a bit of that would probably be okay.

I remembered a story that Geordie had told me once about Cyprus, when he'd tried to teach a Jock unit how to administer the water-treatment. As he'd been instructing them, a Jock, out on patrol, was shot in a street ambush. A little later, a Greek suspect had been dragged in and beaten to a pulp.

Geordie intervened to save his life, because he thought the prisoner might have some useful information.

'Try some waterboarding,' he'd said to the Jocks, 'like I've just taught you.'

Geordie described how he'd then stood back, as the Jocks had spread-eagled the prisoner on his back on the floor, with soldiers tightly holding his arms and legs.

After throwing a minging old towel over his face, a file of soldiers then surged forward and stood in a circle around the prisoner's head.

'The Jocks then undid their flies,' Geordie told me, 'and pulled out their pricks and started pissing on the cloth over the prisoner's face.'

When he described it, Geordie had started chuckling.

'One little runt of a Jock took out an enormous cock an' let fly,' he said – then added, in a mock Jock accent, that the soldier had been yelling: "droon in ma pish ya wog cunt'.'

With some difficulty, Geordie had managed to rescue the Greek again and take him back to the prison camp.

'We got quite a bit out of him,' Geordie said, 'because every time he kept stumm, I threatened ter send him back to the Jocks – an' he'd then sing like a canary.'

Now, with the mick, all we needed was a confession and we travelled to the green team unit's fort to get it. Soldiers had already roughed the captive up and we told them to tie him, face upwards, firmly on a table. Geordie then got the soldiers to prop-up the legs of the table on one end, so the captive's head was lower than his body.

'A fucker drowned on me once, I got a right bollocking,'

Geordie explained. 'They were angry I'd not gotten anything out of the cunt first.'

He wet a large cloth and placed it tightly over the prisoners face and we slowly poured water from a bucket over the material. The mick started coughing and choking, but we only stopped when we felt the prisoner was about to breathe his last. Then we let him rest for a minute or so, before continuing pouring again.

After a bit, I jokingly asked Geordie if we should get our plonkers out and piss on the cunt – and he grinned back.

'Na, we're civilised, we're no sweaty socks,' he said.

After the session, the mick would have signed anything, which showed how effective the treatment was. We then handed him over to the plods to get his signature for the confession.

That was the last time Geordie and I worked together. True to his word he refused to sign on for another spell. He was still angry about things like Kincora and I consoled myself with the thought that it was probably for the best that Geordie got out.

After all, while the green team lads did specific tours of duty, we'd few breathers and seemed to be in Ulster continuously.

'Perhaps, we all need a break?' I thought.

Round about the time Geordie had left for good, Stone Eyes also disappeared for several months. It was just after the coup in Chile, when General Pinochet seized power. And the rumour was that Stone Eyes had gone to the US to do a course with the Yanks at Fort Benning in Georgia.

A short while after he reappeared, I bumped into him and he chatted away in a friendly manner.

'I've just been in the States,' he told me, 'the School of the Americas, with the Yank Special Forces and other similar outfits from South American countries.'

Seemingly, at the end of his course, some of the Yanks had invited him to join one of their Condor teams, who were just off to Chile.

'It was just after that red cunt, Allende, got his,' Stone Eyes said, 'and the boss gave me permission, as it was only for a short while.'

Stone Eyes then delved inside his jacket and snatched out a handgun, which he thrust into my hand.

'It was cushtie – I helped them in Chile with their commie problem, and they gave me this,' he said proudly.

As I examined the pistol he explained that it was a steel-framed Smith & Wesson, Model-39 Mk 22 Mod 0, which had been produced for use in South-East Asia.

The handgun, which had a modified suppressor with a side lock to minimize firing noise, was used during Project Phoenix to bump off tens of thousands of commies, who were on CIA death lists.

'It's a stonking shooter,' he said, 'I'm gonna use it instead of my Browning, the Yanks call it a Hush Puppy.'

'Why'd they call it that?' I asked laughing.

'Officially, it was supposed to be used for shooting guard dogs,' he replied beaming, 'but really they killed a loads of gooks in Vietnam and reds in Chile with it.'

Grasping the gun back, his gaze bored into my eyes.

'I intend to add to its quota here,' he said.

Stone Eyes went on to tell me about the elimination of lefties in Chile after their interrogations. Many were drugged and flown by helicopter over the sea, then stripped naked and thrown out. He also told me about two young women he'd seen dealt with in this way. Before they were pushed out of the helicopter a razor-sharp knife had been used to disembowel them, which ensured they would sink immediately and their bodies would never be found.

Stone Eyes was grinning as he recalled it.

'The red bitches were gutted from their quims to breakfast time,' he said.

I'd thought of myself as pretty thick-skinned, but his words made me feel a bit uneasy.

'Was Chile anything to do with us?' I couldn't help thinking.

Obviously, though, he thought it was.

In some ways, with Geordie now gone, I felt safe and glad to have Stone Eyes as a friend. Even if I was somewhat disconcerted at times, about some of the things he'd say, or do.

Anyroads, I was only bumping into him now and again, as our work normally took us in different directions. I found that I was having a bit of success in procuring informers – and in obtaining useful information from them. So, under the Major's orders, my job was to concentrate on that and the odd interrogation from time to time.

I couldn't help remembering, though, that once before Stone Eyes had told me the way he felt about our job in Belfast.

'We're the fuck'n wolves, who'll descend from our lair onto the city and rip the scum apart,' he said.

He'd then taken in the quizzical look on my face.

'Kill the mick fuckers, it's all them cunts understand,' he added for effect.

'Well, for sure,' I thought, 'he and his men are certainly up for that.'

PTSD-LAND

The evil that men do lives after them;
The good is oft interred with their bones.
William Shakespeare (1564 – 1616)
Julius Caesar

When Eddie had left the army after Aden, Amy realised that he was in many ways different from the way he'd been before. He did peculiar things, appeared distant and would sometimes disappear for days. It was almost as if he was living in another dimension – a world of his own. He clearly saw it, however, as the real one.

In bed Eddie's sleep was frequently disrupted by nightmares, during which he would often thrash about and kick or lash out. After Amy had been struck for a third time, they decided, for her protection, to sleep in separate beds. When Eddie later sought solace in drink, Amy recognised that his behaviour was beginning to prove a threat to their marriage.

Before they'd talked and laughed together, now he sometimes did not speak for days and appeared surly and withdrawn. At the slightest provocation, his anger could quickly rise. Once, after Eddie punched another man who had accidently bumped into him, Amy had felt at the end of her tether.

'Sort yourself out, or I'm off,' she'd raged later.

He'd apologised, but his manner did not change for long. And then, when he kept disappearing, Amy couldn't help wondering if he was seeing another women.

So, as a last resort, Amy decided to try to find out what was wrong and endeavour to fix it. This proved easier said than done, as she received little help from the army, MoD or a host of ex-forces organisations. A man from one of the latter groups had glowered angrily at Amy.

'What's the matter with you fuckers?' he'd said. 'Look, some of the lads throw a wobbly when they return from combat – so frigin what? Just give your man a bottle of whiskey and let him ger on with it.'

Needless to say, she did not comply.

In the end Amy got the help she and Eddie needed from the US, when she wrote a letter to a Vietnam Veterans group, outlining Eddie's behaviour and asking for help.

'Lots of our boys have a touch of this,' they responded in their return letter.

They also included a pack of information about post-traumatic stress disorder, outlining how, while it might be difficult to shake off the condition, you could learn to live with it.

At first, Eddie still refused to believe there was anything wrong, and strongly resisted any suggestion that he could be suffering from a psychological condition.

'I haven't gone fookin' mental,' he'd shout.

The doctors in Civvy Street also proved of little help, mainly because they knew little concerning the condition – and especially about how it might affect a veteran soldier.

One item in the pack sent by the Vietnam Veterans, however, proved to be decisive. It was a copy of a page, taken from Shakespeare's Henry IV, Part One. In it, Lady Percy, in Act II, Scene III, had expressed concern about her warrior husband Harry Hotspur, especially his troubled sleep.

Shakespeare's words had her saying she was: 'A banish'd

woman from my Harry's bed.'

'Just like me,' Amy muttered, when she saw it.

After managing to get Eddie to read it, Amy saw the first inklings that he was now starting to understand.

'My god, it goes back to then – and Shakespeare knew about it,' he whispered.

Later on that day, Eddie had turned to Amy.

'That's it,' he said, 'now I'm starting to see what you're on about.'

Eddie and Amy then set to and read all the other papers in the pack and afterwards discussed their newfound understanding and all the things they had learned.

'Perhaps, your PTSD will never go away totally,' Amy said, 'but now we have some understanding of it, we must learn how to live with it.'

Over time they gradually found their own way to handle Eddie's condition. Although he did have relapses from time to time, often triggered by incidents from the conflict in Northern Ireland, or later the Falklands. But working together the couple found they could overcome these setbacks and gradually get the veteran back onto the straight and narrow.

Now, over two decades later, the couple found it somewhat therapeutic to work on the layout boards for the forthcoming strike commemoration. It was also forcing them to face facts about the wider issues in society, which came trickling out as they tried to uncover the background to the struggle around the pits.

'Look, the photos, cuttings and that will evoke the memory of the strike,' Amy said, 'so, what we say should reflect the history and politics – especially the hidden bits.'

'Rather than just say things that's been said loads of times before, or list the happenings,' Eddie said in agreement.

The couple felt there was a connection between the Falkland's war and the miners' strike two years later. They knew that Thatcher and her government had been very unpopular before the conflict in the south Atlantic, but afterwards, the victory had transformed her reputation and destiny. So, they decided to look at that and make it the focus for the text on their next board:

At the end of the Falklands War, our victorious troops were welcomed back by vast crowds in Britain. Behind their backs, however, a revolution was about to take place. As they waved their Union Jacks and cheered the soldiers and Mrs Thatcher, the population were not to know that the 'Iron Lady' would use her new popularity to overturn the gains made for all working people in the post Second World-War period.
The defeat of the miners, and then the ascent, under Thatcher, of the new monetary-driven global capitalism, amounted to a right-wing coup d'état; though one undertaken politically, within capitalism, with stealth and obscured by distractions – the greatest of which were the conflicts in Northern Ireland and the Falklands.
The immediate casualties of those wars lie in graves in both those areas. However, many more people, throughout the world, were destined to become the economic and political victims of the new neoliberal dogma.
In addition to finance capital, the winners of this victory for pure capitalism are the giant corporations and banks and those who own and control them; especially the ten-per-cent at the top – and even more specifically – the one-per-cent of the ten-per-cent – at the very top.
THE MINERS ARE AMONG THE LOSERS

In Mugsfield General, for some time now, Elsie had noticed that Kate was flirting with Jack, one of the MoD cops, who was guarding their bomb victim patient. Thinking an affair might now be in progress, Elsie thought it prudent to have a word in Kate's ear.

'Ginge has a couple of friends in Bloodworth,' she said, 'and they've told me that when they tried to visit, the police refused them entry to his room.'

As Elsie hoped, Kate offered to ask her cop why Amy and Eddie had been stopped. A few days later, Kate came up with the goods.

'Only those on an approved list are allowed to visit Ginge,' she whispered, 'my Jack told me this in the strictest confidence, mind.'

Elsie smiled. 'Thanks, now we know,' she said.

'If you want to know something,' she was thinking, 'they always say pillow talk is a sure way.'

'The order came from the Major himself,' Kate had also divulged.

'So, that's the man I've seen visiting Ginge,' Elsie thought.

She was glad to hear it confirmed, that the wounded soldier had not stopped Eddie and Amy from visiting him.

'The cops are protecting Ginge, but he is their prisoner too,' Elsie reasoned, nodding in recognition of what she had suspected for some time.

The next day, on the A&E ward, the nurses learned that Alec, the porter, was in hot water again. Roger, one of the top hospital managers, was leaving and Alec had been overheard saying discourteous thing about him.

When he was hauled up before his manager, Alec cursed the unknown 'bloodeh tout' under his breath. But he knew his job was on the line, so resorted to a bit of pleading.

'Someone must have heard me wrong,' he claimed, 'in fact, I swear I'd been praising Roger.'

'In that case you can write an article for the magazine,' the manager had told him, 'for Roger's leaving, saying what a good chap he is.'

When news of this leaked out, it led to a good bit of piss-taking from the nurses.

'You gonna start brown-nosing the management now?' Kate asked Alec.

To the porter's further discomfort, the article, which appeared in the next edition of the *National Health Beat*, was eagerly looked forward to.

Many of the staff, therefore, made sure they read it: 'We all now know every really great manager has to finish one day, so, before he goes, I would like to list some of Roger's qualities. Teacher, observer, scholar, scribe, ebullient, rocksteady, these are just a few of the things that we will remember him for.'

Alec, who had a reputation for dishing out the verbal's, now came in for lots of banter himself. Being called 'Sell out,' 'brownnose' – and even 'boss's batty bwoy' by Gwendolyn, augmenting her Jamaican accent.

Taking it all in good part, but anxious to regain his good name, Alec later edged up to Elsie, Gwendolyn and Kate.

'Look, I don't give a continental fuck what the rest think of me,' he whispered, 'but I do care about you lot. So please circle the first letter in the first six words of each sentence, because that's what I really think of that prick.'

The nurses had to go back to the bin to retrieve a copy of the journal and roared with laughter as they circled the letters and 'wanker' and 'tosser' leapt out at them.

LOG 10: PARANOIA & PSY-OPS – 1974

The Major had been missing from Belfast for a while and a rumour went around that he'd been posted. I didn't believe it and Stone Eyes had just laughed, when I'd mentioned it.

'The boss is setting it up, just in case,' he said, with a grin.

'Setting what up?' I queried.

'Chile comes to Blighty,' he muttered, passing over a copy of the *Daily Telegraph*.

'Troops and Police ring Heathrow,' the headlines cried.

'Under Military Assistance to the Civil Power a joint exercise is taking place around London's main airport,' the article stated, 'some of the soldiers are deployed in armoured vehicles.'

'MACP – it's just like us here,' Stone Eyes said. "It will keep that Wilson chappie on his toes,' the boss told me – he's doing liaison, between our green team lot and the plods.'

As I run those times through my mind, I remember that this had been a strange period for us, when suspicion and mistrust had seemed to hang heavily in the air. There'd been a bit of paranoia in the sixties too, but that had been the Cold War – about external enemies. Now, it seemed to be a great deal worse, with whispers and mutterings about a commie takeover in Britain itself.

We'd even got a little touch of it in Belfast from time to time. After Geordie left, I'd often had a drink with another of my oppos, who, like me, was running a team of mick informants.

To put it bluntly, he was an ugly looking cunt – and on the sly I'd tagged him 'Shagnasty'.

'I've done a bit of boxing in the past,' he once told me.

I kept this opinion to myself, mind, but I didn't think he could have been very good, because his nose was twisted to one side and his face looked like a piece of tin-plate hammered into shape.

Anyroads, during a drinking session in the camp one night, Shagnasty whispered to me about a job he'd done recently.

'I was ordered to sort out a Q car and ride shotgun for some bloke around the city,' he said.

He then ascertained that the man was 'a psy-ops type geezer' from the Army Headquarters at Thiepval Barracks, Lisburn, and was travelling about Belfast briefing journalists.

'Probably just HQ giving them the Brit point of view,' he'd thought.

Then the man had asked him to stop outside a newsagent, so he could hop out and buy a few papers. Shagnasty said he'd then had a quick dekko at one of the briefing papers, which the man had left on the passenger seat as he'd got out.

'What'd it say?' I asked, 'anything interesting?'

'That's the thing,' he whispered back, 'it weren't saying anything about us, it were going on about Heath and Wilson, saying all kinds of things about them.'

I can't say I had much interest in any of the fuckwits, but these two pricks kept swopping over as prime minister.

'Yea, what?' I then asked, half bored, half interested.

'It were saying that Heath was a poof – and Wilson was a Soviet agent being run from Moscow,' he said.

'You cunt, you're pulling my plonker,' I replied, sure he was having me on.

But, he swore blind it was true.

'For fucks sake,' I said, 'these are our prime ministers. What the fuck was that cunt doing?'

Shagnasty just grinned and shrugged his shoulders.

'Fuck knows?' he said, 'but it's your round. Just get the pints in, you tightwad.'

In the main, as far as our own little conflict in Ulster was concerned, things were in deadlock. We were filling the prisons with micks, but the PIRA just went out and recruited others to take their place. They'd do bombings and shootings and claim they'd force us out soon, while we dug in and extended our strongholds and surveillance networks.

After Operation Motorman the green team now had a network of forts and on-going patrols in all Nationalist areas, while we were just as busy collecting intelligence and doing the undercover work. And at Westminster, the fuckwits claimed that we were 'beating the men of violence.' The truth was that while we were becoming more entrenched and tightening the grip of our occupation, the micks were becoming better terrorists, killing more and more of our lot.

On the mainland, at the start of the year, the Tory government, with Edward Heath as PM, had been in power. But he was constantly fighting running battles with the unions – especially the miners.

'The reds in the trade unions are outta fuck'n control,' I heard Stone Eyes saying, 'and the cunts need to be taught a lesson.'

Heath, under pressure from the unions who were working three day weeks, then instigated the 'who rules Britain' election.

Labour narrowly won and the new PM, Harold Wilson, immediately made an accord with the miners and gave them a big pay rise. All that incensed some of our lot even more.

'Wilson is a commie,' the Major said angrily, claiming he

had this 'on good account – from his friends.'

'Who are your friends?' I remember wondering. 'And do they include that psy-ops type geezer, that Shagnasty mentioned?'

The previous year, I'd thought things might be looking up in Ulster, when Heath and the Tory fuckwits had appeared to be doing some good work at last. They'd produced the Sunningdale Agreement that promised a power-sharing solution. Extreme Unionists and loyalists, though, opposed it – and tried to bring it down.

Initially, our orders were to support this accord, but that was all to change after Labour and Wilson got elected. Suddenly some green team units began to covertly help the loyalists rather than oppose them – and, I'm sorry to say, the security services and some of our people went even further. It's more than my life's worth to tell about it in detail, but I will say that we became partners with some in the UVF and the UDA. We not only turned a blind eye to their actions, but also often actively encouraged them.

I also gathered, through the grapevine, that an MI5 run agent had brought in a weapons shipment from Holland to arm the loyalists.

'I bet that's one of the buggers from Kincora,' I remember thinking.

I knew, though, that often the weapons used by loyalists came via their friends in the UDR and RUC. And, under the counter, we also were giving them a hand with information, targeting, assassinations and bombings. We even instigated a few actions ourselves and galvanised the loyalists to carry them out.

I then heard whispers that sometimes these extended over the border and even down to Dublin – to warn the micks in the south to stop their meddling in Ulster. The word was that the loyalists did the jobs, but we provided the bombs and facilitated the planning and planting of them. It'd even got to the level where we issued 'out of bounds' notices to the green teams and RUC, to keep their patrols away from areas of loyalist actions that we had approved.

All in all, it put enormous pressure on the Sunningdale Agreement, so, in the end, the accord was fucked and Wilson made to look a twat. Peace was off the agenda again, and the micks and us got on with the conflict. The Major and Stone Eyes appeared to be delighted, but I just carried on with the job and shrugged off any feelings of regret.

There had also been a turf war going on between MI5 and MI6, about who should be running agents and have jurisdiction in Ulster. We were sheltered from this to some degree, because we were already in 5's stable – and, anyroads, the Major appeared to be on good terms with both of them. But in other places, MI5 was gradually taking over and didn't seem to be too worried about how they did it.

Tragically, some of our informers and agents got exposed and burnt in the process. I heard the sad news about Seth late one afternoon and I went back to my bunk and got rat-arsed on whiskey. He'd been liaising with MI6 and running agents with them, when MI5 started muscling in. As a result some of his informers were compromised and, subsequently, punished by the PIRA.

Seth must have felt that he was – at least in part – to blame, because he took his revolver and went to his bunk and shot himself. It was all swept under the carpet, and we were all ordered not to speak of it. They even gave him a gong, but I think that was just a part of the cover-up.

At the time I tried to put thoughts of Seth out of my mind.

So, the next evening, I went down to the docks in my Q car and picked up a whore and fucked her silly. It was a stupid thing to do and could have got me killed, but I kept it to myself and, thankfully, none of my lot twigged it.

It was a sad and crazy – fookin' crazy – time. You just had to keep your head down and try to endure. A few days later, I fucked up again, because I'd been scratching at my long hair and I guess I just got pissed off with it.

'Fuck it,' I thought, and I went to the camp barber and got a number one.

I asked him to leave enough, though, so I had a fair amount of stubble all over. My reckoning was that there were quite a few fellows hanging around in the baddies' areas with skinhead hairstyles. So, in my civvies, I thought I'd still fit in and pass as a local.

The Major wasn't best pleased, though, and I had to admit that my head's thick covering of ginger fuzz gave me a rather unusual appearance. He gave me a right bollocking and the other lads had a good laugh at my expense. Then Stone Eyes crept up behind me and laid a hand on my noggin.

'My girls a ginger too,' he smirked, stroking my head. 'Last leave, I persuaded her to get her bush trimmed. Your hair reminds me of her minge – lovely jubbly.'

After that, for a bit, I was called 'Ginge the minge' by all my mates – the bastards. So that was my last short haircut for a while.

Back in Blighty, Wilson survived the fall of Sunningdale and even went on to win another election later in the year. This seemed to incense some of our lot even more.

'It's time for a cleansing of the Westminster stable,' the Major muttered.

'Don't worry, everything will be cushtie boss,' Stone Eyes

promised, 'when that commie cunt gets his!'

It was just about then that, out of the blue, I got a call from Geordie. He was enjoying his retirement he said, but then hurriedly told me that he'd heard that at hush-hush meetings in Britain, top people were cheering and clapping after being told 'that a period of military rule might be needed to sort out the nation'.

'Is anything like that happening in Belfast?' he then asked me.

'Nothing that I've heard of,' I said, and then I remembered Shagnasty's disclosure about the psy-ops type bloke.

'But I've heard,' I blurted out, 'that a section of our lot over here is secretly putting out information attacking Wilson and Heath.'

'Operation fucking Orange,' Geordie muttered disgustedly.

I was intrigued that he was still taking an interest in all of this. But Geordie was now free to show concern; I had to be a lot more careful. You could easily get yourself killed, if you made a mistake in our line of work. You have to be alert at all times and keep your eyes open – and I didn't want to have to be looking over my shoulder too.

Anyroads, I didn't know what to make of it all. Besides, I wasn't political, I'd never voted in my life. I just knew about my work and concentrated on keeping myself safe.

'Perhaps for my own sanity, though,' I thought, 'I should know a little of what is happening.'

So, on my next leave I made contact with Geordie and arranged to meet him. While he'd been serving, his wife had always stayed in England, whereas he'd often been abroad – so I'd never met her. It was the same now, as Geordie would only meet me in a pub well away from his home.

'He's always liked a drink,' I thought, 'but now he's supping like a full-blown piss artist.'

As we sat there downing pints, I quickly brought him up to date with the recent events in Belfast.

'Look, don't get me wrong,' he said, 'I hate that cunt Wilson, but it's the same pricks, who're running Kincora, that are trying ter fuck him up the arse too.'

Geordie then told me about an old intelligence acquaintance that'd contacted him out of the blue a few months ago.

'We worked tergether once or twice in the past,' Geordie said, 'and the cunt always fancied himself as James Bond.'

This ex-Int man was now in Civvy Street too.

'He's the type that would insinuate he knows more than you do,' Geordie said, 'an' he'd always acted the secret squirrel – so, on the QT, I'd tagged him SS.'

Now SS had gotten his eye on Geordie, because he was seeking to recruit ex-military Special Forces and our lot into a new civilian organisation, run by former brasshats. Their objectives were to combat commies and agitators in industry and prepare the country for a state of emergency and martial law.

Geordie said that the ex-Int man was usually buttoned-up, but could be very talkative after a few drinks. So, after a session initiated by Geordie, SS had whispered that he'd had some contact with another even more secret organisation called Shield. And, accordingly, he'd found out that some of their people had already toured around a few selected officers' messes and Conservative Party Associations in Blighty – and received resounding cheers for the concept that a 'spot of military rule' might be required.

They'd also been working with a top Tory, codenamed 'Colditz,' who was arranging to 'get rid of the poof' and replace him as Tory party leader with 'the Lady.' Apparently, some critical voices had been raised about the thought of having a woman as PM. But Colditz had put their minds at rest.

'The Lady's a formidably operator,' he'd asserted, 'who'll become Britain's General Pinochet.'

Geordie said he'd feigned interest to find out more and SS had indicated that Blighty was awash with cloak-and-dagger organisations that had similar objectives in mind. Their collaborators included many of the great and the good, as well as stretching back into the security services and the military. Their common message was that 'the good ship Britain is sinking' and that drastic action was called for 'to keep her afloat'.

According to Geordie, SS had then said he'd been told by one of the Shield lot that 'some of our boys on active service in Ulster are playing their part'.

When I asked Geordie what he intended to do about this situation, he just shrugged his shoulders.

'Nothing,' he said. 'What can I do? Perhaps they're wrong, perhaps they're right, but how the fuck would I know?'

This was more or less what I thought too. Whatever was happening, it was well above our heads.

We both expressed the wish to keep in touch, though, and agreed, that in the meantime, we'd both try to find out all we could about what was going on. I knew Geordie wouldn't give the conspirators in Blighty any help, because of his niggles about Kincora. As for me, I'd similar concerns, but mine were about the conflict in Ulster.

'Are the Major and Stone Eyes,' I wondered, 'fighting the same war as Geordie, Seth and I?'

Until I could resolve that, my mind would still have doubts. I'd known for some time that Geordie was seeking answers to a few questions and now there were things I wanted to find out about too.

TRAUMATIC-LAND

These are men whose minds
the Dead have ravished ...
Pawing at us who dealt them
war and madness
Wilfred Owen (1893–1918)
Mental Cases

Eddie was overseeing the bookkeeping at a shop in Mugsfield, after the proprietors had requested help to put their paperwork in order. It had taken a few days, but he was now close to completing his task. Now and again, usually during tea breaks, he'd chatted with the couple who owned the shop.

'They're good company,' Eddie thought, 'but I can't help feeling there's some sort of sorrow hanging over them.'

Today, there had been a small item in the local paper about Ginge and the bombing – and Eddie noticed the shopkeepers reading it avidly. The update mentioned that there were quite a few local lads in the army. So, Eddie casually mentioned that he'd served in the local regiment too.

The woman looked close to tears and shot him a quick glance.

'So did our son,' she said tensely, 'he served in Northern Ireland.'

'After my time,' Eddie retorted, 'I got out before that lot started.'

'Our boy did two tours of duty over there,' the man said,

'but he bought himself out because he didn't want to go again.'

'He wasn't the same person, when he came back the first time,' the woman said, 'and the second time, he was even worse.'

'We tried to help him, his mother especially,' the man said, 'but it wasn't any good, we didn't seem able to connect with him at all.'

Eddie remembered his own difficulties settling back into Civvy Street, and thought he should offer to have a chat with their boy.

'Is he around?' he asked, 'perhaps it might help, if I had a word with him.'

They went silent for a minute or two.

'No, I'm afraid you can't,' the mother said, 'he's in prison and he won't be out for a while.'

Eddie could see the pain etched on their faces and tried to resist probing, but he couldn't stem his curiosity.

'What happened?' he asked softly.

They looked at their feet, and then the mother glanced back at him.

'Ten years ago, he killed someone – over here,' she uttered, choking out the words. 'He's now doing a life sentence.'

They went on to tell Eddie that their son had been living with his girlfriend and little daughter. The relationship had been fraught 'because of how he was'. But it was still hanging together when a young single man had moved in next door.

'He was a dropout,' the father said bitterly, 'probably on drugs. He was a good-for-nothing, anyway.'

According to the father the newcomer had 'played loud music – which blared out, especially at night'. Their veteran son had 'gone mental' over this one evening and decided to go and sort the neighbour out. After an angry exchange he returned – and then the music was turned up even louder.

'His girlfriend said "he lost it completely then",' the mother muttered.

'Our boy went round again,' the father cut in, 'and just laid into the waster, when he opened his door. Fists, head, feet, everything.'

'The girlfriend had to drag him off,' the mother said.

'But the chap was dead by the time they got him to hospital,' the father added.

In prison their son was trying to come to term with what he'd done – and what had made him do it. He wrote that his prison 'now seems to be full of ex-servicemen, mostly Northern Ireland veterans'.

'Everyone in here, including the screws, thinks it's a scandal,' he told his Mum and Dad during a prison visit, 'but nobody is doing anything about it.'

When he got home, Eddie told Amy about the veteran and how he'd ended up behind bars. The memory of Eddie's problems remained vivid in Amy's mind.

'There is a battle in the heads of some soldiers,' she thought, 'between civvy values, where killing is the worst thing you can do, and military ones, where you're trained and expected to do just that.'

They both felt that the ex-soldier's experiences had been much the same as Eddie's. They knew that these difficulties could often lead to alcoholism, divorce, homelessness, prison and even suicide. And Amy looked at him fondly as he told her about the Northern Ireland veteran.

'There, but for the grace of god,' she said, 'glory be, you've come back to the real world.'

Eddie grabbed her hand.

'It were your help and concern that saved me,' he said.

Although his memories of the army and Aden had not gone, he considered that he was now in control of them – rather than them of him.

'It isn't full redemption,' he thought, 'but now we can get by.'

The little business they'd built together and their joint quest for the knowledge about how their world worked was not only consuming their time, but also helping him, he felt, to stay on the straight and narrow.

The news of the veteran in jail, however, disturbed and angered Eddie and forced him to consider this issue again.

'It's the cannon fodder syndrome,' he said to Amy, 'the bastards recruit these young lads and use them in conflicts. But don't give a fuck about what happens to them afterwards.'

In the past, Eddie had told Amy about his own training for Aden, but now said that he'd heard from other veterans that the riot drill and other types of training they did for Ulster was even worse.

'The army's built 'Tin City' complexes in all garrison areas,' he said, 'and the drills are repeated and repeated till the soldiers talk about going 'on auto' when violence flares in Northern Ireland.'

'Do you think the shopkeepers' boy went on automatic?' Amy asked, 'when he killed his next-door neighbour.'

'I don't know,' he replied, 'but, if he did, then some of these veterans are walking time bombs. They've been switched-on, but not off. And now, even in civvy street, their training is just waiting to kick in.'

'Sounds like they're on a hair trigger,' Amy said.

'Liable to explode at any time,' Eddie added.

The parents of the veteran in prison had told Eddie, how at first they had thought they would only need to alert the authorities about the problems with their son – and it would soon be sorted out. But they'd raised it again and again with politicians and the MoD to no effect.

'Those in authority know very well about the problem,' they said, 'but they only want to sweep it under the carpet, bury it from public view – and that's the only conclusion we can come to.'

Thinking about their own experiences, Eddie and Amy could only agree.

At Mugsfield General, when Kate had a few days off, it allowed Elsie to spend a bit more time with Ginge. He appeared to be as well as could be expected, but was becoming increasingly morose. Then, she heard him muttering something about 'my man' and 'helicopters' and gradually realised that he was remembering something from his past.

Elsie considered that a bit of a bond had now been forged between them. So, she tried to engage Ginge in conversation about what was concerning him. Like in the past, though, this was more or less a futile exercise.

She did discern, however, that soon the anniversary of an event in Northern Ireland was coming up. It was something Ginge was disturbed about and which he wanted to banish from his mind. But, for some reason, he didn't seem able to.

Elsie could see she was getting nowhere fast. So, she decided to stop beating about the bush and ask him straight out.

'Tell me what happened?' she asked directly.

But Ginge remained silent for a while.

'In Belfast I'd a mate,' he then said, before stopping and correcting himself, 'a contact, anyroads.'

He paused again.

'Did something happen to him?' Elsie probed.

'Yes,' he whispered, after another long silence.

He looked at Elsie and smiled wearily.

'It was only a bit of housekeeping,' he said. 'It was sorted out by the Major.'

Once again, Ginge was silent for a while, until he suddenly burst out laughing.

'My man was a fucking idiot anyway,' he spluttered, 'knick knack paddy whack, turn him into bone, my man SB went swimming home.'

He seemed to find this very funny and lapsed into a fit of giggles. Elsie, however, was familiar with outbreaks of dark humour among hospital staff, especially on occasions when patients had been in a bad way, or died. She could, therefore, recognise Ginge's behaviour as a coping mechanism, to bring relief from some awful event lodged in his memory.

Although she tried to prise it out, he would not reveal anything more about the incident that was troubling him.

LOG 11: MY MAN SB – 1975

After Geordie had left I continued working hard, mainly in the procuring and running of mick informers. Soon I'd built up a little group of them and, although they were mainly low-level sources, every now and again they'd come up with little bits of useful information. Nothing spectacular, but putting a few tads together was often all we had – and sometimes that could pay off.

One day I was given a tip-off by a plod contact about a young druggie who was located in a hard-line nationalist area. I knew I shouldn't have wasted my time on him, and, to tell the truth, I'd been reluctant at first.

'Probably prove to be a liability, or at best, just a dead loss,' was my first thought.

But we were under pressure to get a few more micks on the hook.

'What the fuck, you never know,' I thought, 'I might as well add him to my stable.'

So, we arranged for him to be arrested for possession of drugs and, after he was charged, I took over his interrogation. As we spoke, he kept sniffing nervously and then blowing his nose into a soiled hanky. Reservations beset me again as I stared at his cheeky boyish face and long unkempt brown hair.

'Is this a mistake?' I again wondered, but he clearly fancied his liberty, rather than jail.

So – when I offered him the bait of his freedom, with a

regular supply of drugs plus our protection and some bunce – in exchange for little bits of information, I soon had him on the hook.

The code letters I used for him was SB. I kept it to myself, but in my mind this stood for 'Silly Bollocks'. Still living with his Ma, he was really just a tousled haired snotty nosed kid, with a mouthy gob – getting his highs from drugs and occasional joyriding.

Like I'd thought, though, mostly he was a waste of time. And he kept getting on my tits, because he was so unreliable. But one day, after I'd put on a bit of pressure, he mentioned some night-time activity that he'd noticed, in an uninhabited house in his street.

This was an area of interest for us, in the heart of Indian country and the local green team there at that time were the marines. After my discussions with them, the bootnecks created a diversion, with an early morning search of houses, then infiltrated a three-man surveillance team into a burnt out ruin, a little down the street from the house SB had put us onto. The men were left there for a couple of days, before being extracted one night by having them join in behind a passing patrol.

They'd seen some activity in the derelict house and the descriptions of some of those involved matched the profile of a couple of local PIRA players. The bootnecks waited for a time, hoping to catch the micks at it, but sadly this was unsuccessful. So, they raided the derelict house and carried out a thorough search and, under the floorboards in an upstairs room, they found three rifles, a handgun and a supply of ammunition.

Two of the rifles were old guns, but the other was an Armalite, an AR-18, that was linked by forensics to the fatal shooting of one of their own soldiers. The marines were, of course, delighted with the arms find, which boosted their records. And, although no arrests were made, the bootnecks kept the identified micks in mind and took one of them out with a sniper, just before their tour had ended.

The whole incident was held up as a good example of joint co-operation and it had been congratulations all round, including for me. And SB, being a cocky cunt, pestered me for a reward.

'Come on, I got yous a widowmaker,' he pleaded, referring to the AR-18 by its mick nickname.

In the end, I got permission to reward him with a bit of extra bunce, just to encourage him. The stupid cunt, though, started to splash the cash and act like James Bond – although I'd specifically instructed him to keep a low profile.

After a time SB got himself a girlfriend; it was probably the first time he'd gotten his end away and he became besotted with her. Anyroads, she soon got fed up and left him – probably because he was a fucked-up druggie. But, in a desperate attempt to impress her, he told her a little about his spying activities.

She still left him, though, and eventually he told me about his indiscretion.

'You stupid cunt,' I said, 'but we'll keep an eye on you and if anything looks like kicking-off, you must flee to us straight away.'

Nothing happened for a while, though, and he kept reporting little bits of information. While some were interesting, none matched the arms find.

Then the girl had taken up with another local, who turned out to be on the fringes of the PIRA and acted as a dicker for then from time to time. The new boyfriend was the jealous type and quizzed her about previous lovers. She kept stumm about my man for a while, but had angrily mentioned him during a tiff one day – and also let slip a little about his work for us.

Well, my man was lucky, two days later a Marine patrol happened to come across him being frogmarched down the street by two men. SB was struggling, so the lead bootneck knelt down and fired a shot over their heads. The two micks ran off, vanishing up a back alley – and unfortunately the fuckers had gone to ground by the time the follow-up search got going.

SB, though, was rescued and taken back with the bootnecks – who then called me. I quickly pieced together the story from what my man told me and from others. So, we now had a dilemma, if SB went back to his area, he would soon be picked up again, interrogated and then stiffed.

The Major called me to a meeting to discuss this and he then proposed something that had made me very angry. He said that MI5 had a mole high up in the PIRA, and I should try to persuade my man to go back to his area, promising that we'd protect him. The Major described how he'd then arrange for MI5's agent to abduct SB and have him shot as a tout.

'This will kill two birds with one stone,' he said, 'the mole will get the kudos, enhancing his position in the PIRA. And our immediate problem will also disappear – your chappie is of no more use to us, in any case.'

'Sweet,' I heard Stone Eyes chortle in the background.

Up to then I'd had a very good reputation in the unit as a good and obedient operator. But I then did something very stupid; I threw a wobbly and angrily refused to send SB back to his death. I pointed out that it was his information that had led to the arms find – and this was a reason why we now had a responsibility to protect him.

It was now the Major's turn to get upset, angrily saying that I was not acting professionally and had committed the cardinal sin of making friends with my agent. Not treating him as just an asset.

'The second their covers is blown, all agent chappies are past their sell-by date,' he added, shrugging his shoulders.

To cut a long story short, I stood my ground. In the back of my mind, I remembered that Seth had tried to protect his agents. So, I just felt I should do the same.

'How can we recruit more informants, if it gets out we treat them like that?' I argued.

I don't mind admitting, though, that I was shitting bricks, especially after Stone Eyes got a bit shirty with me and started to call me 'Ginge the whinge'. But it all quietened down after a while and the Major said that he'd make 'other arrangements'. In the meantime he ordered me to keep SB in the special area for 'Freds', in the barracks.

A few days later the Major told me that the only other arrangement they could make was to set up my man abroad, with a false name and a new life.

'This will cost the British taxpayers a lot of money,' he said, looking daggers at me, 'but I'll arrange it.'

He said that, as I'd caused the problem, I had to help out by getting SB to write a letter to his mother – to explain what had happened, and how that meant he now had to go away. The Major ordered me to help him write it, and also to get him to include three more shorter letters, which would suggest he was happy, living a new life with sun and good living – but in an unspecified place.

The other letters would then be posted every year or so to his mother, from countries he was not in – to throw any PIRA pursuers off his trail. I thought this was a bit over the top; I mean Silly Bollocks was hardly a top agent? Okay, because of the arms find, I knew that if he was to go back to his area he'd be picked up and whacked. But surely it was stretching things to believe that the micks would waste a lot of time chasing a fookin' druggie around the world.

I was happy, though, to go along with the Major's new suggestions, because he'd dropped his original plan. A few days later the Major told me that a helicopter would arrive the next day and whisk SB off to Blighty. He said he'd go with my man to liaise with the local Special Branch and the security services, who'd sort him out with his new life.

'Best you don't know about that,' he said, 'but it's all being arranged.'

That evening I went to say my goodbyes to Silly Bollocks, but I spent most of the time trying to placate him. He was so distraught at the thought of leaving his local area and everything he knew.

The next morning he'd got worse and my man was saying he wanted to go back to his home and throw himself on the mercy of the RA. I managed to talk him out of it, but he was adamant that he wouldn't get on the helicopter.

'Its now or never,' the Major said, adding that it was up to me to persuade SB to go through with it.

I did as I was told and I was partially successful, but my man obstinately stated that he would 'only board the 'copter', if I came with him. The Major balked at this to start with, then a kind of grin spread over his face, and he acquiesced.

Just before we boarded, I was surprised when Stone Eyes and a couple of his mates joined us.

'Just in case we need a bit of back-up,' the Major muttered, by way of explanation.

I couldn't help laughing, because one of Stone Eyes' blokes was carrying a large pack on his back, while Silly Bollocks clutched a black plastic dustbin bag containing his few remaining bits and pieces. I sat beside my man, hoping to keep him quiet. And soon we were airborne and heading for the mainland.

After a bit of time, when we were over the sea, one of Stone Eyes' mates delved into the backpack and brought out some sandwiches and flasks of coffee. He seemed to fuss over the provisions for some time, before turning and passing a couple of cups of coffee and a few sandwiches to SB and me. He then dished out the rest to the others.

After we'd scoffed the sandwiches and drunk our coffee, SB seemed to settle down – and in fact started to nod off. Given his agitated state just before, this surprised me, but the wocker, wocker noise of the helicopter blades seemed to become louder and more hypnotic. And I suddenly felt very tired, then found myself nodding off too.

I don't know what wakened me, but when I glanced up I saw a sight that horrified me. Stone Eyes had my man near the sliding door and was stripping him of his clothes, while his mates held SB up by his arms. My eyes felt heavy and kept closing and I suddenly realised we'd both been drugged.

I dropped my head and closed my eyes to just a slit – so I could still see, although not very well. It all felt just like a nightmare and I could feel myself slipping in and out of consciousness. SB was now naked and facing the door and one of the men, holding him up by the arms, shifted his grip on him to one hand – then reached out with the other and slid the door open.

Stone Eyes moved close up behind my man and I saw something was glinting in his right hand. As I suddenly realised it was a knife, Stone Eyes pushed his left hand around SB's chest, hugging him tightly, before quickly moving his right hand around SB's other side to about the area of his groin. He then ripped upwards with the knife.

Raising his left hand above the door to steady himself, Stone Eyes now quickly placed his right foot into my man's back and, as the other two men let go of his arms, kicked out. Silly Bollocks just vanished. His clothes were then stuffed into his black plastic bag, on top of his pathetic collection of belongings and, in turn, squeezed into the backpack.

I knew I wasn't meant to see this and that I might follow my man out the door, if I let on. So, I just fully closed my eyes and drifted off to sleep again. But, as I did so, I heard the Major congratulate Stone Eyes and his mates.

'It's only a bit of housekeeping,' he said, 'well done.'

They woke me when we returned and joked that I must have been totally shagged-out, because I'd slept through the whole trip – there and back. They said that on the mainland SB had tried to wake me up to say goodbye, but I wouldn't open my eyes.

'Anyhow, don't worry,' the Major reassured me, 'he's now in good hands and off to a good life of sea, sand and …'

'Leg-overs boss, the dirty cunt,' Stone Eyes cut in, to great laughter.

By the next day I'd recovered, but still had difficulty remembering all of what I'd witnessed. Even now, I still wonder if I'd dreamt it. Sometimes, I even started to think that the Major might be right – why should taxpayers' money be spent giving my man a good life abroad? Also, I knew that SB wouldn't now be able to make any trouble over our actions, or tell tales about how we operated.

Then, I started to think about the Major sending SB's letters to his mother every year and her, at home in Belfast, thinking her son was safe and dreaming of one day meeting up with him again. This did make me angry with the Major and Stone Eyes again – and also increased my apprehension about them. I now knew what they were capable of – and that they'd not hesitate to remove anyone who stood in their way.

OLDBOY-LAND

*Flags are bits of coloured cloth
that governments use to shrink-wrap
people's minds
and then as ceremonial shrouds to bury the dead.*
Arundhati Roy
A novelist and peace campaigner
War Talk

Kate's affair with the MoD policeman ran its course and then, after a few weeks, crashed into the buffers. She now set her sights on Bob, a new doctor, and was pursuing him relentlessly.

'He's a real heart-throb,' she'd muttered one day, and the other nurses took to calling him 'Bob the throb' and teased Kate about her love life.

One day, as Alec joined the nurses, Kate was undoing a second button on her blouse and with a little shimmy repositioned her Wonderbra.

Alec glanced at Elsie.

'Ayup, Kate's getting her tits out again. Who's coming?'

'New doctor on rounds,' Elsie replied.

'Agh! Let me guess, Bob the throb?'

'You've got it in one.'

'He's lovely,' Kate tittered, as she adjusted the back seam of her fishnet stockings, which highlighted her fake-tanned legs. 'Mae West said good girls go to heaven, but bad girls go everywhere.'

Alec chuckled.

'Looks like you've booked a lifetime of travelling then.'

He then turned to Elsie and Gwendolyn.

'Is it true, she's had more doctors than the average hypochondriac?'

'Oooh! Maatron,' Gwendolyn replied, 'it's like a Carry On film, with her high jinks and your jokes.'

Elsie now had ten of Ginge's secret tapes tucked away at home. She still tried, on occasions, to draw him out on the happenings he was recalling and taping. It was all to no avail, however, because, while Ginge was happy to chat, it was never about anything of consequence.

Now and again, a tiny bit of something intriguing would come out. But when Ginge realised he'd made a slip-up, he would quickly clam-up – or, at other times, attempt to bury it again. When it happened, Elsie would sometimes smile.

'Secret squirrels,' she'd think, or occasionally, 'man of mystery,' after he'd gone silent. But she knew by now that if she probed further he'd immediately turn his head away.

Elsie wanted to tell him about her meetings with Amy and Eddie, but still held it back in case Ginge would disapprove. On her next meeting with the couple, Elsie mentioned that Ginge could be difficult to deal with, especially if asked a question.

'Tell me something I don't know,' Amy said.

Eddie tried to explain to Elsie how the military trained its recruits and indoctrinated them to enhance their group cohesiveness.

'We wore the same uniform, had the same short haircut and learnt to march together,' he said.

Eddie then described how the regimental system bound soldiers to their particular corps, and how it also promoted competition within the army structure, while encouraging loyalty among soldiers to their own unit.

'You distrust outsiders and are more at ease with your own lot,' Eddie said. 'Its like being in a tribe or clan, you have your own dress code, flags and history – and next they sent you off to kill or die.'

Amy could see Eddie was getting agitated.

'Sounds like the bad old days,' she cut in, 'when we just had lords and peasants.'

'Yea, it's like being back in the feudal system,' Eddie resumed, 'you have to swear your allegiance to the crown, not the people or the government. It's a rigid hierarchy of officers, NCOs and other ranks. We called the officers Ruperts, as they'd nearly all come from the public schools.'

After Elsie left, Amy and Eddie continued to discuss the issue.

'Its not just the army,' Eddie said, 'the whole country is still run like that – with the toffs at the top and the plebs at the bottom.'

'I was chatting to Doris at our last meeting,' Amy said, 'and she was saying much the same. Wouldn't it be interesting to see how many public school old-boys were in positions of power in the run up to the miners' strike?'

'Yea,' Eddie agreed, 'but let's see if there's a history to this too.'

They agreed to attempt to find this out and identify its evolution from the past, then make this the issue for the words on their next layout board.

They scoured the local library for any books that might help. And few weeks later, after endless drafts and many crossed out words and sentences, Amy began to type out their final text:

In 1835, John Wade's 'The Extraordinary Black Book, an Exposition of Abuses in Church and State' stated about the MPs of that time:
'It is apparent that the vast majority were connected with the Peerage, the Army, Navy, Courts, Law, Public Offices and Colonies. And, in lieu of representing the people, only represented those interests over which it is the constitutional object of a real House of Commons to exercise a watchful and efficient control.'

In 1841, six years after Wade's Extraordinary Black Book, Charles Dickens wrote a satirical new version of the song The Fine Old English Gentleman:

'The bright old day now dawns again;
The cry runs through the land,
In England there will be dear bread –
In Ireland, sword and brand;
So, rally round the rulers with the gentle iron hand,
Of the fine old English Tory days;
Hail to the coming time!'

From the early days of Empire, both at home and abroad, Britain's establishment had its 'old boy' system to help perpetuate its power and control.
It still continues, because in the early 1970s, a survey of Britain's elite found that the following percentages were 'old boys' from public schools:
Army – 86% of officers of the rank of major-general and above.
City – 79.9% of directors of clearing banks.
Church of England – 67.4% of assistant bishops and above.

Judiciary – 80.2% of high court judges and above.
Ambassadors – 82.5% of heads of embassies and legations.
Civil Service – 61.7% of under-secretary level and above.

In 1979, of Margaret Thatcher's first Tory Cabinet, 19 of the
21 ministers were public school old boys, 6 had been at Eton.
Five years later these 'old boys' set out to destroy the miners.
Fine old English Tory days;
Hail to the coming time!

Elsie knew that over a million people worked in the NHS, and this made her and Mugsfield General a tiny part of a very large organisation. Most of the nurses recognized that the NHS was far from perfect and some changes were needed. But the reforms imposed so far, did not seem to have helped in any way, shape or form.

The cleaning of the hospital had already been privatised, amid much hoo-ha and assurances of better standards. Now, however, there were fewer cleaners and the new ones were poorly paid. Their tight schedule meant that fewer hours were spent on specific jobs, and their equipment was run-down and sparse.

'We're having to do clean-ups too, now' Elsie said.

'I told you it would all go down the pan,' Alec replied.

'Yes you did, clever-clogs. But what can we do about it now,' Kate asked.

'Oppose it!' he replied, 'but our first problem is that after the miners lost the strike, it's become like all of our unions have been sent to the vet and had their nadgers removed.'

The hard-pressed nurses increasingly found themselves diverted from tending patients to do quick clean-up jobs. To the new managers, however, the changeover was a triumph and woe betides anyone who suggests anything different. The forward march of the NHS towards a new system would not be halted, and any person who was thought guilty of trying to do so was to be marginalised and then kicked into touch.

As to the future, rumours were rife of further staff cuts, or proposed changes in work patterns, and of more services being moved to private companies.

'Talk about throwing the baby out with the bathwater,' Elsie said.

'There's a plan behind what they're doing,' Alec replied. 'If the NHS seems to be failing, then the patients and the public will demand change – and then the politicians will claim: 'We're only doing what the punters want'.'

'It's all happened before,' Gwendolyn responded, 'divide and rule was used in the Empire and now it's being used here.'

It was difficult, however, to dwell on such matters for long, because she and the other nurses were now worked off their feet. Indeed, they'd hardly any time to reflect on, or make sense of, the issues that concerned them.

'Even if we were to confront any of this,' said Kate, 'would it be worth wrecking our careers to try and put it right?'

'Kate's right,' Ginge, who had been listening in, muttered. 'In the army, if you stick your head above the parapet, you're liable to get it shot off.'

'Is that by the enemy, or your own lot?' asked Elsie.

'Who knows?' He grinned back, 'it could be either, or both.'

LOG 12: WILSON GETS SHAFTED – 1976

In Palace Barracks there was jubilation in the air about the news from the mainland. Harold Wilson, our Prime Minister, had given up and resigned.

'That commie cunt's got his UB40 at last,' Stone Eyes said gleefully. 'He's gone doolally, claiming there's a conspiracy against him. Little does he know – hee, hee hee.'

'We have to get the Lady in now,' the Major quickly cut in, 'and then we might have our country back again.'

It was as if he was confident that further changes would happen and that all the things he wanted would come to pass. To tell the truth, to me it seemed to be more than confidence; it was actually as if some project the Major had a hand in was about to come to fruition.

Perhaps my paranoia was compounded because this was just a couple of months after Geordie had been in touch with me again. Over the phone, he'd poured a jumble of words about Wilson into my ear. And I remembered about me telling him the things Shagnasty had said about the 'psy-ops type geezer,' with the information he'd been putting out about the PM being run by Moscow.

Geordie said he'd had a few meetings with SS, the ex-Int source, who'd given him good information in the past. And he'd asked him about the Wilson stuff being put out by our spooks.

'According to him,' Geordie said, 'there was a top bod in

the Yank's CIA, who was codenamed 'Christ,' an' he debriefed a Ruskie defector, who named Wilson as one of their agents. This turncoat commie was then passed on ter 5, an' his whispers about our PM were dispersed through a few of their clandestine networks. Now, if Shagnasty's stuff is hunky-dory, then some of our Int lot were more than happy ter spread some of this dirt about Wilson too.'

'My god, do you think it's true – is he a red agent?' I queried.

'Well, I've done a bit of checking, this end an' it all looks like bollocks ter me,' he replied – 'a bit like Kincora, really. The Ruskie took a lot of bunce off the Yanks an' 5, an' ter my mind, this defector was looking for an easy life with big bucks, an' tells 'Christ' an' our lot what he thought they wanted ter hear. This was then passed around ter all our spooks as gospel. Now, there are some around who believe it, both among the Yanks an' our lot – the reds under the bed crowd. There are a lot more, mind you, who divvint believe it, but some of them are happy ter go along with it, because they want to see Wilson brought down. An' they are the ones who are really driving this.'

'But, why, what's their agenda?' I asked.

'I divvint know why,' Geordie muttered, 'except that they want Wilson kicked into touch. That's the problem with all this, you think you've got the answer ter one question, an' then another pops up.'

Thinking about it later, my mind was churning over.

'With all that stuff about Wilson and him giving up as prime minister, and Heath before, getting fucked over for the Lady,' I thought, 'could this be something that the Major and Stone Eyes were mixed up with?'

I also remembered the old days in Krautland, when the emphasis had been on the Cold War and a possible conflict against communist Russia. Then, with the new edition of Land Operations in 1969, and our involvement in Ulster, the priority for us in the army had changed from external foes to internal ones. So, we started to seek the enemy within and perhaps it can be argued, that here in Belfast – which is a part of the UK after all – that is what we're doing.

I was caught in two minds. On the one hand I didn't like any of the fuckwits, so I didn't feel much sympathy for Wilson – just as I hadn't for that poof Heath before. On the other hand, with their going, unlike Stone Eyes and the Major, I didn't feel any sense of elation either.

'Basically, I don't give a fuck who's in charge at Westminster,' I thought, 'and I don't think Geordie does either.'

My concern was our war against the micks in Ulster, because to me that was the only thing that was real. I felt that only an honourable end to the conflict could vindicate the death of Seth and all the others. So, it disturbed me to think that some of our lot seemed to be more absorbed by events in London, than by what was happening in Belfast.

Anyroads, although Wilson had gone, Labour was still in power, and they started implementing a tougher policy against the micks. We were happy to oblige, of course, and the conflict stepped up a gear. At the time our intelligence reports in Belfast were suggesting that the PIRA were reconstructing their organisation and tactics to fit in with a new long-war strategy.

Their old system, based on hard-line areas with battalions and companies, was to be scrapped, because it'd become increasingly vulnerable to our detection, infiltration and capture. Instead, they were intent on introducing a cell system of new active service units – ASUs – each made up of a small team of PIRA members focused on a specific activity, who would be able to operate anywhere.

The micks were also setting up a new internal security unit, which later became known in Belfast as the 'nutting squad'. Working directly for the PIRA leaders, this section was to quickly build up a fearsome reputation – hence the nickname. Its main job was to sniff out, and then kill, informers.

I knew, therefore, that our agents would be even more in the firing line and I could see our work getting more difficult and dangerous too. So, I was surprised to find that the Major seemed somewhat pleased by this news. He glanced at me and must have seen the look of concern on my face.

'Don't you see?' he said, 'if we can get an agent into that part of their organisation, think of the information we'd get – and the mischief we'd be able to do.'

By now, the Royal Ulster Constabulary had been fully reorganised, re-armed and were building their own special forces. Except for a few hard-line places, the plods were now patrolling all nationalist areas, although they often required green team backup. The Ulster Defence Regiment, now integrated into the British Army, was also active, although many of its members were local part timers.

Both the RUC and the UDR were almost 100 per cent prod and tensions worsened between them and the micks. I was concerned and somewhat fearful by this turn of events, as the conflict became more of a civil war. But once again the Major appeared to be delighted.

'We now have a full-blown crisis,' he said elatedly, 'but fewer of our lads are getting killed.'

'The Yanks told me how in Vietnam they got their good gooks to fight the commie gooks, boss,' Stone Eyes chipped in, 'Vietnamisation they called it, perhaps we've now got our version of that here?'

'Yes, Ulsterisation!' the Major muttered.

He then recounted how 'That less than happy chappie, Wilson,' had actually considered 'withdrawing the army,' when the fuckwits back home had become scared by the 'troops out sentiment' among the mainland population.

'This has now lessened,' the Major claimed, 'now that fewer of our boys are going home in boxes.'

Stone Eyes and most of his men had been absent for long periods, training the local plods' special units in weapons use and ambush techniques.

'We all know which micks are at it, but sometimes we have difficulty proving it,' Stone Eyes said to me one day. 'So you can beat a confession out of them and get them put away in clink, or me and my RUC mates will just shoot the fuckers.'

In the latter case, he said they'd ensure that no witnesses were left around 'so that our version of events will be the only one'.

I'd seen some stuff in the papers about 'shoot-to-kill' operations, which were causing concern. But all this seemed to please Stone Eyes, especially the fact that in his estimation: 'The plods are well up for it.'

I couldn't help thinking, though, that it was like all of us – the micks, the prods and us Brits – were all strapped into some sort of madhouse, with wheels fastened on, which was heading straight for the abyss. Somebody needed to be putting the brakes on, but I knew it wouldn't be the Major, Stone Eyes or any of our lot, who'd do so.

I remembered Geordie saying that in Kenya there'd been nobody reporting on what the army had been doing there. So, they'd been able to just get on with things. In Ulster, there were reporters everywhere and often they were very happy to write articles criticising 'the Brits'. Our type of undercover work, especially, often came under attack from the hostile media;

usually put out by agitators, or other fuckers, who were talking through their arses.

That was one of the reasons all the soldiers engaged in our line of work kept changing the names of the units we operated under. At first we were a Q squad, then the muscle arrived and we became the MRF – which stood for the 'military' or 'mobile,' 'reconnaissance' or 'reaction,' force – depending on which journalist you spoke to.

We were all quite happy with the ambiguity, which we'd helped and covertly encouraged. It's just that the first part didn't mean jack-shit anyroads, and reconnaissance and reaction were separate parts of the same job. To us it all made sense, so whatever name we used, our operations had a purpose and continuity, which we all understood.

Next, we were 14th Intelligence, which we called 'the Det,' and then the Force Research Unit – FRU. Various other names have also been used, or mentioned, but I don't intend to divulge them here – or say if they are correct. Let me just say that we knew who we were, who we were working for and the objectives we were expected to meet.

We were quite happy, though, to see shit-for-brains outsiders getting their nickers in a twist attempting to decipher it all. At the same time, we had regular updates and courses – often back in Blighty. And our training and techniques were becoming more comprehensive and specific.

Frequently, we'd be issued with some ground-breaking pieces of kit and technology. Sometimes our needs pushed us into coming up with a few spanking bits of the new stuff ourselves. At all times our weapons were regularly modernised and some were procured especially for us.

Our Q cars still looked like local motors, but were now all armoured with communications and cameras added, the engines souped-up and the lights rewired. We even took to the air, when Stone Eyes and his lot started using the 'Bat flights,' as we called them. These were Army Air Core Gazelle helicopters, which could follow suspects using sophisticated surveillance gear. This was carried in the pods on the underside of the fuselage – and trailing players could be done, even when high up and out of sight and sound of those below.

Perhaps our biggest advantage against the micks, though, came through our ever-expanding network of concealed listening devices and cameras. Gen from these augmented the stuff from stakeouts, informers and agents. It was all a bit cumbersome to start with, but when we began using computers, it was gradually all linked together into, what became, a vast surveillance, information and communications network.

Another change, which was welcomed by all of us, occurred because in the early days our men on duty in hostile areas were sometimes spotted, or at least tended to attract unwanted attention. This made a lone man, or a few men, vulnerable to detection and hostile actions. A male and a female, on the other hand, hardly drew a second glance, especially if they were holding hands, or kissing.

Consequently, we started recruiting female soldiers, mainly for Stone Eyes' squad. Most were easy on the eye and often got our testosterone levels jumping. We'd used a few lumpy jumpers in the past for specific jobs, like the Four Square Laundry and the Malone Road knocking shop, but now they were being recruited regularly and used on many of the dangerous jobs in mick areas.

All our staff, including the girls, had to pass a rigorous selection process. So, we were all expertly trained and well tooled-up. And, I'm glad to say, that when it had come to a bit of action, the ladies had quickly proved themselves able to handle it too.

One, we all called 'Babs,' made herself really useful. Her blond hair was cut pixie style, making it shorter than most of ours.

'She's more than a match for most of my lads,' Stone Eyes had said, after she'd done a few jobs with him.

I reckon he'd taken a real shine to her, because he continued to use Babs on many of his operations. And she proved to be a disciplined and ruthless operator.

So, among lots of changes, we'd even become a unisex outfit. As far as we were concerned, though, through all this time – and even though our name had changed from time to time – we hadn't gone away. We'd just became better trained, organised and equipped – plus we were integrating ourselves into the background better.

What really mattered was that, all the time, we were becoming more professional and that Ulster was now the most watched and controlled place in Western Europe – if not the world.

'We still aren't winning, though,' I thought, 'but then, neither are the micks.'

COMMON-LAND

When Adam delved and Eve span,
Who was then the gentleman?
John Ball (1338-1381)
A radical priest who was hung, drawn and quartered
for his part in the Peasants' Revolt of 1381.

A new rumour was sweeping through Mugsfield General and causing consternation among some of the staff.

'Alec's kicking off again,' Elsie remarked, as the nurses were working on the A&E ward.

'Who's rung his bell, this time?' Kate asked.

'Ach, the same as usual,' Elsie replied, 'he's heard that both the laundry and the porters' jobs will be sold off soon.'

The nurses knew that cleaning had already been privatised and that they now had to compensate for this deteriorating service with frequent clean-ups of their own.

'If its true, we'll all end up washing sheets, cleaning bogs and at the same time having to push a trolley around with our arses,' Gwendolyn snorted.

'And in our spare time do the nursing,' Elsie agreed.

Alec appeared and quickly joined in with the carping.

'We are back as fucking peasants again,' he said. 'At least they knew in the old days what was happening, even if they couldn't stop it. Now they just call it something else and before we realise, it's done – and we've all been banjaxed.'

Kate grimaced and burst into song.

'Knock, knock, knocking – that's all you ever do,' she trilled. But Elsie, Gwendolyn and Alec ignored her.

'In the old days,' Alec continued, 'the ordinary people had a saying: 'The law locks up the man or woman, who steals the goose from off the Common. But lets the greater felon loose, who steals the Common from off the goose.' And that's what the Tories are doing now, conning us, giving us all this bullshit – while their pals in big business steal the NHS.'

The next day, as Elsie was tending to Ginge, he said he had a special favour to ask of her.

'Could you fetch me something from my home?' he asked.

'Yes,' she agreed, 'happy to help.'

'It might be things to do with the tapes,' Elsie thought delightedly. But since this was Ginge, she suppressed her excitement and a hint of caution entered her mind as she remembered that his cottage was right on the edge of Bloodworth, next to the woods.

'However, it might be a few days before I can do it,' she added.

Ginge smiled and handed her a couple of keys.

'Yea, that's fine,' he said, 'there's a box file I want, it's marked 'Psy-ops Crap' and it's in the cupboard under the stairs.'

'Around him there are always questions,' Elsie reckoned later, 'but often no obvious answers.'

She had arranged to visit Eddie and Amy again that evening, anyway, so she mentioned Ginge's request to them, which, because of her doubts, she now wanted to sound them out about.

'Some people thinks I'm nosey,' Amy said, with a pointed look at Eddie. 'But I like looking in other peoples' houses – so you do it girl.'

But Eddie did not agree and instead urged Elsie to be cautious.

'If the army crowd think the IRA might come back,' he said, 'they might have surveillance on the cottage too.'

'What, like the policemen who're guarding Ginge now?' Elsie asked.

'Yes, something like that,' Eddie replied, 'I'll tell you what, in order to be sure, I'll take a stroll out there tomorrow and give Ginge's place a quick once-over.'

The following evening he met Elsie and told her that he was pretty certain there was concealed scrutiny being kept on the cottage.

'I must admit I didn't see anyone,' he said, 'but I could sense it.'

When Elsie did not say anything, Eddie thought she might be unwilling to turn down Ginge's request.

'Normally, it might not matter,' he continued, 'but with Ginge, I have a feeling that things are a lot more complicated. There is something a bit off about all this. If you go to the cottage, there might be SAS men there and you don't want to be tangling with those fuckers.'

He looked at Elsie and thought she might still require more persuasion.

'Look,' Eddie said firmly, 'I suggest you tell Ginge that you think surveillance is going on there – and see what he says?'

The next day Elsie did confide these fears to Ginge. She only gave him a somewhat pared-down version, however, not mentioning Eddie or Amy. Instead, Elsie said she'd walked passed his cottage and felt there was a concealed presence about the place.

Ginge shot her a sharp glance, but said nothing.

'He's thinking, what the fuck would I know about

surveillance?' Elsie thought. And she was about to say something placating, when Ginge suddenly slapped his hand to his head.

'Of course, the plods outside,' he said, 'they might well have some at the cottage too.'

'It would make sense,' Elsie said. 'Was your car there, when the bomb was attached?'

'Must have been,' Ginge replied, then thanked her for 'being smart,' about having 'a good shufti at the cottage first.'

'If you'd gone in and got my gear, it might have alerted the Major,' he said, before lapsing into a bit of mock Irish, 'and that wouldn't do at all, atoll.'

After work, on her journey home, Elsie was running their exchanges through her mind. She figured that Ginge still felt there was something fishy about her story – even if he'd shown no sign of this. She was still mulling it over in her brain, even when she sat down to the evening meal with her Mum and Dad.

A few years after the pit strike, Elsie's Dad had sunk into a depression and started to drink heavily. The family were worried for a while and this had increased when he'd started to disappear for long periods and no one knew where he went. Then, while visiting the library one day to get a book for a nursing course she was on, Elsie had discovered her Dad in a corner, with his head stuck in a history book.

When she'd approached, he'd glanced up at her.

'We lacked knowledge,' he'd said, 'that's one of the reasons we lost the strike. Most of us don't even know our own history.'

After coming to this realisation he'd taken to spending time in the library, studying books and making notes. Elsie wasn't sure if his newfound wisdom would be of any use, but she felt it was a lot better than moping about and drinking.

As they ate, Elsie mentioned about Ginge and his request to her, and her Dad started to talk about the conflict in Northern Ireland. He told her that during his studies he'd come across something from an early period of British and Irish relations. It was from the writings of Sydney Smith, a British clergyman, who, in the early eighteen hundreds, had written *The Letters of Peter Plymley*.

'The moment the very name of Ireland is mentioned,' one of the letters stated, 'the English seem to bid adieu to common feelings, common prudence, and common sense, and to act with the barbarity of tyrants, and the fatuity of idiots.'

Elsie's Dad said he was against violence, but he'd just been studying the partition of Ireland and considered this to have been a stupid and despicable act, which had occurred about a hundred years after the Peter Plymley letters.

'I defy anyone to look at Partition and the facts from that period of Anglo-Irish history and not come to the same conclusion,' he said.

'How'd you mean?' Elsie asked.

'Don't get him started,' her Mum cut in to no avail, as he'd already started to explain.

Later in bed Elsie tried to recall how he'd outlined that situation. He's said that just before the First World War the Liberal government at Westminster had put forward a Home Rule for Ireland Bill. At that time Ireland was not divided and the country as a whole was part of the United Kingdom.

The Liberals had introduced two other Irish Home Rule bills in the past, which were both defeated. But this one was thought to have a better chance. The Tories, however, viciously attacked it, because they thought it would weaken the Empire – and they also saw it as an opportunity to defeat the Liberals and evict them from office.

The Tories then formed an anti-Home Rule alliance with right-wing elements in the British establishment, who'd been prepared to instigate and use violence to get their way. They helped fund, form and arm the Ulster Volunteer Force and supported this illegal militia when it threatened armed resistance to Home Rule. Then, when the Liberal government ordered British troops, stationed in the south of Ireland, to move north and face down this threat, some senior army officers had held a secret meeting and refused to obey.

'That was mutiny,' her Dad said, 'and if, in other circumstances, ordinary soldiers had done the same, they'd have been taken out and shot.'

The Liberals, however, were so shaken by the scope and force of this establishment treason that they backed down. The Home Rule bill was then postponed as Europe entered into the conflagration that would become known as the 'Great War.'

'Home Rule for Ireland, the policy of a democratically elected British government,' her Dad said, 'was stopped by a mutiny of the officer-class in the British Army and the threat of armed resistance from the UVF, an illegal Unionist army. Both were generated, organised and directed by extremist elements inside the British establishment.'

According to her Dad this led directly to the Easter Rising, the Anglo-Irish War, the Irish Civil War and then to the partition of Ireland.

'It also ensured that Ireland's English problem would persist,' he'd added, 'and that the violence would continue.'

'At least all of that was in the past, surely such things could never happen today?' was Elsie last thought, before dropping off to sleep.

LOG 13: THE MAJOR'S SECRET – 1977

I remember thinking that it hadn't been too bad a summer and we'd been seeing a bit of sun at last. It was a fine day in the middle of August and I was out in my Q car waiting to meet an informer. I felt full of life, but after the tout arrived, he told me some sad news.

'So, the king is dead then,' he intimated, after the usual: 'how's she cuttin?'

'What's the stupid fucker on about?' I thought, flashing him a quizzical look.

'Elvis!' he spat it out, after clocking my expression. 'I mean, he's popped his clogs – that's what you Brits say, isn't it?

'It's just been on the radio,' he added.

Realisation dawned. Seemingly Elvis had been found on the floor of his lavvy in a pool of vomit, his now podgy body bloated with fast food and a cocktail of prescribed drugs.

'The king of rock 'n' roll,' I thought, 'and the cunt dies having a shit!'

'What a fookin' waste,' was all I muttered, though.

That evening I kept playing *Lonesome Tonight* – to me Elvis represented our break from our parents' generation. It felt like your youth had died with him. Deep down, though, I knew that my youth had died a long time ago.

After telling me about Elvis, the informer whinged on about the state of his finances.

'Some of my touts have a bit of character,' I thought,

glancing at him, 'but too many of them are snivelling toerags.'

'Don't take me for a poxy social worker, you cunt,' I said angrily.

I had to do the business, though, so I took a wad of notes from my pocket and waved them under his nose.

'Money talks,' I whispered, 'now you talk for money.'

He glanced at the bunce, hesitated for a minute or two, and then poured out the details of a conversation he'd overheard in a mick drinking-den about 'the RA setting up an active service unit.'

I peered at him closely.

'Is he bullshitting me?' I thought.

But it all sounded spot on, so, after I'd quizzed him on some of the details, I pealed a few notes from the wad and deposited them in his top jacket pocket.

'Elvis has cashed in his chips, so you have a pint on us for the king,' I then muttered dismissively.

Any information about a PIRA ASU was valuable to us. So, when I got back to HQ, I quickly jotted down all he'd told me, so it could be passed on.

A few weeks before, the Major had said that the top brass wanted better integration between the various sections of the Security Forces; especially those involved in surveillance, agent running and other undercover activities. Consequently, we were all working hard to minimise the problems and tensions. And sought to increase harmonisation, between the main information seekers, providers and users.

After a while, I can't say we become best friends, but at least our lot, plus the plods and the security services, did improve our coordination. A lot better than before, anyroads. And the info from my informer, about the new mick ASU, was an example of the sort of thing that could be shared around.

It was about that time, when our operations in Ulster were running as smoothly as could be expected, that the Major found some safe quarters in a prod area and brought his wife across from the mainland.

'Married life in bogwog land?' Stone Eyes queried, as we watched him disappear one evening. 'Hope the boss finds it worth the bother.'

I kept stumm, because I was hoping that the Major's missus might turn out to be a bit of a harridan and give him some of the hairdryer treatment he'd often dished out to us.

When they got settled in, the Major started to use the office safe to lock away his briefcase, rather than take it home.

'Just in case,' he often said.

He kept the combination numbers secret. But I clocked him on quite a few occasions, flipping the dials to open the safe's steel door – and I reckoned I'd sussed out the numbers. At the time I'd zilch in mind, it was just a useful exercise in observation and memory.

For a while I'd been keeping a sleeping bag and a roll of polystyrene stashed under my desk. And sometimes, if I was working late on running an agent, or toiling on some information, I'd stay over and sleep in the office. It could be a bit uncomfortable, but I usually managed fine.

'In times of strife,' I'd think, 'a kip in a good dossbag can work wonders.'

So, one night, after I'd been working late, I decided to get the sleeping bag out. But, as I settled down to sleep, I found that my mind was fixed on the Major.

'There's something driving him,' I thought, 'but I can't work out what.'

I then remembered about Geordie – and him saying about trying to find out what was going on. And suddenly a thought surged into my brain.

'Perhaps there might be a clue to the Major's secret in his briefcase?'

After twisting and turning for a while, the idea still persisted and got stronger. In the end I got up, turned the key to lock the office door and switched on the side light next to the safe. I felt a flush of pleasure, after my second attempt, when I'd turned the numbers and the door swung open.

'Hurrah, I've still got the skills,' I thought.

Then, glancing nervously over my shoulder, I gradually eased the briefcase out of the safe. But it was the dead of night and nothing moved. Most of the Major's papers were the usual military ones and I'd been given copies of most of them myself. There were a few I'd not seen, but nothing of any great concern.

I removed them all very carefully and returned the papers to their exact position. As I prepared to replace the briefcase, I noticed a slight bulge on one side. On closer examination I uncovered a concealed zip on the inside, and after undoing it, I found a couple of folded documents inside. They appeared fairly old and looked like they'd been read and reread several times.

The papers were folded in two – one was on two sheets and the other on a single piece. They were both closely typewritten in black and had: 'Read then Destroy' stamped across the top in heavy red.

'Is this the Major's secret?' I pondered.

It certainly was heavy political shit, so I took the papers to our newfangled copying machine and made a print of each. I then returned the documents exactly as I'd found them, and took the same care returning the briefcase to the safe.

I kept my copies hidden and took them home on my next

leave. When I'm better, I'll be able to retrieve the documents and quote them in full. In the meantime, because I've read them a few times, I think I can give a good account of what was in them. The first paper was dated 1969 and compactly typed on two pages.

It was titled – The Army and Ulster:

'As our Nation stands in need again, in this new time of perfidy on the mainland, we remember that in times of adversity in the past our troops in Ireland became England's Praetorian Guard. This last occurred in the run-up to the First World War, when the Conservative Party wanted to oust and replace the ruling Liberals – who in April 1912 had presented a Home Rule for Ireland Bill to the House of Commons.

This foolishness could have beckoned the end of Empire, so to bring the Tories back to power, a committed group of far-sighted men then launched an offensive against the Liberals. This included forming an alliance with the Ulster Unionists to stop Home Rule.

Lord Alfred Milner secretly raised large amounts of money to set up and arm the Ulster Volunteer Force, which threatened to use armed force to stop Home Rule. Then, in an action organised by the military friends of Milner, army officers based in the Curragh Camp near Dublin refused a government order to move their units north and face-off the UVF. This fatally undermined the authority of the Liberals and they backed down soon after.

Lord Milner had worked with Cecil Rhodes in South Africa, having been a member of his 'Society of the Elect,' which advocated an aggressive Empire building policy, to be run by the English-speaking world. Back in England, Milner was determined to protect this vision from anyone who threatened to ruin it.

His members, like ours today, were ready to do anything to save the nation. They also came, like us, from the top echelons – landed gentry, business, banks, politics, security services, armed forces and the media. Milner and his 'Round Table' followers, after saving Britain, became the power broker in our country for many years after.

Now that our nation is in trouble once more and the Irish are acting up again, perhaps the situation in Ulster can again be used to help sort out the current problems in Britain. To this end, a new Praetorian Guard needs to emerge. Like Lord Milner before, work has already started with a select group of Ulster Unionists. If a crisis was to flare again in the Province, against an old external enemy, then use could, and should, be made of it – to assist in making the required changes on the mainland and once again to take on and destroy our internal enemies.

Our friends in the MoD are about to produce a new version of their Land Operations Manual, which will be called Counter-Revolutionary Operations. This will be used to prepare the Army for use within the UK – and Ulster will be the training ground. Our armed forces will then become central to the project for the changes that can lead to a New Britain.'

The second paper was shorter than the first and was on one page. Headed Clockwork Orange (part 2 of the Orange Project), it was dated 1974. I haven't read this one as many times as I have read the other one, so I can only give the gist of it:

'This operations' part one – Activate Orange, was started nearly a decade ago, to instigate, control and direct Loyalist paramilitary groups (in part this was conducted in conjunction with some leading Ulster Unionists). It was an integral part of the larger mission to help initiate a conflict that would affect the whole of the UK and provide cover and a mobilisation platform for required changes on the mainland.

This has mainly been successful, so congratulations all round. But now it is time for the second phase – Clockwork Orange – which will be in two parts.

First: with the leeway given to it in fighting the war in Ulster, some of the army's intelligence sections are uniquely positioned to distribute the truth about the wets and reds running things at Westminster, which will greatly aid their removal.

Second: the attempt by Wilson to broker the Sunningdale Agreement must be stopped, and sections of the army joining together with the Loyalists and Unionists to bring it down could accomplish this.'

At the moment, that is all I can remember. I hope I've not left anything out.

'This is all politics,' I was thinking, after I'd read the papers and that was something I hated. Perhaps, because I never bothered with it, that was why I'd always had difficulty getting a handle on such things. But I couldn't help remembering about Geordie and his doubts, though.

'What he uncovered, did that fit in with this?' I thought.

A few evenings later I phoned him and found him distressed because he'd just received a surprise visit from his old ex-soldier RUC contact, which he proceeded to tell me about.

'The cunt appeared at my door,' Geordie muttered, 'out of the fucking blue.'

'A lot of the stuff I mentioned before, about Kincora and that,' the source had told Geordie in hushed tones, 'had come from a Catholic RUC man. I got to know him quite well – and recently he told me he was going to raise a lot of the bad goings-on with some of the high-ups, to see if someone would put a stop to it.'

'Did he have any luck?' Geordie asked.

'No! He was shot dead,' the source replied, 'outside his police station – by the IRA they said, and the RUC buried him as a police martyr, with a full honour-guard.'

'Fucking hell,' Geordie said, 'typical, trust the micks ter fuck things up.'

'But I don't think it was them who done it,' the source had cut in. 'I've done a bit of digging and everything points towards the Jackal.'

Geordie said he'd been astonished, because he'd recognised at once the name of the loyalist's most feared hit man. And he knew that the killer, Jackson, did jobs for the RUC Special Branch and the security services.

'Surely, yee don't think they'd kill one of their own?' Geordie asked.

The source, though, nodded his head vigorously.

'Well, I'm fucking sure they did,' he'd replied, 'and that's why all I've said to you must go no further. Otherwise, I might end up with that bastard on my doorstep too.'

With that he'd left, after getting Geordie to promise to keep stumm about all the information he'd provided.

'The cunt was shitting himself,' Geordie said to me, describing how his source was nervously glancing over his shoulder as he'd sped away.

I then told Geordie a little bit about the Major's papers. I thought he'd enough on his mind right then, so I left out a lot of the detail.

'I'll fill him in sometime later,' I reasoned, 'after I've considered it a bit more myself.'

'Perhaps I've a too simple view of our service in Ireland,' I thought afterwards.

As far as I was concerned, we were in Ulster to fight the micks and nothing else.

'But if others were fighting another battle?' I thought, 'then, conceivably, the Major's papers might shed a bit of light on some of our lot's actions that have puzzled and perturbed not only me, but also Geordie – and perhaps a few others too.'

LEVELLER-LAND

How contrary this is to the common interest
of mankind let all the world judge,
for a people that desire to live free,
must almost equally with themselves,
defend others from subjection ...
John Harris, a Leveller
Writing about Cromwell's conquest of Ireland
Mercurius Militaris

The episode about his cottage and Elsie had made Ginge uneasy and caused him to reflect. He now felt unsure about whom he could trust, and for the first time he became conscious about how confined he was, within the walls of his hospital room. Before, he had regarded it as a sanctuary – now it felt more like a prison.

When she was next tending to the bomb victim, Elsie noticed that Ginge appeared withdrawn and was no longer his chatty old self.

'Having an off day?' she asked him.

But he did not answer and just seemed to withdraw into himself a bit more.

'Best to let it go,' she thought, knowing that all patients could sometimes get a bit cranky from time to time.

After her shift, Elsie decided to visit Eddie and Amy once again, and quiz them some more about Ginge, soldiers and the army.

'Why don't you come with us on Sunday?' Amy inquired, 'we are going to the Levellers' day event.'

Amy explained how every year a crowd would gather in Burford, near Oxford, to commemorate the Levellers, who'd fought with Cromwell in the English Civil War.

In 1649, after the King's head had been chopped off, a New Model Army regiment, who'd refused to fight in Ireland, were trapped at Burford by troops loyal to Cromwell and imprisoned in the church. Three of the mutineers, who refused to recant, were then taken out and shot. This acted as an example, and a warning, to the rest of the dissenting Leveller troops, who watched the executions from the roof of the church.

'I don't know anything about this,' Elsie said, 'but it sounds interesting, so I'd like to join you.'

On the Sunday she cursed a little about having to get up early, but on arrival, they were all pleased to see a large crowd had gathered. It was a pleasant day and the sun was out and tea and antique shops thronged the picturesque little town. Burford dated back to the Saxons and Normans and was about the same size as Bloodworth had been, before the mining started.

Most of the crowd supporting the Levellers congregated near the church and many had attached rosemary sprigs, or green ribbons, to their shirts and blouses.

'They'd women in their movement too,' Amy said, before warbling to Elsie: 'We are the Bonny Besses – in our sea-green dresses.'

'Those were the Leveller colours,' she explained, as they settled down to listen to the speeches.

The first speaker was an ex-soldier, who described how Leveller supporting units in the New Model Army had elected representatives called agitators, who put forward the rank and file's point of view.

'At the Putney Debates in 1647,' the veteran said, 'the Agitators sat and debated with the senior officers, or Grandees as they were known, on the General Council of the Army.'

He went on to describe how the Agitators stood for the rights of the ordinary soldiers and civilians alike. They argued for true democracy and 'An Agreement of the People,' while Cromwell and the other Grandees made their stand 'For property rights and a hierarchy.'

The Agitators won the debate, but the repression of them and the Levellers started soon after.

'The war in Ireland became a part of that,' the veteran explained, 'instigating patriotic feelings against 'papist plots' and providing a diversion, behind which the repression could be carried out.'

The next speaker was the Labour MP Tony Benn, who said there were links between many modern struggles for democratic rights and those of the Levellers centuries before.

'The fight of the Levellers is still going on,' he proclaimed, 'and we have to decide – which side are we on?'

Elsie noticed Eddie and Amy making notes as Benn continued with his speech.

'The ordinary people in Britain are still held in bondage,' he said, 'by the way our society is still organised.'

After their return to Bloodworth, Elsie took her leave and made her way home. Leaving Eddie and Amy to settled down and consider their latest layout board. They'd learned a lot during the visit to Burford, but they knew a lot of changes needed to happen before a new Leveller movement could be built.

'It's like climbing a ladder, doing these boards,' Eddie said. 'We started out near the bottom and now we're halfway up. But we've still a long way to go.'

'Aye, we still don't understand it all,' Amy replied, 'but if we can get everyone else halfway up too, then a least we can all have a decent discussion.'

'So, we need to concentrate on getting them up that first bit,' Eddie said in agreement, 'and hope we can all kick on from there.'

After days of considering and discussion, they decided that their next text should contain some of what they had learned at the Leveller's day event. They also wanted to set out a challenge to those who would read it:

We all know what happened during the strike of 1984/5. And about the tragedy of the mining industry, the greed of the financiers and the arrogance of the bankers. But often people say:

'we agree that is terrible, but never mind eh!'

or 'we agree, but we can't do anything, can we?'

In Britain, our minds are numb, because the educational system, TV, and the papers instil subservient beliefs about 'our betters' and have built in us, from a young age, an attitude of respect for the status quo.

Then a host of media and professional placemen, including politicians, civil servants, academics, clerics and counsellors – who bewilder and pacify us

– continue to augment submissive attitudes throughout our lives.

If our minds remain numb, we will never challenge the wrongs being thrust upon us – never mind overturning them. We need to shake the cobwebs out of our brains and challenge, first as individuals in our own minds, the media and other spin-doctors statements, views and attitudes. Only then will we be able to join with others to combat and overthrow

Back at the hospital, Alec's nightmare was starting to come true. The management had officially stated that the laundry and catering jobs were to be outsourced, and the ones of the porters would follow. The union, who opposed this, issued a statement.

'Staff doing these jobs will have to transfer over, but should retain their wages and most of their old agreements. New staff, however, will be employed on totally different pay and conditions.'

'I told you so,' Alec said. 'Here we go, here we go, here we go!' he then chanted, adding: 'That was the miner's mantra.'

'Well, I wouldn't do what the miners did,' Kate said, 'they took on the bosses and look what happened to them.'

'Dad said he once went on a Vietnam War demonstration in the 60s, with a couple of other miners,' Elsie said, 'and he recalled that some of the others were chanting: 'Dare to fight, dare to win, Ho, Ho, Ho – Ho Chi Minh'.'

'I bet they were students,' Kate cut in, 'what would they know? Young, privileged, idealists – losers!'

'At least they showed concern!' Elsie snapped back. 'And you know what – Ho Chi Minh did win.'

After a short silence, Alec said he'd gotten into a stormy confrontation with his new NHS manager over the jobs issue. They exchanged angry words, with the last ones going to his boss.

'I guarantee the first thing your new company will do,' he'd threatened, 'is get rid of all the agitators – like you.'

Elsie winced, thinking back to what she'd just learned about the Levellers and the Civil War.

'Just like Cromwell did in 1649,' she murmured.

But no one heard and Kate just laughed.

'He knows you only too well,' she said to Alec.

He smiled in return.

'I suppose,' he said. 'But if we don't fight back, these fuckers will destroy the NHS and we'll all be kyboshed.'

LOG 14: THE FALSE FLAG – 1979

For some years now the law had been tailored to make it easier for us to get convictions and more and more micks were ending up behind bars. The IRA then made the prisons a focus for their protest, which eventually was to escalate into a hunger strike. First, though, they refused prison work and garb and commenced a dirty protest.

Shagnasty and I got a first hand account of this from two prod prison officers, who we occasionally had a pint with in the KAI Arms. One, who we nicknamed Dragarse, was short and squat; while the other, who we called Lurch, was tall and lanky. They'd clocked that Shagnasty and me were Brits one day and joined us for a pint and a natter.

Now we sought them out at the pub and asked them about the events in the jails.

'Ach you know, our eejits were too soft on the fuckers before,' Dragarse muttered, 'letting them be political prisoners and wear their own clothes.'

'When that was rightly taken from them,' Lurch said, 'tha taigs refused till wear prison gear and went about stark bollock naked – or with a blanket draped over them. So we taught them a few manners, when they went till tha bogs, or that. They learnt that a blanket isn't much use against our boots and batons.'

Dragarse leaned forward and laughed.

'Dead on, there's nothing like a steel toecap in tha bollocks to bring a taig till their knees,' he said. 'But that's how they should be anyway.'

'What the fuck is this dirty protest, then?' Shagnasty inquired.

'Ach, they're all mingers – you must know what tha taigs are like,' Dragarse replied. 'When they got scared of going till tha bogs, they started decorating their cells with their own shite.'

'Bloody hell,' I said uneasily, 'they're living in their own crap and piss?'

'Catch yourself on!' Lurch replied. 'They're all ignernt bastards, shite goes till shite, they probably decorate their own homes like that.'

As the protest intensified, fewer soldiers were being killed, but the micks stepped up their murders of prison officers and more and more RUC and UDR men.

While we carried on with the good fight in Ulster, back on the mainland it was clear that Labour was hanging on to government by the skin of its teeth. Strikes, stoppages and disputes occurred all through the winter and another election seemed imminent. The Major was ecstatic, and appeared sure that the Tories, with the Lady at their head, would walk it.

I can't say I had the same excitement – and I certainly didn't know what to make of it. So, one night, I decided to phone Geordie to see what he thought. He'd appeared uninterested in all that, though, because something else was bothering him.

'Colditz was murdered,' he uttered, 'some micks done him in his car with a mercury-tilt job.'

'The top Tory who brought the Lady in!' he then added, as if I needed an explanation.

I'd known all about that, though, since it was the micks in the Irish National Liberation Army that had blown him up – and the eyes of the top brass had then turned towards us to seek some explanation for how it could have happened. My mate, Shagnasty, was one of the first in the firing line, because lately he'd been specialising in running INLA agents. I'd bumped into him a few days after the bombing and enquired what had happened and he'd appeared distraught and shaken by the event.

He'd gotten even worse when I told him about the new mick slogan, which I'd just spotted.

'You got out of Colditz,' it said, 'but you couldn't get out of the House of Commons car park.'

I explained how I'd seen it, while out for a spin in my Q car. It was freshly painted along a wall on the Falls.

'How the fuck could these micks have killed him – like that anyhow?' Shagnasty suddenly muttered, 'well, not without some of our lot knowing about it.'

Later, he said something similar in the office, when a crowd of us were there.

'Button your lip,' the Major said quickly.

'Or, you'll have your mouth shut for you,' Stone Eyes threatened.

I couldn't get anything more out of Shagnasty after that.

Another issue became evident at that time, when it came to our attention that some of the more devious micks had been learning and increasingly using Irish. We realised that this was a bid to keep us in the dark, as it was making phone tapping and listening in to conversations difficult.

'Some of our chaps need to learn their lingo,' the Major said, by way of a solution.

Consequently, a few of us, including me, were put on Irish language courses, which took place back on the mainland. They lasted for three-and-a-half weeks and on my course, besides a couple of our lot, the intelligence officers from the green teams made up most of the personnel. I can't say I became fluent, but I did learn some key words and phrases.

While I was over, I'd arranged to take a few days leave and I decided to set up a meeting with Geordie again. It took place on the Sunday following the course, at a pub he suggested. After a bit of chat, he got quite agitated, when I told him some more details about the Major's documents.

I didn't tell him everything, though, as I still was somewhat cautious. But he seemed to think that what I did tell him fitted in with what his ex-Int contact, SS, was saying. I also told him what Shagnasty had said about Colditz and that got him even more excited.

Geordie intimated to me that his instincts were telling him that something was wrong about this. He also said that SS had gone silent after the Colditz bombing had been mentioned. So Geordie had decided to ask him straight.

'How the fuck could those micks have done that?'

But his source still remained stumm, he said.

Later, after many more drinks, SS had eventually indicated that some sections of the security services were worried about Colditz's future intentions towards them. They knew that the Lady would give him any job he desired in her future government and he'd said he wanted: 'To sort out the corruption in the security services.'

'Some of the spooks weren't keen on that,' SS told Geordie.

To tell the truth, I wasn't sure if I liked the direction Geordie was going with this.

'But surely the INLA killed him because of his attitudes on Ulster,' I stated indignantly, 'you're not suggesting that our lot had a hand in it, are you?'

'Stranger things have happened,' he replied, shaking his head. 'An' what yee've said about the Major's papers adds ter this. I've had my eyes opened an' I wouldn't put anything past those cunts in the security services.'

I fell silent and Geordie took a long sip from his pint.

'I've come across a few articles over here about the Colditz' bombing an' they aal make the wrong assumptions,' he continued. 'Basically, they insinuate that because the INLA did the bombing, no one else could be involved. But that's aal bollocks.'

Geordie glanced at me, as if to see how I was taking this.

'Remember how our lot operated wi the prods,' he resumed, 'we used them ter take out micks we saw as targets. Sometimes, we just turned a blind eye ter things the loyalists were doing anyway, but on others, we used agents ter suggest a target. We even provided the mick's whereabouts information, an' facilitated the whole procedure at times. We might as well have painted a bullseye on their backs.'

He looked at me again.

'Who's to say, we haven't used some of the micks, now an' again, ter do the same?'

Now my head was spinning, arranging the killings of a few micks I could understand. After all, they'd have done the same to us.

'But getting them to kill one of our own – in Blighty?' I just couldn't bring myself to believe that.

Anyroads, I quickly changed the subject and told Geordie about my Irish course.

'Tricky buggers, the micks,' he said, grinning. 'We often had ter do the same in the past. Mind you, I always made the wogs speak English. But then I usually had their goolies connected ter the electric system – an' I was ready ter flick the switch.'

I got back to Belfast at the end of April and it was just a few days later that the Lady came to power in Blighty. It was celebrations all around after her election victory and the Major brought in a couple of bottles of bubbly and a few nibbles. To tell you the truth, I wasn't sure what we were celebrating. I joined in though, but mainly just to scoff the goodies.

Still, Stone Eyes and the Major, more than compensated for the absence of joy on my part. It was the only time I saw the Major a little pissed.

'Out with the old, in with the new,' was his take, 'it's all systems go, from now on.'

Stone Eyes patted the area of his jacket covering his Hush Puppy pistol and grinned at the Major.

'Perhaps, I'll now get a few scalps in Blighty too, boss.'

A month or so later, I was working late again trying to sort out a meeting with one of my informers, when I remembered that Geordie had asked me to take a look in the Major's briefcase again.

'If ever you have a chance,' he'd said.

I'd let it go for a while, because I'd been worried about doing it. That evening, though, I hadn't realised how late it was, so just after midnight I got the dossbag out again.

As I was settling down to sleep, Geordie's request suddenly popped into my mind. I tried to dismiss it, but the thought persisted and I got up, locked the office door and switched on the side light next to the safe. The combinations were still the same and the safe door was soon open.

I carefully lifted the Major's briefcase out again and this time I went straight to the hidden area. Pulling back the zipper, I discovered a new two-page document there, which I removed and copied. Then I carefully returned the papers to their hiding place and the briefcase to the safe.

I took the copy home on my next leave, where it joined the collection of other bits I'd liberated. The document –

Operation False Flag – was an update, produced in 1978, for the paper I had seen before called 'The Army and Ulster'. It was for a select few in the armed forces, and once again 'Read and then Destroy' was stamped across the top in heavy red.

As the copy I made is now at my cottage, once again I will have to do my best from memory – and this is how I recall it:

'I have it on good account that our work in Ulster is greatly appreciated and congratulations have been sent "to our new Praetorian Guard".'

To do their work back home, our friends required an ongoing crisis in the UK and we enabled one. We assisted in replacing Heath and bringing down Wilson. Our Orange Operations – Activate and Clockwork – abetted greatly with that.

Above all, we must now persevere in running and managing this conflict in Ulster in a way that continues to help our friends on the mainland. It must persist in acting as a false flag, to keep people's eyes back home off the real targets, as well as building up support for strong government and its authority.

To this end, the internal security project is moving forward well. The cooperation between the army, police and the security services are at its best for a long time. Both here – and also between us in Ulster and those on the mainland – from where various police top brass, and others, have come to look and learn from us.

Our systems have developed until we now maintain a vice-like grip on this province. New laws, techniques and equipment have strengthened our arsenal. And public support, in the face of the substantial terrorist threat, remains high.

We were confronted by political and military threats and we provided answers on how to manage and control them. These can now be applied anywhere. And if we are ever required to act in the same way on the mainland, or overseas, we are both up for it – and are fully capable of doing so.

Many of our colleagues in the army are not aware of our plans, or intentions. So, we still have to be very careful and should seek to recruit only those who we are certain will support us.

Besides our secret aims, however, there are very good military arguments for managing this conflict in the way that we do. The army has never been so well equipped, as every regiment is provided with new kit before a tour of duty. Now, any good CO can get most of the weapons and equipment he wants. An infantry officer said to me the other day: 'Seconds of incoming fire on the Falls Road teaches my men more than any amount of time in a classroom can do.'

So, we now have armed forces that are better equipped and trained than most others in the world, ready for the impending conflicts that are sure to come – either on the mainland or abroad.

Another bonus is that our arms firms are also making a killing, by selling the new weapons and internal security kit to our friends around the world.

Overall, we are heading towards a happy conclusion – that Britain will soon have the 'Great' back in it. So hold fast, keep going and stay vigilant. Then we can be sure that good things will come to pass and our dreams will be fulfilled.'

When I read this paper, like the one before, my main problem was that I struggled to understand what all the crap in them meant. I wondered if this might be because there was something missing.

'Could there be another document,' I reasoned, 'that outlines their overall plans?'

Of course, I could understand some of the stuff, perhaps

most of it. But the full implications? – No.

'Who the fuck was this Praetorian Guard?' I queried as well.

So, I made an effort to find out, and from what I could gather they were elite units of Roman soldiers who were tasked to guard their Emperors.

The problem with them was that they'd got too big for their boots. They'd started to interfere in policy and became involved in conspiracies and sedition. In the end they'd been got rid off by the bigwigs, after their subversive role in the making and breaking of the rulers became clear.

'Hardly a great aspiration, then,' I thought, 'to be like them?'

So, like Geordie with Kincora and Colditz, my instincts were telling me something was wrong. But what, when or how? Fuck knows.

'On the other hand,' I thought, 'perhaps the Lady will actually do a good job – just like the Major thinks. Lets face it she can't do much worse than those Labour cunts Wilson and Callaghan – can she?'

I also had another burning question to do with those documents.

'Who the fuck was writing them? Was it the Major, or one of his mates? Or were there others, higher-up, who did it?'

Even today, I'd like to know, but I don't even dare admit I know about them, never mind ask who is scripting them.

PRICK-LAND

A truth that's told with bad intent
Beats all the lies you can invent.
William Blake (1757 – 1827)

It was now three months since the explosion and gradually Ginge was leaving the memory of the pain and trauma behind. His moods were now mostly optimistic, although his mind could occasionally become beset by doubts.

'It's like a lifetime,' he thought, 'since 1970, when I first set foot in Belfast.'

He felt that he was on the mend at last, with tiny signs indicating that feelings might be returning to the tips of his toes.

'I hope it's not just wishful thinking,' he thought later, remembering that every so often a doctor would turn up and push a pin, or needle, into his legs, or feet and ask: 'You feel anything?' Unfortunately, he never did.

That morning Gwendolyn had plonked a paper down on the bed beside Ginge. She'd then got on with her nursing duties, without indicating that there might be something of interest for him in it. Ginge could still remember his shock, when a bit later he lifted up the paper.

'IRA declares Complete Cessation of Military Operations,' the headlines screamed.

'Was it over?' the thought spun around in his mind. 'Was it really finished?'

He recognised that the hospital staff had contributed a huge amount to his recovery – especially the nurses. And Ginge felt he'd got on well with them all, but today, Elsie, his favourite and secret helper, was beginning to piss him off. He didn't want to have a go at her; after all she was the one who was enabling him to do his recordings – and was keeping the tapes for him.

Elsie was, however, wittering on and on about Cromwell and the English Civil War. She'd also mentioned levelling something or other – and even more fuckers called agitators, who seemingly had been in the army of that time.

'You'll get me shot,' he said at last.

Seeing the peeved look on her face, he quickly added, 'well, that's what they'd do to agitators in the army today'.

'Not much chance of you doing something like they did, then?' Elsie asked, with a hint of sarcasm.

'Nah,' he stated flatly, 'you can be fookin' sure I wouldn't.'

Although for the life of him, he couldn't remember what she'd said they'd done in the first place.

Elsie bit her lip and smiled back.

'I get the message, here endeth the lesson for today,' she said.

'Thank fuck for that,' he replied, 'it were beginning to be a right pain in the arse – even if I can't feel my bum at the moment.'

'It's like trying to flog a dead horse,' Elsie thought, 'attempting to interest Ginge in politics or history. Perhaps all soldiers are like that.'

Then she remembered Eddie had become very interested and involved since he'd bought himself out.

'And what about that officer, the Major, the one who visits Ginge? Does he ever get involved in anything?' she thought.

'Or is he like Ginge – is it strictly army business only, with him too?'

Later, after taking the bus back to Bloodworth, Elsie had bumped into Eddie as she made her way home. He asked her how the hospital was going and Elsie shook her head.

'From bad to worse,' she answered.

'No change there then, just like everything else,' he said, before inviting Elsie home for a cup of tea with Amy and him.

'You can tell us what you think of the layout boards we've done so far,' he added.

While Amy put the kettle on and rummaged around to sort out a plate of biscuits, Eddie pulled the boards one by one from their stack and placed them around the room. Seven were completed and another nearly done, and Elsie slowly went around them, taking in the contents.

'They look great,' she said, 'but I would need a bit of time to take in all the stuff, especially in the written bits.'

Amy and Eddie both noticed Elsie having to stoop to read the words.

'We'll have to make sure they are secured to the wall at exactly the right height for people to read them properly,' Amy said.

'And hope the punters take it all in,' Eddie agreed.

When back at home, Elsie told her family about meeting Eddie and Amy and seeing their exhibition boards for the strike commemoration.

'They're not finished yet,' she added, 'they've three more still to do.'

Elsie's Mam and Dad were full of praise for those working on the commemoration and the effort that was going into it, but Sean was his usual negative self.

'Yea, well done and that – but what good will it do?' he scoffed.

'Probably none,' Elsie answered 'but at least they're trying. Remember the spider, if at first you don't succeed – try, try and try again.'

Her Dad nodded in agreement.

'We need to be off our knees to fight on,' he said, 'we lost a battle with the strike, but we haven't lost the war.'

'No, but we've lost the pit,' Sean muttered, 'anyway, we've other things to be worried about now.'

He passed across a local paper he'd just been reading.

'Drug Wars come to Sherwood,' was the headline.

The paper went on to say that there had been 'a murder by gunfire and a couple of knifings locally'.

With the shooting, a man had been parked in a side road and was dealing drugs from his car window. The killer had come up behind the motor and thrust a sawn-off shotgun into the side of the dealer's head, and pulled the trigger.

'We're keeping an open mind,' the paper reported the police stating. 'The murder could have been a vigilante action, but more likely was the result of a drugs war between two gangs.'

The knife crimes were viewed in a similar light – and according to the police: 'had probably resulted from local youths fighting over the control of territory.'

'We didn't have problems like this when the pit was going,' Elsie's Dad said.

'Idle hands!' her Mum agreed.

'Thatcher said there weren't any society,' Sean said, 'well, there certainly isn't any now.'

At the hospital, the next day, two of the nurses began to prepare Ginge for a bed bath. While Kate was sorting out the washing gear, Elsie snatched the tape recorder and sneakily moved it out of sight. They then gently pulled the bedding and pyjamas off the wounded soldier and placed a waterproof cover below him.

As Kate was washing him, she sponged between his legs and they laughed together.

'There will be a time, before long, when your winky will burst into life as I do this,' she promised, before collapsing into a giggling fit.

Ginge chuckled back.

'I can assure you, the desire is there – but the flesh is still weak,' he playfully replied, ogling her ample cleavage, as the nurse bent over him.

Elsie joined in the laughter.

'I'll be throwing that bowl of water over the pair of you,' she said, 'to cool you both down.'

After Kate had finished towelling him dry, Elsie helped her to clad Ginge in fresh pyjamas and change his sheets.

'Who's a pretty boy, now then?' Kate asked friskily, as they finished.

The three nurses, Kate, Elsie and Gwendolyn, had grown fond of the bomb victim and they all wished they could spend a bit more time with him. But they also felt this about most of their other patients – and all of them had to make do with less attention.

Later, in the A&E ward, when Elsie and Kate were working with Alec and Gwendolyn, they could all see that more and more punters were coming in for treatment. But the numbers of nurses were getting fewer and fewer and the pressure to get their work done greater and greater. At the same time the number of managers had grown and grown.

'There are some right pricks among them too,' Alec said.

'Takes one to know one,' Kate retorted.

'That's a little unkind,' Gwendolyn said, 'surely, we can all see what's wrong. But the question is, how can we fix it?'

'That's easy,' Alec said with a grin. 'First we replace the economic system – get rid of the market-is-king crap – across the world. Then we change our government and the top bods in the NHS. After that we kick the management in this hospital into touch.'

'It does your head in, just thinking about it,' Elsie said.

Kate snorted.

'Well, I'm having the weekend off. Can you have all of that done by Monday, when I'm back?' she asked.

LOG 15: LOVE, HATE AND BLINKERS
– 1980-81

The Major had taken to visiting the mainland quite a bit; officially on army business, of course, but really I think he'd been trying to help the Lady and her backers to forward their agenda. Perhaps, it was all as described in the documents that I'd discovered in his briefcase. That was probably the case, as far as I could tell anyroads.

Certainly, the Major often looked quite worried and harassed when he appeared in Palace Barracks.

'It would have been a lot easier,' I lip-read him muttering to Stone Eyes one day, 'if we'd just gone ahead and done a Pinochet.'

'Well, I reckon the lady would have been up for that, boss,' Stone Eyes replied, 'we needed someone with balls and she's our man.'

With the Major away from time to time, Stone Eyes took a bit more interest in us and often came around for a chat. One day he told me about his interest in the British days in India, during the Empire, and our soldier's service there.

'That's where he gets some of his sayings from,' I thought.

I was glad he was being friendly, though, but I think he was probably just doing it to keep an eye on us.

When you're constantly on duty in a place like Belfast, you don't really notice many outside happenings. The green team boys and us are like one of those horses in the Grand National, with flaps around its eyes. But our blinkers are invisible, fashioned by circumstances and military-thought processes, rather than fabric.

Like the horses, though, our vision and concentration has to be one hundred per cent. Otherwise, a horse might get distracted and not win. And we might drop our guard and get whacked.

Around this time, my blinkers were definitely on, and I was just getting on with the job and protecting myself. The things from the mainland that I vaguely remember were events like Blunt being exposed as the fourth man, the SAS storming of the Iranian Embassy, and the riots in Brixton and Toxteth.

Probably the only things that really registered with me were Elvis dying and John Lennon being shot in New York. Today, here in hospital, I'm finding it difficult to recall any of those external past events. So, as I now have a lot of spare time, I got Elsie to buy me a book listing world events over the past twenty-five years.

I've subsequently been looking at the global news over those times. Amongst a lot of other things: I noted the Yanks leaving Vietnam and the commies taking over, a hundred black protestors being killed in Soweto, Chairman Mao dying, Soviet troops entering Afghanistan, and Ronald Reagan becoming the US President.

To me, though, internal happenings were much more vivid and I remember Geordie talking to me about how it felt, serving in Ulster.

'You walk down a street here an' Coronation Street will be blasting out on the telly, an' they'll have a Man U sticker in the window,' he'd said. 'But the micks will want you gone, even dead, aal the same. Just like the wogs did in Kenya an' Cyprus.'

Those countries, though, are distant lands to me, but, while in Ulster, I felt all was personal – everything was real. We'd lived through events like the micks killing Mountbatten and eighteen green team soldiers on the same day. Not to mention the other constant attacks on us and the plods and the many day-to-day bombings, shootings and other bits of mayhem.

I'd have to acknowledge, though, that Ulster does get under your skin and I have a hate-love relationship with the place. Perhaps it's to do with the intense life and death experiences we've all had here. And when you go on leave, you'd be so glad to get away – but after a few days back at home I'd feel out of kilter.

'I don't fit in here,' I'd begin to think, because civvy preoccupations can appear so stupid and different from ours.

In Blighty, my mind is always alert and, out and about, I'm scanning for danger, calculating risks and I don't like anyone walking behind me. In a pub I need to sit with my back to a wall, in a place where I can scan the entry and exits. Sometimes, I'll get funny looks, as if I am a nutter.

'Civvie cunts,' I'll think in disgust, and then realise that I want to return to Belfast and duty.

Back in Ulster, when the hunger strikes by the PIRA and INLA prisoners started, we'd already dealt with something similar the previous year. This time, though, it was a whole lot worse and the security services set up a secret link between the fuckwits and the micks. The Lady, though, stood firm against any pressure to do a deal, but every time a hunger striker died, the atmosphere got tenser and the dissent intensified.

As well as terrorism, the micks started contesting and winning elections and their street protests escalated. We were on full alert, constantly processing every bit of information from agents, informers, phone-taps, bugs, whispers and overheard conversations. It was one of the most intense periods we had – and this chaos around the hunger strikes was to bring the Major back, full time, to Belfast.

In the middle of the turmoil, I had to step up my own security, when I learned that the micks' nutting-squad had pulled in one of my touts. He was never seen again.

'Fuck knows what he told them,' I thought, 'before he'd gotten a bullet in the back of his noggin.'

Although I felt sorry for him, I knew I could do fuck all about it. My priority was to keep myself safe, so I subsequently changed all my routines.

The hunger strikes also seemed to make the micks even crazier, and those outside seemed intent on delivering retribution. They were not the only ones, though. Because, as I was having a chat with Stone Eyes one day, he'd implied that some of the fuckwits in London: 'Had put two and two together and come up with five,' in regard to the Colditz bombing.

'Subsequently,' he'd added, 'some groundless rumours reached the ears of the Lady and her circle – and this cast something of a cloud over the security services, and also us. But now, under cover of the mayhem created around the hunger strikes, we've a chance to redeem ourselves.'

Then Stone Eyes let slip that he was working with some loyalists, who were intending to strike back at the supporters of the hunger strikers.

'The boss asked me to help them – and also steer them towards the micks who did the Colditz job,' he said.

From what I could make out these loyalists were the Ulster Defence Association, who were setting up a special killing squad to carry out this work. According to Stone Eyes this would secretly be posited back home as: 'Revenge for Colditz' – and he said this would help: 'To get us back into the Lady's good books.'

Did it work, did it happen? I'm fucked if I know, but I don't think Stone Eyes was pulling my plonker. It certainly was true that some people associated with the INLA were killed in these UDA operations, where, if you were in the know, it looked like our lot had played a big hand.

Remembering all that now, though, put this disturbing thought into my mind.

'What Stone Eyes claimed to be doing, was it greatly different from our normal methods and objectives?'

These were to identify possible hostile actions, or people who were in opposition to us, either physically or politically – i.e. PIRA members, and their active supporters. And sometimes, the info we'd produce would put someone, or several people, in the frame as being players. On the one hand, their details might then go onto lookout lists for general circulation throughout the Security Forces – to aid their detection and arrest. On the other hand, they might be passed on to Stone Eyes and his men for exterminations with extreme prejudice, either directly, or by loyalist groups, like the UDA, we'd agents in.

At the start of the next year, Geordie phoned to tell me he'd again heard from his ex-soldier RUC source, who'd been excited because a man had been questioned by the plods in Belfast over the Kincora abuse issue. This top loyalist, who among other things had been instrumental in setting up the Tartan Gangs and the Red Hand Commando, had said openly that if he was to be in any way implicated over Kincora – then he'd spill the beans on all those involved. Three days later two INLA gunmen had entered his shop in east Belfast and shot him dead.

'At least one of the trigger men was connected to our lot,' the source had told Geordie, 'and the rumour was that both were being run.'

'Shades of Colditz,' Geordie said, 'another one out of line, stopped an' shut up.'

Personally, I wasn't sure I could see much of a connection, but perhaps that was just me being naive.

The hunger strike ended after the tenth prisoner died. The Lady had faced them down and she got a lot of praise in the papers for that. What was not mentioned, though, was that most of the prisoners' demands were then quietly granted. We also seemed to forget about all of the other people who'd been killed during that period.

Our media, though, regarded it all as something of a victory for the Lady. But, in my humble opinion, the micks had got stronger, not weaker. The 'hunger-strike martyrs' were potent symbols for them and the PIRA was now combining the winning of elections with their military strategy.

SCAB-LAND

The present is the past
rolled up for action,
and the past is the present
unrolled for understanding.
Will and Ariel Durant
The Reformation

In A&E, Alec was having a bit of a laugh with the nurses, as they helped him to lift a patient from the trolley onto a bed.

'How many managers does it take to change a light bulb?' Alec asked. Elsie and Gwendolyn shook their heads and Kate shot him a sardonic look, winking at the others.

'Don't give a toss,' she retorted, 'but I've a feeling you are going to tell us, anyway.'

Alec was determined to continue his joke and manfully tried to show he was not put off by Kate's put down.

'Five – then a nurse and me,' he said.

Kate just giggled, as Elsie and Gwendolyn looked at him inquiringly, waiting for the punch line.

'The five administrators hold a series of seminars and brainstorming sessions at luxury hotels and decide that the light bulb needs changing,' Alec said grinning, 'then they tell a nurse to fetch me and I change the bulb.'

'Ha, ha, very funny,' Kate said mockingly.

Gwendolyn sighed.

'The sad thing is, it's not too far from the truth.'

Elsie laughed. 'Except, there'd probably be ten managers, not five.'

The nurses were happy that Alec seemed so cheerful. They all knew, however, that it might not be long before he was no longer pushing his trolley or changing light bulbs. Because the porters were next in line for privatisations, after the cleaners, laundry and canteen services who'd gone before.

'Of course, he could transfer to the firm who got the contract,' the nurses all thought.

'But, given what he was like, how long will that last?' some wondered.

When Elsie returned home that evening, her brother Sean mentioned he had seen Eddie and Amy down in the village.

'I went across to say hello,' he said, 'and they asked me to pass on their best.'

He went on to say that they'd tried to interest him in the layout boards they were doing for the commemoration. But he'd fobbed them off and rejected their request for him to view their efforts.

'I'm not interested,' he'd said adamantly, 'look, I was on the strike right through and on the picket lines for most of it. So, I know only too well what happened – and I don't want to be reminded of it.'

Although disappointed, Eddie and Amy went home and continued their work on the text for their next board. Amy wanted to return to local issues, so they agreed to try and put in context the changes that were happening in their village, which were now affecting everyone:

In Bloodworth, the pit shafts were constructed deep under Sherwood.

A long time before, Robin Hood had roamed the forest above and fought for the poor against the rich. Was Hood real, or just a myth?

No one really knows. We remember him because, in our folk memory, he represents the battle of the native peoples against the foreign Norman overlords.

Just a little while ago Bloodworth had a working pit with a big bank on the high street. The state ran the pit and provided work for most of the people. It provided protection for the bank as well – to make sure it was not robbed. The state also regulated the bank to make sure it played fair with its clients.

So, they protected the bank – and protected the people from the bank.

Now, the Tory government has shut nearly all the pits, imports coal from abroad and has put everyone out of work. It has also removed the regulations from all financial institutions.

So, the banks are still protected from thieves, but they are now free to rob the people.

And rob us they do, because, after deregulation, people who are little better than spivs and gangsters are running them. That is what the new neoliberal political and economic system does to the ordinary people who live under it.

Robin Hood used to rob the rich and give it to the poor. Now, instead of robber Barons we have robbing Bankers. And the hoods that run the banks, with the politicians who support them, rob the poor and give it to the rich.

When they'd finished Amy and Eddie sat reading their words.

'I hope the punters get the Robin and robbing bit,' Amy said.

'Aye, they will,' Eddie replied, 'we need a bit of humour, here and there. Otherwise, it might all be too heavy.'

'There weren't many laughs when it happened,' Amy said. 'But they say laughter makes the world go round, and we certainly need a few turns from it now.'

At the other end of Bloodworth, Elsie couldn't help feeling worried about her brother. Before the strike Sean had been happy-go-lucky and positive. Since then, especially after the shut down of the pit, he'd become increasingly cynical and morose. Occasionally, he managed to get a few labouring jobs from time to time, but nothing that ever lasted.

In better times, with a crowd of mates, Sean had gone religiously every Saturday to support the Stags – or Mugsfield Town FC, to give his football team their full name. The strike and then the closing of the pit had put a stop to that, but now and again he still managed to take in a game. This Saturday was to be one of them and Elsie could see he was looking forward to it, especially as it was away to local rivals Chesterfield.

When Sean returned in the evening, however, Elsie could see her brother was looking very dejected.

'How many did you lose by?' she asked sympathetically.

'We didn't,' he replied, 'we won two nil.'

'Well, I'd hate to see your face if you ever get beaten some time,' she retorted.

'No, it wasn't the result,' he said, 'it's the Chesterfield lot, they were chanting 'scabs' at us the whole match.'

Sean described how he'd found himself on the away section of the terracing, beside a lot of ex-miners from Bloodworth. Many of them had not been on strike and others had gone back to work before the strike was ended. They had all, therefore, been able to work on till the pit was closed.

Sean and his Dad, however, had both stayed on strike right to the end. Subsequently, they were both dismissed for being militants, when they tried to go back after the strike had ended. Even now, there was still much bitterness between those who had stayed out, and those who had never been out, or returned before the end.

When the chants of the opposition supporters had reached their ears, most of the Stags' fans next to Sean had complained loudly.

'I'm the one who should be complaining,' Sean said he'd shouted at them, 'you lot were fuckin' scabs.'

Sean explained that before the strike it was not unknown for the supporters of the two clubs, although rancorous rivals, to sometimes stand together on the same terrace.

'There's no chance of that now,' Sean said, knowing that the end of the strike had been accompanied by a deep hatred, and this would linger on for a long time yet.

'We used to put 'Coal not Dole' on our placards, well, those against the strike are all out of work now too,' he added bitterly. 'So striker or scab, we've all ended up on the dole.'

He cheered up somewhat, however, when he mentioned that the only divergence from the 'scab' chants was when the opposition fans had launched into one of the old strike anthems.

'Maggie, Maggie, Maggie – OUT! OUT! OUT!'

Everyone, including the Stags' fans muttered along with that one, although the Tory PM had been out of office for nearly four years by then. The Chesterfield fans had also produced a new jingle about the Iron Lady.

'When Thatcher dies, and this we crave,
we'll volunteer to dig her grave.
While toffs and traitors ring her bell,
we'll dig it so deep, she'll go straight to hell.'

LOG 16: TO KILL A SPIC OR TWO – 1982

In the spring of '82 I found myself sitting on a converted liner drinking beer with a load of Marines. We were all sailing towards the Falklands and the bootnecks were giving an old Cliff Richard's hit big licks, especially when they added their own words.

'We're all going on a summer holiday,

we're all gonna kill a spic or two.'

Just a few weeks before I'd been sitting in our office in Belfast, when the Major and Stone Eyes had approached and asked if I wanted to go on an adventure.

'Don't ever volunteer,' was the advice that had rang loud in my ears.

But I felt I needed a break.

'Anywhere must be better than here,' I'd thought.

They say hindsight is a wonderful thing and, even as I said okay, I just knew the bastards were spamming me into something. I nearly fell off my chair, though, when the Major said he'd been tasked to provide a small team to go to the Falklands and interrogate Argentinian prisoners. My surprise was compounded, because so far there was no war and certainly not any prisoners.

'But sir, I thought that was all going to be sorted out. A leaseback deal or something – with the fuckwits on both sides sitting around a table and having a natter?'

The Major looked me in the eye.

'Well you thought wrong,' he replied, 'the Lady is having a hard time at the moment, and it's time she showed her metal.'

He went on to intimate that a victory in the South Atlantic would do wonders for her future in England.

'And you'll be able to get yourself a medal for twisting the goolies off a few spics,' Stone Eyes jeeringly suggested.

The Major said the rest of those selected for the job were Blighty based. He wanted someone 'who'd been up the sharp end,' though, to run the team. He then claimed that he would have sent Geordie, if he'd still been around – but, as he was gone, I'd make a good alternative.

'I'll have you made up to sergeant,' he then promised, 'and you will run the team.'

Thinking back on it, I reckon the stuff about Geordie had been said just to butter me up a bit. After all, he'd been gone quite a few years by then. But the Major must have known that mentioning him like that, would have flattered my ego.

Anyroads, I was now in the frame for the job, so I had the three stripes sewn on all my gear. I then shifted to the mainland and the next two weeks were just a blur as we hurriedly sorted out our equipment and supplies. After that we made our way to the docks at Southampton and our awaiting troop ship.

I used to think that our journeys to Ulster could be a little hair-raising. After all, your vehicle might be ambushed, or bombed. The micks, though, did not have an airforce, or a navy – while the Argies did – and if warranted, they would be sure to use them. So, we all knew we could be sailing into a D-day situation, with death and mayhem coming at you from every angle.

There were only five of us in my team, made up of four corporals – and me, with my three stripes, in charge. Luckily, the four others all spoke the spics' lingo. We'd have been fucked otherwise, because I certainly didn't. Unlike them, though, I'd practical experience in interrogating prisoners.

Our brief was clear, we'd be required to follow any landings, or advances, and extract any relevant information about numbers, locations and equipment from any captured Argies. We'd also have to try and uncover any other bits of enemy military gen that we could. We were promised full cooperation from any of our green team regiments, including the use of soldiers for guarding prisoners.

Before I left, the Major had given me some advice.

'If you read military history books, you will know that bad information can get men killed,' he'd said. 'Good information, however, not only saves lives, but can also help to bring victory.'

With this in mind, I managed to find a tiny space on the ship, where I could brief the others.

'We will have to do the interrogations subtly,' I said. 'If we just beat the fuckers, break their arms or legs, or twist their goolies – they'll talk, but probably only give us what they think we want to hear. We need them to be fearful all right, but not scared shitless. Then, if we use our brains and fuck-up theirs, they might give us information that's hunky-dory.'

I detailed the corporals to do the interrogations, but said I'd supervise this process.

'We'll need to work fast,' I said, 'but still get into the prisoners' heads and extort the info.'

I also laid out the way we'd process and evaluate any information we managed to extract. So it could be passed on immediately to the brass, to help them plan future operations.

When we were more than halfway down, I heard about the Argy ship, the Belgrano, getting banjaxed. I knew then that the talking was over and there was no way out anymore. The war was on and the Argies would be coming to get us – and us them.

To tell the truth, I wasn't surprised. Because, the way I'd figured it, the Generals in Argentina needed a diversion from their internal troubles and the Lady and her coterie, back in the UK, needed a victory.

'Perhaps I'm getting cynical,' I thought, 'but the Major himself had hinted at it. Hadn't he?'

As we got closer, we'd sometimes seen our Harrier Jets streaking towards targets on the islands. Then we started to see planes that were not ours – that had come to do us damage. After Ulster, most of us knew what to do. Our blinkers went on and we started to gee each other up.

One joke in particular did the rounds.

Question – 'How do you grease your Volkswagen?'

Answer – 'Run over that spic cunt Ossie Ardiles.'

That one went down well with everyone, except the Spurs supporters of course.

My chaps had been perfecting their Spanish, including some of the local variations, when we all heard the gunfire as we entered San Carlos Bay. Special Forces had already landed and were engaging the Argy defences. Soon after, the Marines and Paras went ashore and quickly secured the beachhead.

When we landed, a bit later, we immediately set out to construct a holding and interrogation area. We set it up in record time, with a bit of help from some of the locals, or 'bennys,' as we called them.

'It's fairly rough and a little bit wonky, but it will do,' I thought.

It needed to be, because we'd hardly time to draw breath, before the first prisoners started to arrive.

They were a poor looking lot, bewildered and helpless. I was very happy, though.

'There're ripe for our interrogations,' I thought.

So it proved. There were a few regulars, but most of the Argies were conscripts, and some began to spew out vast chunks of info. We'd problems keeping up at times.

A lot of it was unspecific stuff that we already knew about. When anything important came up, though, I insisted that it be confirmed from various mouths before we accepted it. I knew from my Belfast experiences that this was required.

The green teams then moved east towards Port Stanley and we followed on behind. First, though, the Argies – dug in on the high ground of the Two Sisters and the two Mounts, Harriet and Longdon – had to be winkled out. The battles on the mountains were often fought hand-to-hand and a lot of Argies were bayonetted in their trenches.

During the aggro on the mountains, we sourced a holding base for prisoners close to one of our heli-pads and we then started to see the medics with their stretchers. A lot of the wounded were theirs, but there were a few of our boys too. They were treated and flown out for more comprehensive doctoring back at base, or on the ships.

The ones who didn't make it, though, were just sheeted over. Things like that stick in your mind, but it was all over, soon after that. And we all let out a big cheer, when we heard that the Argies had raised the white flag in Stanley.

One thing I remember during our interrogations, occurred after a few prisoners had been handed over to us. My team couldn't understand two of them at first, and then one of the corporals turned to me.

'These fuckers are Taff's,' he'd said.

'This cunt's taking the piss,' I'd thought. But then he convinced me that they were speaking Welsh. Seemingly, they were descendants of a considerable number of Taffs who had moved to Patagonia a long time ago.

These ones had been conscripted and found themselves fighting for their lives on the Malvinas, as they called the Falklands. I had to borrow a Welsh-speaker from the Welsh Guards in order to interrogate them. In other words, we had our Taff quizzing their Taffs.

All in all, I like to think us Int boys gave a good account of ourselves during the war. Due to our interrogations, we passed over a fair amount of information, and in a coherent form. I'm sure some of it must have been helpful.

We departed from the Falklands a few weeks after the Argies surrendered, leaving the fresh dug graves containing the fallen. Going out, we passed the incoming units, who'd soon be starting the reconstruction. Now, we've one soldier for every two bennys over there – to protect the islands from further attack.

'The whole fookin' thing could have been sorted out,' I couldn't help thinking, 'by the fuckwits, on both sides, sitting down together and finding a solution.'

A few of the green team lads, though, were jubilant. On our boat going back there were some of the bootnecks we'd travelled out with.

'It was a close run battle,' a Marine Colour Sergeant told me, 'a lot closer than most think. If their army had fought like their airforce we could have been fucked – but their soldiers were often like frightened rabbits. We were sharp, better trained and organised. We were also experienced, well up for it and fine-tuned for the aggro. We won it on the back of Ulster.'

On our return to Blighty, massive crowds greeted us. Cheering and waving Union Jacks, they hailed us and Maggie as their heroes.

'The Major's gonna be chuffed to bits,' I remember thinking.

Before the war the Lady's support in opinion polls was going down and down, after our victory it rose and rose.

SODALLCO-LAND

War is nothing but a continuation
of politics by other means.
Karl von Clausewitz (1780 – 1831)

Ginge has spent a restless night, as across his mind had flickered troubling images from Ulster and the Falklands. He awoke tired and disturbed, but suddenly a big smile came over his face and he laughed out loud. He was remembering that in Belfast a good few years after his Falkland adventure, he'd again bumped into the Marine Colour Sergeant – now on an Ulster tour of duty.

'We got our knuckles wrapped for calling the Falkland islanders bennies,' he'd told Ginge, 'and we were ordered to pick another name for them.'

'Our bootnecks thought about it for a time,' he said, 'and then came up with the name 'Stills'.'

'That's a lot better,' an officer said. 'But 'stills,' what does it mean?'

'They're 'still' fucking bennies sir,' the bootnecks replied.

As Elsie journeyed to the hospital, she was thinking about the conversation with her Dad last night, when they'd talked about the Northern Ireland Troubles. He said he'd been upset by the killings and was happy peace moves were now being made. But then he mentioned something interesting about the early days of the conflict.

'When you were still in nappies,' he said.

Seemingly, in the early 1970s, as British troops first patrolled the streets in Northern Ireland and a lot of bad things were happening, there was a programme on TV called The Comedians. He explained that the comics had come on one by one and told jokes for a set time.

'Some were good and some were bad,' her Dad said, 'but the lazy ones knew there were easy laughs to be had.'

'The main butt of their jokes were the Paki and the Paddy,' he added. 'A comedian just had to say, 'there was this Paddy,' and the audience would burst into peals of laughter – the comic didn't even need to deliver the punch line.'

Her Dad said he'd thought that this – 'the Irish-are-stupid attitude' – as he called it, needed to be pervasive to attain that result.

'Therefore, it could only have been achieved,' he said, 'after there had been the drip, drip, drip of systematic stereotyping in the media – at a national and local level.'

'The jokes were a part of that, of course,' he continued, 'but, while this was good for bad and lazy comedians, it also shows how the top people manage to exert their domination.'

Elsie screwed up her face.

'How? – Why?' She asked, trying to take it in.

'In times of conflict, when laughter burst forth at the mere mention of someone's ethnicity – that is control, that is power,' he explained. 'Because, rather than 'political opposition,' it was 'Paddy's stupidity' that was then used to explain the hostility to British soldiers on Irish streets.'

Elsie also remembered something that had happened during the pit strike, which Sean had told her about. One of the NUM leaders had arranged a trip to Westminster and Strasbourg to lobby MPs and MEPs. He'd wanted to take a striking miner with him and Sean had been selected.

'I was amazed, both places were buzzing with people that I took to be members of the parliaments,' Sean had said. 'But the NUM bloke put me right in Strasbourg: 'They're only a few MEPs here, most of this crowd are lobbyists for vested interests. They're here 24/7 and take the elected members to lunch or other junkets and whisper in their ear about what else they can get – if they prove useful'.'

'I protested of course, said it was corruption,' Sean divulged, 'but the NUM bloke just said 'Now you know what we're really up against'.'

'It might be how the state works, but it's hardly democratic,' Elsie had thought, when he'd told her.

Thinking back on that and what her Dad had said about the Paddy and Paki jokes, Elsie felt anger welling up.

'Talks behind closed door, wheels within wheels and everyone else locked out,' she thought, 'and then the bastards use their media to get into your head and divide and rule you.'

As Elsie arrived for the morning shift, she bumped into Gwendolyn. Then Kate suddenly appeared from A&E and came running towards them.

'I've just heard, Alec's been fired,' she burst out, trying to get her breath back.

Kate explained that his new boss, in Hospital Services, was saying that Alec had been caught with his head down during the night shift, in one of the rest rooms.

Elsie snorted in disbelief.

'Well he told us 'he knew for certain' that he was on a list of staff they wanted rid of,' she said.

'He did say: 'It's only a matter of time',' Gwendolyn muttered in agreement.

Many of the nurses decided to go to Alec's leaving do at the end of the week – the ones who were not on shift anyway. One of the managers, however, had got wind of this and was trying to discourage staff from attending, pointing out: 'that Alec has been sacked.' But this cut little ice, because everyone believed he had been fired for political reasons.

Even Kate appeared angry and upset. She said she was sure she knew what Alec would have said if he was here.

'I don't give a continental fuck, what them cunts think,' she whispered to much laughter.

They all knew that this was one of his favourite sayings.

'I asked him once,' Kate added, 'what's a continental fuck then – when it's at home? But he went a bit red and struggled to give me an answer. Must have been the only time the bugger was tongue-tied.'

On Friday, after their shift, Elsie, Kate and Gwendolyn made their way to the Robin Hood pub to say their goodbyes to Alec. As part of the old staff, he'd been transferred over after the contract started, with his pay and conditions relatively intact.

Over a few drinks Alec explained how, before he was sacked, he'd been investigating his fresh employers – and finding out about the situation of the many new workers.

'A lot are double jobbing, mostly the foreign ones,' he told the nurses. 'Its not that they're greedy,' he added, 'it's just they get shit pay and many want to send a bit home, so they need another job as well.'

He also discovered that Hospital Services was part of a huge conglomerate, called Sodallco, which operated all over the world. This giant corporation specialised in securing and running outsourcing contracts, from which it made vast profits. The global free market system was forcing country after country to privatise all their services; only to find Sodallco and others waiting, like vultures, to gorge on the process.

'They're ace at winning contracts, but shit at running them,' Alec said despairingly.

In Britain, as Prison Services, Sodallco ran several prisons, a tagging facility and some Immigration Detention Centres. As Transport Services they'd a hand in running airports, trains and buses as well as providing both clamping and parking-meter services. As Sports Services they ran sports centres and provided schools with physical training facilities.

'And that's just a few of the things they do,' Alec said, 'they're annual turnover is larger that a lot of countries.'

Now, as Hospital Services, they were sniffing around the NHS, and were already running Care Homes as well as various other services, including the ones just privatised at Mugsfield General.

'Remember the end of the Falklands War?' Alec asked. 'We were all dead chuffed and we were all out cheering on Maggie and the troops. Thinking back on it all, what we didn't know then was that, behind our backs, a revolution was taking place. As we were out waving our little Union Jacks, Maggie's friends were organising to outsource our services, prune our wages, pillage our pensions and overthrow our welfare state.'

'What an old cynic you are,' Kate said, 'we were only supporting our boys.'

Alec sighed, as if it was painful to run those times through his mind, and downed another pint.

'There was this old Prussian general, Karl von Claustwitch, or something like that,' he muttered, 'and he said that war was the continuation of politics by other means. By politics he meant the ruling policy, but what if you turned that around, does that mean that sometimes the policy the bastards impose on us is the continuation of a war by other means?'

217

Alec saw the bemused look on some faces.

'I mean our politics is all bent nowadays,' he added quickly, 'the political parties are all tweedledum and tweedledee, they're all stitched-up before we get anywhere near them. It's class warfare and it's the toffs at the top who are running all of it – and winning hands down.'

LOG 17: THE ENEMY WITHIN – 1984

During my time in the Falklands, I'd needed to get a regular haircut once more. As a result, on my return from the south Atlantic, my head again had a topping of ginger fuzz. So, when I got back to Belfast, I was greeted with the usual squaddie type of congratulations and piss-takes.

'The sheep must have been in moral danger, while Ginge the minge was on the mountains,' claimed that bastard Shagnasty, who was supposed to be a mate.

'Yea, but I bet he needed to elbow the bennys aside first,' Stone Eyes laughingly agreed.

The Major looked delighted, but his take on our victory was somewhat different.

'Well done,' he muttered, as he clapped me on my back, 'the Lady's gained the nation's support, now she can move forward with her programme – double quick.'

In Ulster, things appeared to have been ticking over in my absence. But, as I took over my stable of touts again, I realised from my sources that some changes were happening. The new younger mob, who'd consolidated themselves at the head of the micks' organisation, were adopting the 'Armalite and ballot-box' strategy.

This meant they were getting more involved in politics, although the bombings and shootings still went on. So, for us, it was much the same as in the past. But, once again, the Major seemed to be preoccupied by events on the mainland, where the Lady had used her popularity from the Falklands war to win another election.

'A landslide,' he said delightedly, 'now she can go full steam ahead.'

I remembered those documents of his that I'd seen.

'Yes, it's going exactly as you wanted,' I thought.

The Major, though, calculated that the Lady still faced some formidable obstacles. The foremost of which was opposition to her policies from the: 'fuck'n commies and union trouble makers,' as Stone Eyes called them.

'There's going to be a reckoning and it's coming soon,' the Major revealed.

What I didn't know was that some of the aggro would happen in Bloodworth, my home village. I knew the miners had faced down Conservative governments in the past and that had riled the Major and his chums big time. And now the Lady, as the hero of the Falkland's War, was setting up another confrontation with them.

'And this time we'll win,' I heard the Major predicting.

The day after the strike started Stone Eyes and Babs appeared with a photo of Arthur Scargill, which they'd cut out of one of the tabloids – and they pasted it onto our office dartboard. But I didn't see why events in Blighty should affect me, so I just got on with the job in Belfast. By now, I was well ensconced once again – running informers and obtaining information.

The aggro with the miners was a few months old, before the Major summoned me.

'I've got a special job for you,' he said.

He explained that from my records he'd seen that I came from a mining area, and he wanted to send me home for a bit, to provide info for the police and the security services.

'Officially, you'll be on leave,' he said, 'but unofficially, you'll actually be there to provide our people with data about the strikers.'

Of course, over the previous decades, I'd been home quite a few times. I especially remembered the funerals of Mam and then Dad, who'd left me the cottage, which I then had all to myself.

Now I was to be on leave there again, but this time still on duty. And that gave me a funny feeling; not that I was much bothered about informing on my home lot – well, not to start with anyroads. It would, though, be a reversal of roles for me.

'Now, I'll be the informer,' I thought, 'with some other fucker handling me?'

And I wasn't sure I liked that idea. Perhaps, at the back of my mind, this was because I was aware of what could happen to touts. Nevertheless, I knew that I'd upset the Major once in the past and I'd no intention of doing so again. So, at the start of May, I found myself back at home again.

'Welcome to Belfast-Bloodworth,' I thought, as I walked through the cottage door. Because, this time, it was my village that was being split asunder by internal and outside forces.

Nearly all the miners in Yorkshire were on strike, but in Nottinghamshire only a few were out. That made Bloodworth a main battleground of the scrap, because we were just a short distance from the border. And pickets from Yorkshire kept coming across, trying to close our mines.

I moved around and started to get myself known in the area again and some recognised me from my boyhood days. Mainly, though, I traded on my Dad's name, as he'd been a miner here all his life. After a bit, I started to have a drink in the local pubs and even in the Miners Welfare.

Soon I was on friendly terms with a few locals and I'd been home less than two weeks, when I got wind of some interesting information. A large group of Yorkshire pickets had just arrived in the village and were being put up by the locals who supported the strike. I quickly phoned my plod controller and informed him of the arrival of the protesters – and I promised to try and find out more about it.

The fucker didn't give me any time to do so, though, because the very next day a huge force of police invaded Bloodworth and carried out door-to-door searches for the pickets. I walked through the village to take a look and a feeling of dread came over me. The plods had gone in hard, just as I'd seen the green teams and the RUC do in Belfast.

They were breaking down doors and rushing into houses, and clashes were occurring between them and some locals in the streets. Some of the plods even turned on me as I walked by.

'Commie bastard,' they called me, and told me to: 'Fuck off back to Moscow, where you belong.'

There were scores of police vans and hundreds of police in full riot gear.

'This is fookin' crazy,' I thought, 'what do the cunts think they're doing?'

I became so angry, that I started to have some outlandish visions.

'I'd like to see a mick with an Armalite pinging a few of these plod fuckers,' I even thought.

And to cap it all, it was me who'd started it all. Some of my informers in Belfast must have felt like that, when our lot had gone in with all guns blazing, based on something they'd told me. Don't get me wrong, I knew the plods had got a few of the Yorkshire pickets and I didn't feel much sympathy for the cunts on strike.

'But, why alienate everyone?' I agonised.

When I rationalised it, though, I could see that we'd done much the same in Ulster. And I remembered Stone Eyes telling me about the saying he'd gotten from the Yanks at Fort Benning: 'If you have 'em by the balls, their hearts and minds will follow.'

'Maybe Stone Eyes is right,' I thought. 'Perhaps, that's the only way to get results in situations like this?'

I was also reminded of Ulster in another way, because there was already civil strife going on in the village between the miners on strike and those who worked on. Many of the latter belonged to a new union that someone conveniently started. Somehow, it all reminded me of the sort of work our psy-ops crowd did back in Belfast – stirring aggro between the prods and micks.

After that first bit of informing, I was in my-lot's good books again. I reckoned, though, I'd be more careful after that – about the information I was passing on. I then made a list of militants, as requested, but a lot of those names were just blokes who shot their mouths off in pubs; I also passed on the number plates of a few cars, which I thought might be being used by pickets. All in, it was just enough to show I was still playing their game, but not enough to do too much damage.

Having some spare time, I took the chance to sort out a few problems at the cottage. Like mending the dodgy plumbing and fitting security locks and bolts to the doors and windows. I also collected up the copies I'd taken of the Major's documents and placed them together in a box file, which I labelled 'Psy-ops Crap' and hid in the cupboard under the stairs.

During this time the Lady's lot were gradually winding up the aggro; there was little doubt in her mind as to who the main enemy was. Her home secretary started to use the criminal law, rather than civil legislation, against the strikers

– just as we'd done in Ulster against the micks. Then the Lady herself weighed in.

'We had to fight an enemy without in the Falklands. We always have to be aware of the enemy within, which is more dangerous,' she told a bunch of Tory MPs.

The next time I put fifty pence in a striker's collecting bucket, I was handed a sticker to wear.

'I am the Enemy Within,' it proclaimed.

'Maggie's declared class warfare,' some of the lads in the Miners Welfare claimed.

They also told me about the pitched battle at the Orgreave coke depot, between thousands of pickets and police. From what they said, it was clear to me that the police had been ready, well equipped – but also very organised and proactive. Mounted police had smashed through the picket lines and then units of plods in riot gear had streamed into the gaps and set about the strikers.

It was like one of our lots big operations in Ulster and I knew the scope of the planning and backup required, in order to have everything in place to secure a victory.

'As a contest,' I thought, 'it's so one sided it's like Man U facing Mugsfield Town FC in the FA Cup.'

I knew then, there was only going to be one winner – and that was Maggie's boys.

Towards the end of that summer, the Major ordered me back to Ulster. Seemingly, in his circles, the word was that the miners wouldn't last out much longer.

'Well done,' he said, as I reported back for duty, 'but there's work for you here, and I've been told the strike will be over soon anyway.'

I could now see things from the perspective of the informer, seeing as how I'd just been one. That whole thing back home had left a bad taste in my mouth, but now, in Belfast, I'd be facing a real enemy again.

'I'll just put the episode down to experience,' I thought, 'and make good use of it – in my continuing work in Ulster.'

HELL-LAND

I will not cease from Mental Fight,
Nor shall my Sword sleep in my hand:
Till we have built Jerusalem,
In Englands green and pleasant land.
William Blake (1757 – 1827)

It was now nearly a decade since the miners' strike and many in Bloodworth were remembering, in solidarity and sorrow, the ten-year-old events. The village had become a cockpit of the struggle, suffering division and social strife in the process. Some local families still remained bitterly divided between the strikers and those who had worked – wounds that might never heal.

Just under half of Bloodworth's miners had backed the strike; but many believed their pit would never be closed, so just over half had worked on. Five years after the strike they'd all been forced out of work anyway, as the triumphant Tory government ordered the closure of the pit.

'After the Tories shut the pit, they'd a thousand tons of rubble poured down the mineshafts,' Jed said, as he sat with Amy, Eddie and Doris in the Miners Welfare.

'Dad said the bastards were making sure it would never be used again,' Amy said.

'Aye, the village's like a ghost town now,' Doris said, 'its hearts been torn out with the pit machinery.'

'An' its soul been lost, along with the shift sirens,' Jed added.

Amy's Dad had been a miner and stayed on strike to the bitter end, but then died six years later.

'Dad passed away far too young,' Amy had whispered to Eddie at her father's funeral. 'The doctor said it were the Black Lung that killed him, but his heart were already destroyed after our loss at the strike – and then when the mine was closed, that were it.'

Amy's Dad had been a Methodist, and she followed in his footsteps. At home, from time to time, she'd take herself off to a quiet corner and read a little section of her bible. The Book of Revelation, the final book of the New Testament, especially interested her; John of Patmos's prophetic and apocalyptic descriptions enthralled her, and in his visions, she could sometimes recognise facets of that fateful decade they'd all just lived through.

When she thought of the coming of Thatcher, Amy remembered: the closing down of industry and manufacturing; the freeing of the banks and financial markets; the Irish hunger strikes and deaths; the sinking of the Belgrano and the Falklands War; the miners' strike and the shutting of the pits; the dismantling of the welfare state and the enhancing of the rich and the impoverishment of the poor.

With these images in her mind, Amy rewrote one of John's visions. After jotting it down by hand, she showed it to Eddie.

'Lets use this for our next board,' he said enthusiastically, 'and then we can add a list of all the pits that Thatcher's lot have closed.'

After compiling the list, they counted up the one hundred and twenty-one pits that had been closed across the country in the last ten years. And Amy and Eddie looked at each other in despair, shaking their heads.

'They've shut the pits and put the miners on the dole – and

then import coal from Poland, or wherever,' Eddie said, 'it don't make no sense.'

'Bet it does to Maggie and her mates,' Amy said, as she typed out their latest missive:

And I looked, and I beheld an Iron Lady
and the name that sat with her was Death,
and Hell followed after her.
And Power was taken by them over many
parts of the earth, to destroy and to kill,
with weapons, hunger and with monetary control,
and their rule threatens all who live on earth.

Pits closed from 1984 to 1994:
Bearpark, Cronton, Aberpergwn, Abertillery, Ackton Hall,
Bedwas, Bold, Brenkley, Brookhouse, Cortonwood, Emley
Moor, Fryston, Garw, Haig, Herrington, Margam, Moor Green,
Penrhiwceiber, Pye Hill, Sacriston, St Johns, Savile, Treforgan,
Wolstanton, Yorkshire Main, Babbington, Bates, Bersham,
Birch Coppice, Cadeby, Comrie, Cwn, Eppleton, Glasshoughton,
Horden, Kinsley, Ledston Luck, Nantgarw/ Winsor, Polkemmet,
Tilmanstone, Whitwell, Whitwick/ South Leicester, Newstead,
Nostell, Polmaise 3/4, Snowdown, Wheldale, Whittal,
Woolley, Silverwood, Abernant, Arkwright, Ashington, Cadley
Hill, Lady Winsor/ Abercynon, Linby, Mansfield, Manvers
complex, Seafield/ Frances, South Kirkby/ Riddings, Baddesley,
Barnburgh, Barony, Betteshanger, Bilston Glen, Blidworth,
Cynheidre, Holditch, Marine/ Six Bells, Merthyr Vale, Oakdale,
Renishaw Park, Royston, Sutton, Trelewis, Warsop, Agecroft,
Ellistown, Lea Hall, Littleton, Shireoaks/ Steetley, Treeton,
Donnisthorpe/ Rawdon, Florence, Bagworth, Barnsley Main,
Creswell, Dawdon, Dearne Valley, Deep Navigation, Denby

Grange, Dinnington, Gedling, Murton, Penallta, Sutton Manor, Thurcroft, Allerton Bywater, Bickershaw Complex, Cotgrave, Sherwood, Shirebrook, Silverhill, Bentley, Bolsover, Easington, Frickley/S Elmsall, Grimethrope, Houghton/ Darfield, Parkside, Rufford, Sharlston, Taff Merthyr, Vane Tempest/ Seaham, Westoe, Goldthorpe/ Hickelton, Kiveton Park, Markham, Manton, Ollerton, Wearmouth.
May they REST in PEACE
and all who worked in, or lived among, them
find SALVATION.

When Amy recalled her life as a schoolgirl, she knew she'd been a good but not outstanding pupil. She'd passed most of her exams, but mainly with lower grades. This was enough, however, to allow her to get a job as a junior in the bank.

She had friends of her own sex, but gradually became attached to Eddie and Ginge – and, often as not, would tag-along with them. After becoming engaged and then married to Eddie, her life seemed to be following a predictable path – till the banks, pits and all society changed. For the first time she started to question the life she led and what the forces in society were – that were pulling and pushing her in directions that were not of her own choosing.

'Thatcher must have been having a laugh,' Eddie muttered one day, 'with what she said when she was elected: 'Where there is discord, may we bring harmony.' All she ever brought us was bitterness and conflict.'

'She stole those words from St. Francis of Assisi,' Amy said. 'I prefer William Blake and his talk of arrows of desire and a bow of burning gold. All this neoliberal crowd think about is the banks and money, they've got no heart, or soul.'

Amy resolved to try to unravel the way the powers-that-be

had conspired to change her life – and that of many others. She was happy that Eddie and her were now on the same path, after he'd put the demons from his times in the army behind him. Together, though, they questioned if they were clever enough to fully understand and reveal it all.

'I can't get my head around all this,' Eddie had cried out in despair, when they'd started on their boards. 'First the strike and then these changes that threaten everyone.'

'When I were young, Mam and Dad and me would do these jigsaws, especially on winter nights,' Amy replied. 'Dad would bring back ones that got more and more difficult and he'd always hide the picture of how it should look. So, it were really difficult to get bits you could recognise to appear. Then, gradually, identifiable sections would emerge, bit-by-bit. And, by and by, those isolated segments, that seemed to make no sense on their own, would come together to reveal the whole shebang.'

Eddie looked mystified and screwed up his face.

'What are you getting at?' he asked. 'Are you saying each of our boards could be like one of those jigsaw bits?'

'Aye, each on their own, probably won't mean owt much,' Amy replied, 'but if we get the lot completed and someone takes the trouble to read 'em – it might all come together in their noggins and start to expose the bigger picture.'

They'd both been Christians, then Eddie, after his army experiences, had rejected God and become an atheist. Amy retained her Methodist faith, but like Eddie had grown to hate those who used religion to dominate and control – or as a stick to beat others. About God's existence, they agreed to differ, but sometimes they would tease each other.

'Heathen pagan,' she would mutter, grinning.

'Jesus freak,' he would reply, with a laugh.

In her own mind Amy resolved, that together, they would uncover the forces that had shaped and controlled ordinary people's lives during the strike and afterwards.

'Well, if not all,' she thought, 'at least fragments of it anyway.'

Amy knew very well that some people regarded her and Eddie as cranks. Others considered them to be dangerous subversives. But she had also seen the miners in her own village change from being praised as 'the salt of the earth,' into being vilified as 'the enemy within.'

The subsequent civil war, created between striking and working miners, had destroyed the fabric of village society – ripping apart its cohesion and good will. Then the police, stripped of their usual veneer of affability, had come to visit in great numbers and unleashed their real power and authority. It was then she realised that the powers-that-be and their state forces would stop at nothing to achieve their aims.

Sometimes Amy felt consumed by pessimism.

'Our layout boards verses a Murdoch dominated mass media – hardly a fair contest?' she'd said to Eddie, during one of her glum episodes.

'Well, we've racked our brains for other ideas, but this and going on protests is the only thing we can think of,' Eddie replied. 'After all, most people can't even see what's happening – never mind do summat about it.'

Amy realised she had to stay optimistic. She remembered the Chariot of fire that had taken Elijah directly to heaven and how Blake had used its symbolism to portray divine energy.

'We need a bit of that,' she thought, and she took to saying, to anyone who would listen: 'This neoliberal agenda can be stopped if enough people take a stand against it. We are many, the rich at the top are just a few!'

She knew that the fight back, so far, did not add up to much, but with understanding, she hoped, might come real opposition to what was being thrust upon them.

And in her heart Amy was determined to keep the faith.

'Jerusalem can still be built,' she believed, 'in England's green and pleasant land.'

LOG 18: THE LADY ON TOP – 1984-5

For a time things had been fairly quiet in Belfast, when everything went apeshit again. Although the micks were involved once more, this time it happened on the mainland. The fuckers bombed the Grand Hotel in Brighton, during the Conservative Party conference – and just missed killing the Lady.

The Major was raging mad at us for not detecting that such an operation was on the mick's agenda.

'None of you had a bloody sniff,' he declared furiously. 'If you can't detect something like that, what frigging use are you?'

The truth was, that after the PIRA reorganised, our flow of information had dried significantly. I decided, though, to keep that view to myself. Well, until the Major had calmed down, anyroads.

Other things in Blighty were not going to his satisfaction either. The miners were proving stubborn; many were still out on strike and would not give in. Consequently, around mid-December, the Major ordered me to once more go home for a spell – to provide information about the strikers.

Although I still had reservations, I complied, chiefly because I'd seen the Major's wraths and I didn't want to be the one to upset him again. So, just before Xmas, I found myself back in Bloodworth and making my way to the Miners Welfare. I quickly learned that the miners' attitudes had deepened and got angrier.

'There'll be no presents and little food this Christmas,' one told me. Things were getting desperate and some miners, I felt, were now casting suspicious glances in my direction.

'They've gone through a transformation,' I wrote in my notes, 'they started off thinking this strike would be a bit of a fight and then an easy win – similar to the ones in the past. Now they know they're locked into a life or death struggle and they think all the pits will be closed if they don't succeed.'

A lot of people in the community were against the strike, while others passionately supported it. I bumped into Amy and Eddie and found out they were in the latter camp. I think they were amazed that I appeared happy to chat to them. Not surprising, I suppose, because in the past I wouldn't have done so.

This time, though, I needed information and names for my lists.

'Happy Crimble,' I muttered, as John Lennon used to say.

I also indulged in a bit of small talk; it was the time of good cheer after all. I expect they'd have been upset, though, if they'd known I'd added their names to my list – and then passed it on to the plods.

This time around the Major had arranged for me to make my reports in person to my controller, who was situated about a twenty-minute drive from Bloodworth in an old disused industrial park. I made my first visit to him early in the new-year. After gaining entry from the two police sentries at the gates, I came across rows and rows of parked police vans.

'Plods playing at soldiers?' The query flashed across my brain and made me uneasy.

I knew the police had come from all over Blighty and, in some of the old factory buildings, I saw hundreds and hundreds of them. Some were sleeping and others making ready for duty.

'My god! It's getting more and more like us in Belfast,' I thought, feeling a little gobsmacked. They'd no guns, of course, well not in sight anyway, but otherwise it was the same.

Then, when I went to report, I clocked some of the police brass, who were running the show – and I suddenly realised that I'd seen some of them before. They'd been across to Ulster to learn from us, the experts, how to carry out internal-security operations. And now they were putting it into practice here.

'Dixon of Dock Green, eat your heart out,' I recall thinking, 'this is no coppers' civil order job – what we have here is a military operation.'

I could see that this had all been planned. That they were doing what we did in Ulster: the police acting as a militia; surveillance and phone tapping; agents, informers and provocateurs; the media smearing the miners; the justice system criminalising them; the plods smashing them with batons and breaking down their doors; covert actions and all the other spanners in our psy-ops toolbox.

'The micks in Ulster are different,' I reasoned, 'they've gone from peace to war with us – and we've both raised the stakes along the way.'

I reckoned the micks knew what they were fighting, but that these poor fuckers didn't.

'It's them verses the state – and this time the state is organised.'

I saw then, there could only be one winner and that, sooner or later, the miners would get shafted.

I was back in Belfast midway through February and the strike was over a few weeks later.

'Cushty,' Stone Eyes said, clapping me on the back, 'you've kicked those commie cunts into touch.'

The Major smiled.

235

'Well done,' he said, 'now the Lady has a clear run.'

Soon, I was back running my touts and the Major was happy again, so everything was well in the world.

Before I returned to Ulster, I'd managed to meet Geordie again. He was very interested, when I told him about what was happening at Bloodworth, and my part in it. His ex-Int contact, SS, had told him the strikers would cop it big time.

Geordie, like me, was not really on one side, or the other.

'I can't say I feel sorry for them union cunts,' he said, 'but it's different from when we'd done it ter the wogs an' micks.'

'Yes,' I agreed, 'now, it feels a bit like crapping on your own flesh and blood.'

In Bloodworth, you see, they were my own people and I was part of the system that'd smashed them.

'Perhaps some of my touts in Belfast feel like that?' I later thought. 'Perhaps, in the past, I've taken a very simple view of conflicts and informers? Perhaps in Belfast and Bloodworth both situations are far deeper and more complicated than I've dared to think? Perhaps, perhaps ... ?'

Anyroads, I kept my head down and just soldiered on. I concentrated on my job, and tried to put any negative thoughts to the back of my mind. Deep down, I still wanted to know about things, though, so I listened in to the office chitchat and lip-read passing conversations.

One day I heard 'Stakeknife' – or something like that – muttered. And I twigged that our lot, or the security services, had been successful in recruiting, or placing, an agent, or agents, fairly high up in the micks' organisation. Even, I suspected, in their nutting-squad.

'No doubt the Major's played a role in this,' I thought, and guessed that he'd now be racking-up the mischief.

I also kept in mind his briefcase and that, given an

opportunity, I'd have another look for secret contents. So, the next time I was working late and had sorted out my sleeping bag in the office, I took my chance. Once again in the small hours, when nothing was moving, I did the business with the safe.

There was another paper, this time on two pages and it looked like it'd been passed around a lot. Like before, it was compactly typewritten, but it was crumpled and faded – and had been folded two times.

'This's been kept in someone's inside pocket for a while,' I thought.

At the end of the document it stated that this version was for a select few in the Armed Forces – and that it had been produced in 1967.

'This predates all the other papers,' I thought, 'perhaps it's the prime mover? The one I've been looking for – the initiator?'

Stamped across the top in heavy red, was 'Most Secret – Read Then Destroy,' and underneath was the headline: 'Towards a New Britain.' The document started with the sixties and Britain being in crisis:

'Currently, with the Cold War, the great ideological battle is between capitalism and communism. The fact is, however, that the major communist countries are vulnerable, being weighed down by their bureaucracies – and are threatening to disintegrate, unless they change their economic systems.

What we have to realise is that we are also in a weak position, because of the Keynesian distortions of capitalism, which have made Britain soft – with its welfare state, mixed economy, nationalisation and strong trade unions. The real fight for us now is therefore inside the countries of the West – with this enemy within. We need to destroy this wet Tory and red Labour-movement block – and replace it with pure free-market capitalism.

Internationally, we are rapidly becoming a third rate power and here again we urgently need a strategy and an economic ideology that will thrust us back into the front line. The Empire is mostly gone and our present leaders have lost their way, so, we now need to work in conjunction with firstly the US and secondly with the rest of the civilised world to maintain Western domination. Working together, we can then bring a new order to the world.

Our internal enemies can now be linked to our external ones, so, the Cold War will remain in place. It has proved a useful tool for concealing our motives and actions and should be retained, until something else comes along to do the same in the future.

In the US, forces, equivalent to us, are intent on attacking and changing similar aberrations there, both at home and abroad. The remnants of Roosevelt's New Deal have been knocked on the head and Indonesia is already being sorted out and some countries in South America will probably be next.

In Britain, the main forces that will be our nation's economic salvation reside in London, especially in the City. Our key task will be to make sure that future governments give priority to their interests, by boosting the banks and finance capital and ensuring that the market becomes dominant as well as free from rules and restrictions.

Our first step, on the road to achieve this, will be to radically re-shape our political system: Wet Tories must be removed and a proper leadership restored; Red and militant Labour must be destroyed and a new Labour formed; Do-gooder Liberals must be curbed and a realistic leadership fashioned.

Only when this has been achieved, can we hope to have leaders who will curb Trade Union power, stop the drift and have a Britain that is Great once again.

Our second step will be to prepare Britain for, and ensure the people accept, the new economic order. Perhaps, a period of military rule will be needed to force this through. Our preference, however, would be to bring it about using the existing political system, with a crisis, or a series of emergencies, acting as false flags – deflecting attention and endorsing patriotic feelings.

First we need a zealous leader and a strong state to force this through and then remove the shackles from finance capital and big business. After that, all the politicians, especially the new party leaderships, can be pressurised to follow on and keep coming up with the goods.

Our third step will be to help organise, and ensure our position in, a new order for the world. Realistically, the lead in this will be taken by the US. They will act as Sheriff, but we must ensure that the UK becomes the first Deputy.

A great new age of empire, albeit in a new form, could then come about and the British Army will, once again, play a dominant role in the world. This is all part of a shared global vision. Remember, we are not alone, all around the world people of foresight, like us, are arranging to do similar things in their own countries.

Organisationally, we are connected to esteemed trans-national organisations like the Bilderberg Group, and act as the UK arm of these movements. We come from different fields and areas of influence, but we want the same outcome. Up to now, we have been separated and therefore weak; now our strength will come from united actions. And our inner core will guide and co-ordinate this work.'

At first, after reading the document, I'd felt enthused, because I thought this might be the first document.

'Have I struck gold?' I wondered. 'Is this the Daddy?'

But then, thinking about the contents, I'd felt frustrated and full of contradictory thoughts.

'I'm with the good guys, aren't I?' I questioned, because, up to then, I'd been fairly sure. But, after doing my informer job in Bloodworth and now reading some of the stuff in this text, I was beginning to have doubts.

Anyroads, back on the mainland, with the miners beaten, the Lady had gone ahead and implemented her new economic policies full-whack – the kind of stuff the Major and his mates were after. Those sort of things, though, were all well above my head.

'The Tories are all good business people,' I thought, and assured myself that they would make a success out of it all.

I did realise, though, that this new policy could only have been implemented, because of the conflicts with the enemies without, the micks and Argies – and after the enemy within, the miners, were defeated.

GANGRENE-LAND

Whose game was empires
and whose stakes were thrones,
Whose table earth,
whose dice were human bones.
George Gordon, Lord Byron, (1788–1824)
The Age of Bronze

As she moved around his room, Elsie glanced at Ginge, but his brain appeared to be elsewhere. As the nurse moved from task to task, she was passing over in her mind all she knew about the wounded soldier.

'With other patients, you sometimes know all about them in five minutes,' she thought, 'although, that can include a few things I'd rather not have found out.'

With Ginge, however, when they'd spoken together he'd been guarded, with very little slipping out. All the usual things were known, his name, where he lived, the fact he was a soldier – but nothing in any detail.

'Will the facade ever crack? Will his mask slip?' she questioned. 'Will the real person underneath ever emerge?'

Ginge had been in hospital for over three months now. His head, however, was filled with images of Ulster. That morning, he'd woken with a memory of a day in Palace Barracks, when Stone Eyes had come into the office and started talking about his trip to Chile.

'They had a gathering of their military and some of the

Yanks were invited to it,' he'd said, 'and they let me tag along too.'

'It was evident that Stone Eyes was finding our attention pleasing,' Ginge had thought. 'So the Major, me and all the rest, must have looked suitably impressed.'

Stone Eyes had then grinned – and paused for a second or two for effect.

'It was addressed by the General,' he'd continued, 'who told us why Allende needed overthrowing. 'If you have gangrene in an arm, you have to cut it off, right?' Pinochet shouted out, and we all jumped up, cheering and clapping him.'

Ginge considered it was difficult knowing what to make of far off conflicts like Chile – and his mind kept drifted back to Belfast.

'I can't wait to get back again,' he thought. 'I know the ceasefire is a bit on-off, but I want to get my own back on the micks who did this to me.'

The series of operations on Ginge's back had been completed, and now and again he believed that he could feel a tiny flicker of something at the end of his toes.

'Is it my imagination?' he reflected, 'or am I on the way back?'

His thoughts wavered between despair and hope. With the latter, sometimes his judgement was overly optimistic.

'I'll be walking again soon,' was the thought that popped every so often into his brain.

Ginge also knew he was now getting near the end of his logs and he was glad, because he knew he could be moved on soon to an army hospital, to complete his rehabilitation.

'The logs will probably be impossible then, at least without me being detected,' he thought. 'Anyroads, all I want to do is simply to tell my story and let others judge it – so I'll have the logs completed soon.'

Ginge's mind, however, was already moving on to other things.

'I haven't had any real contact with women for a long time,' he reasoned, 'well, not counting a few whores, of course.'

The thing about Amy, with her preferring Eddie to him, had put him off in the past. He'd gotten it into his mind that women were devious cows – and paying an agreed sum for a servicing now and again had been about as much as he wanted to do with them. Remembering his meetings with Amy and Eddie during the strike, however, he realised that he no longer felt any animosity towards either of them.

Also, after lying in bed for so long in the hospital and being looked after by Elsie, Kate and Gwendolyn, he somehow felt cleansed of all his old resentful feelings.

'Towards women, anyroads,' he thought.

The cheerful goodwill of the nurses and the way they'd looked after him had broken through his armour. Even engendered in him thoughts of looking at the fairer sex anew – and, perhaps, the possibility of a new start with them.

In Bloodworth, it was the warmest day of the year so far and Amy had noticed Eddie was out in the back garden deep in conversation with someone from over the wall. Going out to join him she was annoyed to see the woman of the house next door lying out on a lounger, wearing a skimpy bikini.

'Come on, we've the last panel to finish,' Amy muttered, before dragging Eddie inside.

The strike memorial events, including the exhibition, would happen soon and the couple had been trying to dredge up ideas for their last layout board. That evening, when they attended a meeting of the Commemoration Committee, Amy and Eddie had high hopes that Doris, Jed and the others would be able to help.

'For the last panel, we need to push the right buttons, to tie it all in,' Eddie told them.

'Perhaps, some of the men would be more interested if we pasted up a page three girl instead,' Amy muttered, giving Eddie a pointed look.

Eddie grinned and ignored her words.

'Any issue might help,' he said, glancing around.

'How did Maggie get the support to turn her boot boys on us,' an ex-miner from the back of the room piped up, 'and let them kick our heads in?'

'Ah, how the forces of the state act?' Eddie said, 'that might be something that can be part of the last board.'

Jed then posed them a question.

'How come then, if we have a dispute, us in the union are always accused: 'Of pursuing our own selfish interests to the detriment of everyone else?' Even if the facts clearly show that we seldom do that?'

'Maybe, it's because we're on one side,' Doris chipped in, 'and the supremoes, most politicians and the media chiefs are on the other.'

'And they always help each other out,' Amy said.

'Aye, the bosses do that,' Jed cut in, 'but they're seldom accused of pursuing their own interests – selfish or otherwise – even when the facts show that they are doing that all the time.'

'Before the strike we never really thought about things like that,' Doris said, 'how the bigwigs dictate and the state acts. But after the strike was on, it started to become visible.'

'Yes, the blinkers came off and we all began to see,' Jed agreed.

'We've already done a bit of work on this,' Amy said, 'but it's difficult to understand. How does what the rich want come to be transferred into 'national interests' – and receives the support of everyone – even when it's clear that the only ones who'll benefit are the bosses?'

'I found this book,' Eddie said, pulling a battered paperback from his pocket, 'that quotes something that Marx said about the relationship between England and Ireland: 'A nation that oppresses another forges its own chains'.'

'We've been trying to understand what he meant by that,' Amy said.

'Perhaps he meant that the problem is in our heads – one of ideology,' Doris said.

Eddie glanced at the quote again and rubbed his chin.

'If the big bosses have an opponent, say one who lives a long way away, and the establishment, the prime minister and the media all shout and scream about how this is now a terrible enemy and that they must be destroyed. And if it then becomes in the 'national interest' to do so – and we rush out and support them in this task. Are we then accepting that those at the top can define our enemies for us? If so, when they say there is a new deadly enemy that we must fight, but this time it's an internal enemy – say 'the enemy within' – then are we not already halfway towards accepting them as a foe. And, perhaps, smoothing the progress for the use of the state forces against them?'

'Just like a lot in this country did with Northern Ireland and the Falklands,' Amy said, 'and then joined in with the government, when they turned on the miners.'

'But remember the money men are the organ grinders, the politicians are just the monkeys,' Doris chimed in.

Some in the room looked a bit bemused, trying to take it all in.

'You might have something there,' one muttered. 'Perhaps you're right, but I'll reserve judgement 'till I read you panel.'

Back home, Eddie and Amy set to work, but it took a week before they produced the first draft of their deliberations.

'We've only got a short time left,' Amy said anxiously.

'Aye, we'll need to get it done soon,' Eddie replied, 'but it is the last one.'

They knew that this text would need to catch the essence of what they thought had been happening. The writing, however, required a lot more work before they'd felt that it was pointing in the right direction – and Amy could type out the final version:

In the 1970s, Pinochet in Chile and Thatcher in Britain were chosen to front administrations in their respective countries, which would initiate and then establish the economic programmes of a globalised free-market system. Thatcher and Pinochet had few original ideas, but both had very strong convictions. Guided by hidden hands, they became the ideal leaders of the strong states that were needed to deliver the new agenda.

Although a different route was taken in each, a bit of shock and awe was needed in both Chile and the UK to establish the new dogma.

In Chile, it was provided by a military coup and its repressive aftermath. General Schneider, the army chief of staff, was murdered because he opposed Allende's overthrow. Then, with General Pinochet now in charge, the US organised a military coup d'état, to overthrow Allende, the elected leader. This was followed by years of repressive military rule that murdered any opposition and compelled the rest of the people onto the new economic path.

In Britain, the process was mainly non-violent and much more gradual. It started with a political coup that steadily, over a number of years, rid the Tories of Heath and Labour of Wilson – and then swept the Iron Lady into power. This was following by years of strong government, which included suppressing the miners, the selling off of public owned utilities, running down manufacturing, prompting finance capital and breaking up society and substituting individualism.

The shock and awe was provided by the conflicts in Northern Ireland and the Falklands, which aided and obscured the process of this neo-liberal agenda. Northern Ireland became a testing-ground for – and reservoir of – repressive apparatus, techniques, legislation and ideology, while the Falklands War provided the patriotic impetus that allowed Thatcher to take on and defeat the miners – 'the enemy within' – and start implementing the new monetarist policies.

Amy and Eddie added the images and cuttings from the last days of the strike and pasted them in around their final bit of text.

'Let's hope the boards can help towards a fight-back,' Amy said.

'If we've got this near the mark, perhaps it'll help explain how all this came about,' Eddie said excitedly.

'Well, it's not directly about the strike, but it might explain a lot of the things lurking in the background,' Amy agreed.

They were now happy they'd completed their ten layout boards and hoped their efforts would be understood and appreciated. They could now relax, at least for a day or two, they felt, before having to install their display at the Miner's Welfare – and later at a couple of other places that had agreed to have it.

LOG 19: CHINESE WHISPERS 1986-90

In Belfast the war still went on; the micks would hit us and we'd hit them. To me it looked like stalemate – something that could go on forever. So I must admit to having mixed feelings, when Shagnasty told me he'd heard on the radio that the Lady had met the Irish PM – FitzGerald, or something, his name was – and signed some sort of agreement about Ulster with him.

I wasn't sure what to make of the news.

'Is it just another bit of fuckwit pissing in the wind?' I asked Shagnasty.

'Fuck knows,' he muttered, shrugging his shoulders, 'but it might signal an end to the conflict. That'd be something – wouldn't it?'

'Yea,' I agreed, 'but no doubt we'll be the last to find out. We're just like mushrooms, they keep us in the dark and every so often they'll throw a bucket-load of shit all over us.'

I was intrigued to find out what the Major would make of it all. I knew from his secret documents that he'd sought conflict in Ulster, so surely he'd want the aggro to continue. I was fairly surprised then, when he appeared to be in high spirits and rather blasé about the news.

'Don't worry chaps, we won't be out of our jobs just yet,' he said, 'well, not for a while, anyway.'

'Did that mean he'd known all about this and was happy with it?' I wondered.

Well I couldn't ask him, could I? But I did happen to bump into Stone Eyes at our Q car garage a few days later – and I decided to broach the subject with him. I asked if he knew what this agreement was all about? And if the Lady and the Major were okay with it?

'I don't think she's too keen on it herself,' Stone Eyes answered, 'but the people who are running her are.'

'And the Major?' I pressed again.

Stone Eyes gave me a hard stare.

'I don't know for sure,' he said, 'but as the boss is in with them that runs her, I expect he's okay about it too.'

I took Stone Eyes look to be a warning, so I quickly changed the subject.

'Had a chance to use the Hush Puppy again lately?' I asked.

'Now and again, here and there,' he said with a grin, 'but you know the score – no names no pack drill.'

On my next leave, I again made arrangements to meet Geordie and we met in the same pub as before. After a bit of chitchat, I mentioned my query about the Major and the conversation with Stone Eyes.

'Has it occurred ter you that their Ulster project might be over?' Geordie asked.

I looked at him in amazement.

'But the war is still on. Full on!' I retorted.

But he just nodded.

'Yes, it's all like fucking Chinese whispers,' Geordie said. 'For you, or me, the conflict is all about the micks, but are there people, say the Major an' his mates, who think it's all about Blighty? An', if they do, might they not want an end ter the aggro in Ulster – if they think that their project on the mainland is complete?'

All sorts of things were now tearing about in my mind: our

war in Belfast; the Major's documents; the Lady coming to power; the Falkland's War; the Miner's strike. To me, they'd all been jumbled up. But did they all link together? And if so how? Geordie seemed sure that the first answer was yes, and he thought other links could be uncovered through probing the Major and his mates.

'If you really want ter find out,' he told me, 'you'll have ter keep digging away.'

The mine in Bloodworth was closed for good, during that visit home. Joining all the others, up and down the country, that had gone since the strike.

'The tory bastards kicked our nuts in,' one of the ex-miners in a pub said, 'and now they've ripped out our heart.'

He had a point; even I could see the place was now decaying, going down.

During the strike, I'd found out that I quite liked socialising with the punters in the village. Of course I'd had an ulterior motive then, but I continued to do it because I found I enjoyed it. I even mingled with Amy and Eddie again, from time to time, even though there was this chasm between us; not the thing about Amy and me anymore, but rather my secret, which I could not tell them about – me the spy, who'd informed on them and helped bring down the 'enemy within.'

During the following years, I saw that the Major was increasingly happy with the progress that the Lady was making back on the mainland. The obstructions had been overcome and she'd started on all the things he'd wanted. Selling off council houses, then a load of public companies connected to gas, water, power and this and that. She'd freed the banks and let them soar and London was fast becoming a world finance centre.

There were loads of other things too. There was a boom on.

I could see the Major's point of view.

'What's not to like,' I thought, 'didn't these things need to happen?'

I had to admit to being confused, but I was trying to rationalise ascendant London and crumbling Bloodworth – and my part in it all.

I remembered the old Major and Geordie talking about places like Malaya and Kenya. Then, the Empire had been crumbling, but they'd helped to manage that process.

'To ensure it aal worked out in our favour,' Geordie had said once, 'we took out the bad guys an' our lot were able ter hold on ter most of the goodies. The game changed, but we made sure it was still our fucking ball.'

'Haven't the Major and his mates now done just the same?' I wondered. 'But this time, on the mainland itself.'

And they'd done it to some of our own. I tried to put a positive spin on it, but I still felt there was a fookin' monkey on my back that was to do with me. Hadn't I been a part of it this time?

Geordie was right; it hadn't felt wrong when it was done to the wogs or the micks.

'But to our own people – was that right?' I questioned.

It certainly felt distasteful, just like you'd been enjoying a good scoff and some bastard had said it was rat meat. Perhaps it was bound to leave a bad taste in your mouth?

I couldn't dwell on it, though, because there was still a war on in Ulster and the micks were far from finished. They'd been winning elections and still killing a lot of our crowd. So we set a trap for them at Loughgall and the SAS wiped out a whole pack of them. The Lady had three more of the cunts killed in Gibraltar.

We also had a bit of a cock-up in Belfast – well, a bit of a blip really. It mainly concerned a surveillance task and one of Stone Eyes' blokes, who'd been ordered to carry out. We called him Nobby, he had this swagger about him and you could see he fancied himself, regularly toning up his pecks and abs at the gym.

The job was in a right dodgy area and it was thought that he'd probably require an oppo. Accordingly, to help deflect attention from Nobby, he was partnered with Debs, one of our new lumpy jumpers. Now, she was a bit of alright – and her jumper was more lumpy than most.

Out on the job, all had been going well, until a couple of locals had flashed Nobby and Debs curious glances. So, pretending to be a courting couple, they put on a show of wooing – touching and kissing. That'd worked out fine as far as the attention towards them was concerned, but it'd all got out of hand between them – because tongues were used, passions flared and they'd got horny.

Overcome by desire, they decamped from the job and, jumping in their motor, they made their way to a cheap Bed and Breakfast where they knew they could rent a room for a quick shag. Afterwards, with their urges satisfied, they paid up and left. They were still in Indian country, though, and discovered that their Q car had been broken into and the boot forced open.

A Hockey and a Browning pistol had been stolen, along with a couple of our special maps and other papers. Horrified by their own stupidity, but now fearful for their safety, Nobby and Debs hightailed it back to barracks. They then shamefacedly confessed to the Major, about giving in to their lusts.

He was furious, first at them and then at the micks who'd robbed them. But Shagnasty and me were having a drink a bit later and we were laughing our cocks off about it all.

'Debs must be like that Mrs Slocombe, from off the telly,' he said, 'because her pussy is always a bit damp too.'

'Yea, and for all Nobby's working out,' I replied, 'after his gristle started to throb, he's shown that all he's got between his ears is his prick and two bollocks.'

Stone Eyes wasn't laughing though. He swore he'd have revenge, especially after we learned that the mick culprits were attempting to sell the stolen goods in west Belfast. But, as he said, at least that meant that this gang of micks were hoods and not the PIRA.

Stone Eyes and his top woman Babs then set out to track the fuckers down. They latched on to the culprits fairly quickly and put them under surveillance. After a time, an informer brought news that this gang were now planning to rob a bookies shop on the Falls Road.

Stone Eyes, who'd taken the whole affair as a personal affront, set about planning our payback. On the day, the robbery was allowed to take place. But afterwards, as the hoods sought to escape, Stone Eyes and his lot, who were lying in wait outside, shot them down.

'Mess with us – and you're dead, you cunts!' Stone Eyes yelled.

Babs, especially, was in his good books, because she'd walked up to a wounded robber and fired a further burst into him from her Walther P5 pistol, to finish him off.

Back in the barracks Stone Eyes grabbed Babs's hand and kissed it. 'Lubbly jubbly,' he said, 'you're a better man than I am, Babsa Din.'

The two culprits, Nobby and Debs, were used in a reduced role for a while and then returned to their previous units by the Major. He seemed to take it all philosophically, though, after his initial rage.

'It's the cock-up scenario, this time literally,' he said with a smug grin. 'When it comes to human beings, things will always go wrong from time to time.'

I think he was glad that Stone Eyes and Babs had saved our face, by extracting revenge. We were all well pleased too, because honour was satisfied. And after all, in the middle of a war, nobody's going to get too exercised about a few hoods getting whacked – are they?

Generally, as to how the conflict was going, we were still far from winning; on the other hand neither were the PIRA. At the same time, under the table, we knew there'd been contact going on between the fuckwits and the micks – carried on through the security services and intermediaries.

That left a bad taste in my mouth.

'Talks, notes and secret meetings – how civilised,' I muttered to myself.

Geordie had felt the same about his old wars; I remembered he'd been angry about Kenya.

'That wog cunt Kenyatta,' he'd said to me one day, 'we jailed him for seven years for being a terrorist leader an' then the fuckwits let him out. Before you know it, the country is independent – an' he's become the new president.'

I suppose there will always be differences between the fuckwits sitting safely in Westminster and the blokes, like us, they've sent into the front line. To us, Kenyatta and the micks will always be terrorists. But the fuckwits can scream terrorist one minute and proclaim statesmen the next.

'You bastards,' I thought, 'I'd really like to march you all off to a tattoo shop and have: 'I am a fuckwit cunt,' needled across your goolies.'

DEATH-LAND

It does not take a sharp eye to see the sun and the moon,
nor does it take sharp ears to hear the thunderclap.
Wisdom is not obvious.
You must see the subtle and notice the hidden
to be victorious.

Sun Tzu
The Art of War

There was a consensus among the nurses that Ginge appeared to be returning to fine fettle. They knew it would still be a long road, however, so they tried to keep up the spirits of the wounded soldier.

'You'll shortly be back to your old self,' Elsie said to him.

'That'll be good – but actually, none of us have seen your old self, yet,' Gwendolyn muttered, with a smile.

'Well I think we'll have trouble with this one,' Kate chipped in. 'He'll be chasing us around the room soon.'

Gwendolyn and Kate then had to rush off to A&E, leaving Elsie to finish sorting out Ginge. While feeling better, and relishing the nurses' attention, the bomb victim was still worrying about his logs.

'Is it a betrayal of my oppos?' he agonised.

Deep down, however, he was glad he'd been determined to carry on and complete them.

'I've nearly finished the tapes,' he'd whispered to Elsie a few days ago. And today, after they were on their own, he beckoned

Elsie over and whispered that he'd finished them.

'Can you take the recorder?' he requested, 'my last tape's still inside – and dump them in your hiding place. I'll come and collect them when I'm able.'

Elsie asked him to keep the machine hidden under his pillow till the late afternoon – and said she'd then come and collect it, just before going off shift.

Ginge smiled. 'Sounds like a good idea – and the bonus is that I'll get to see you again later.'

Elsie finished her fussing over him by tucking in the sheet and blankets at the bottom of his bed – and blew him a kiss from the doorway, as she made her way out.

Elsie was pleased, firstly by the progress of her patient and then by the fact that he'd completed the task of recording his tapes. His series of operations were thought to have been a success, and there were hopes that feelings might soon begin to return to his toes and feet – and after, his legs. Full recovery was still a long way off, however, and there was a rumour that Ginge might be moved to a military hospital soon.

Later on that morning Elsie was told that a woman needed to speak to her urgently and was waiting for her at the hospital entrance. When she'd speedily made her way down, Elsie was surprised to see Amy waiting for her, with a troubled look on her face.

'Eddie were feeling a bit down this morning and he decided to go for a long walk into the woods beyond the Druid Stone,' Amy said, a little breathlessly. 'Passing Ginge's cottage, he noticed it were cordoned off by police and saw 'military types,' as he called them, carrying boxes and a computer to a white van.'

Elsie immediately thought about Ginge's recordings.

'I wonder what they were looking for?' She questioned.

'Yes,' Amy replied in a whisper, 'and I wonder if they found it? The bastards must have been clearing him out.'

Elsie thanked Amy for letting her know, although they both agreed that there was nothing they could do about it.

'I don't think I should tell Ginge, in case it upsets him,' Elsie added.

'I agree,' Amy muttered, as they said their goodbyes.

As normal it was hectic on A&E for the nurses, and it was gone two before Elsie could settle down in the canteen with her food. She'd just finished eating, when Kate rushed in.

'Something bad is wrong with Ginge,' she blurted out.

Elsie jumped up and sped after Kate down the corridor to Ginge's room. A defibrillator lay on the side of the bed and Gwendolyn and a couple of doctors were in attendance. They were shaking their heads as Kate and Elsie entered.

'I'm sorry, he's already gone,' muttered one of the doctors.

'His ticker's given up,' added Gwendolyn soulfully, clasping Kate and Elsie to her.

The nurses felt heart-broken; they had tended Ginge with love and compassion. Perhaps, because he was a bomb victim, their feeling for him had exceeded the way they felt about most other patients.

The hospital as usual was very busy, so Gwendolyn and the doctors had to hurry back to A&E arrivals. Before returning to his other duties, the senior doctor asked Kate and Elsie to tidy up the deceased, and clear his room of medical equipment. It was then that Elsie suddenly remembered the tape machine and she insisted on tending to the body and straightening the bed, while Kate went to fetch a porter – as they'd needed a trolley to remove all the now unwanted hospital gear.

As soon as Kate went out the door, Elsie pushed her hand under Ginge's pillow and found the recorder. She removed the tape machine and hid it among a bundle of towels, sheets and other laundry items that were due to be taken away.

'I'll sneak it out, before throwing the washing down the shute,' she thought.

Elsie was starting to clear up the room, when the door suddenly burst open and two men strode in. Although they wore civvies, she noted their military demeanour and then recognised one of them as the Major. His sidekick was powerfully built, with long blond hair, cold dead eyes and a mean look.

'Right, we're now taking over, this is now designated a military area,' the Major snapped.

'All personal effects must be left with the body,' he ordered, before adding that after the hospital stuff had been removed, the room would be sealed and guarded by the MoD police.

'What's this load of crap,' the man with the Major muttered suspiciously, while glaring at Elsie and patting the heap of laundry.

'Just stuff for washing, I'll deal with it,' Elsie said, quickly brushing past the man and moving the bundle of items into the corner.

The two men stood silently watching and Elsie could feel herself breaking into a sweat. She knew how close the mean looking man had come to discovering the recorder and tape. But she hid her feelings by bustling about, seemingly intent on complying with the Major's orders.

When Kate returned with a Porter and his trolley, the army men glanced at each other and then left the room without so much as a bye-your-leave. The two nurses quickly finished their task and loaded the hospital bits and pieces onto the trolley. Hesitating at the door, Kate and Elsie glanced at Ginge for a last time, before leaving his body to the police guards.

At the far end of the corridor, Elsie removed the laundry bundle.

'I'll get rid of these,' she said.

Before throwing the washing down the chute, Elsie furtively retrieved the tape machine and hid it in her locker. Later, at home, she removed the last tape from the recorder and noticing it was not numbered, Elsie followed Ginge's pattern and wrote 'LOG 21' across it, followed by 'Mugsfield General – Oct. 1994'. She then lodged it, with the recorder, among the rest of the tapes.

The next day, the nurses heard that the Major had declared that Mugsfield General had failed Ginge and the hospital staff were denied any further access to his body – which was to be removed to a military medical facility.

'The army will carry out his post-mortem,' he'd added.

It was three weeks, therefore, before the funeral could take place. Many of the medical workers, including Elsie, Kate and Gwendolyn, wanted to attend, but the hospital, as usual, was busy and could not spare the staff. In the end, only a token doctor was allowed to go.

That evening Elsie, Kate and Gwendolyn visited the churchyard in Bloodworth to lay little bunches of flowers on Ginge's grave. As they stood there in silence, Alec suddenly strode up behind them. He hugged them all in turn and gave them a little peck on the cheek. Afterwards, they adjourned to the pub to reminisce about the dead bomb victim and meet Eddie and Amy, who had attended the funeral.

The military, they reported, had done Ginge proud. Smartly uniformed soldiers had carried his coffin, which was draped with a pristine Union Jack. And at the grave the soldiers fired a full military salute over his coffin, before his body was laid to rest.

'In the church, this officer gave Ginge loads of praise,' Amy said.

'A eulogy, they called it,' Eddie interrupted.

'Praised Ginge to the high heavens, anyroads,' Amy continued, 'said he were a great soldier and that a terrorist action had cost the army the loss of a brave and dedicated soldier.'

'I saw him before – the officer,' Eddie said softly, 'he's a major now, he were a captain then. He was in Aden, he's the one who was in charge of the prisoners there.'

It was only later, when Elsie was chatting to Amy and Eddie that little doubts about what had happened began to surface.

'How come the police and military were at Ginge's place, on the morning of the day he died?' Eddie and Amy asked.

'And how come the Major and his mate were on the scene at the hospital, so soon after Ginge passed away?' Elsie muttered in reply.

They concluded, however, that both were coincidences.

'What other explanation could there be?' they all asked themselves.

And none of them could come up with any logical answers.

LOG 20: HOUSKEEPING – 1993

I was working in the office on my own one day, when I glanced up and by chance spotted the combination lock on the safe.

'Are they still the same?' I thought, 'or has the groupings been altered?'

After checking the office and the corridor to make sure no one was around, I quickly moved to the safe and clicked the dials. Nothing, the safe would not open and a feeling of dread came over me.

'Why have the numbers been changed?' I questioned, because the events that led up to that discovery make me shudder – even now.

It all occurred back towards the start of the year, when I'd been in the office working late again. It wasn't long after the micks had exploded a huge vehicle bomb in London, which had caused a vast amount of damage in the City. According to the Major, though, the attempts by the moneymen to make London a world-banking centre were hurt even worse.

I was on leave when it happened, but was quickly recalled. When I got back, we, of course, were getting our bollocks chewed off again about why we'd not detected anything. So, we put ourselves about a lot, trying to get a sniff about how it'd happened – and finding out if the micks had any more jobs in their pipe-line.

Late one evening, as I parked my Q car back in our garage, after a meeting with one of my touts, I bumped into Stone Eyes and Babs, who were just setting out on a job. She grinned, as he patted the area of his jacket covering the Hush Puppy pistol.

'A bit of payback,' he said, 'we're gonna pop another fuck'n mick.'

I waved them goodbye and made my way to my desk to compile my report. But it took a little longer than I thought – and I was shagged-out from being up all hours and burning the candle at both ends. So, I then got my old dossbag out and settled down in the office for the night.

I woke, bursting for a slash, when everything was dark. Coming back from the bog, I glanced at my watch and saw it had just gone 3 a.m. My head seemed to be stuffed full of thoughts and I had difficulty getting back to sleep again.

I was heading for the land of nod, though, when suddenly the Major's briefcase came to mind.

'Will there be any new secret papers?' I thought.

I was yawning my head off, but the thought persisted, so I jumped up and went to the safe.

It opened straight away and I got out the Major's briefcase and went to the secret pocket. Sure enough there was a new paper, this time just a single sheet and I made a copy, which I popped under my pillow. And quickly replaced the paper in the hidden pocket and the briefcase in the safe.

That's when I sensed it; I just knew that someone was watching me and I nearly kicked myself.

'You stupid fucker,' I thought, 'you've forgot to lock the office door.'

I knew not to let it show, though, and just casually closed the safe. Then, as I'd turned around, I saw Stone Eyes standing in the doorway watching me.

'Anything interesting?' he asked, in a seemingly friendly manner.

'Na,' I replied, trying to hide my panic. 'Just checking, to see if I've been put up for a medal.'

His eyes seemed to bore through me.

'Like Seth,' I added, trying to make a joke of it.

Stone Eyes glanced around the room, then again fixed me in his steely glare.

'Yea, well he killed himself to get his gong,' he said, 'you're not gonna do the same, are you?'

Before I could reply he thrust his hand under his jacket and pulled out the Hush Puppy and pointed it at my head.

'Because, if you do, this will make a good job of it!' Stone Eyes spat out in a harsher tone. 'It's already done one tonight.'

I was quite taken aback by his angry change of attitude, so I stayed silent. I stared at the Hush Puppy, though, wondering if it had just been used on one of the micks. He glared at me, but lowered the pistol slowly and then put it away – much to my relief.

'You've been looked at the Major's papers, haven't you?' he accused.

I just stared back, trying not to look guilty.

'Look, that's not the problem,' he continued, 'I've a look from time to time myself. But, I agree with the boss, the problem is you might? Or you might not?'

These were questions I didn't want to answer, so I remained mute.

'You'd better start supporting the winners, not the losers – or you'll become a loser too,' Stone Eyes said, with what I took to be the hint of a threat.

I still kept stumm.

'You care too much about druggie micks,' he then said angrily, in what I took to be a reference to my man SB.

'And look at Seth,' he continued, 'the silly fucker killed

himself because he cared too much about the fuck'n touts he was running.'

Stone Eyes scalded me with a glare and spat out some more words: 'Look, shit happens sometimes in this job, it's a pity Seth didn't wise up, but you need to start living in the real world, or the same's gonna happen to you.'

The things he said about me, I could let them wash over my head, but what he said about Seth made me angry.

'Well, Geordie, Seth and me came here to fight the micks, just as I was in the Falklands to stuff the spics,' I foolishly answered back.

'We weren't interested in all this other crap,' I continued, 'what is that to do with us?'

He fixed his eyes on me again and I could virtually feel them drilling into me.

'Do you think the people who really run Britain give a rat's arse about a load of Irish bogwogs – either micks or prods – or about a load of sheep-shagging bennys in the Falklands?' Stone Eyes asked.

I just shrugged my shoulders and struggled to find the words to reply.

'Well, what the fuck are we doing here?' I eventually asked, 'and why are we still up to our knackers in crap and mayhem?'

'The aggro weren't about Ulster or the Falklands,' he said scathingly, 'but mainly about sorting out Britain. Our lot on the mainland were bloated and weak, after decades of the nanny-state, and needed to be shocked into compliance. Now the City boys are back in charge and that is all that matters. We got the Lady in as PM on the back of Ulster, but before the Falklands her popularity was fucked. Afterwards, with the plebs all out cheering and waving the flag, it shot up and up. It allowed her to take on the fuck'n miners and make the bankers top-dog again.'

I felt I couldn't take all that crap in, because I was still thinking of Ulster.

'And now they're making peace with the mick bastards,' I said accusingly.

'Of course,' he stated, 'the bigwigs don't want the micks bombing the crap out of the City again, so they require our lot to make a deal and push the prods into complying. Look, they really don't care if Ireland is in one or two bits, well not now anyway. But they need the aggro to end – so the finance boys can make a shit-load of money.'

'In that case why didn't we help with that Sunningdale thingy – twenty years ago, rather than join in with the loyalists kicking it into touch?' I enquired.

I felt shocked and must have looked it, because Stone Eyes continued in a lower, friendlier tone.

'Then the top brass needed a crisis or two to get England sorted, and now they need stability to allow the City to get to work. As for us, there will be plenty more wars soon. That's what my mates in the good old USA think, anyway. Our great empire started with Ireland and spread out across the world. Now us, with the Yanks, will be fighting together to have a rerun. And if we can't find enemies, we'll need to construct some – because the bigwigs will still need distractions to keep the common herd's eyes off the real prize.'

After a while, Stone Eyes left. But I knew I'd made a fuck-up, I should have remembered he was out and about that night. He'd left me with two burning questions: How much had the cunt seen? And would he shop me to the Major?

I was also thinking about some of the things he'd said.

'Did any of it make sense?' I wondered, but my mind was all fucked up.

Later, I took the chance to glance at the copy I'd made, which was still hidden under my pillow. It was closely typed on one sheet and this paper was called 'Housekeeping – an update for project members in the Armed Forces.' It was dated 1993 and once again 'Read and Destroy' was stamped across the top in heavy red.

This how I recall it:

'Some of you may have been worried, when the Lady was forced out of office. The fact is, that while we should remember her with affection and gratitude, she was near her sell by date anyway. And our project is going forward full steam without her. Even Labour, while not talking our talk in opposition, will, I have been assured, walk our walk if they ever get back into office again.

Our aim was to change the nation and the world; to have a globalised free market and remove the restrictions placed on it by national governments. And we have now – along with others like the Pinay Circle, Bilderberg and the CFR and TC in the USA (in essence we are the UK arm of these movements) – achieved most of our domestic and some of our global objectives.

This document is called Housekeeping; my dictionary defines the word as 'maintenance of home affairs.' That we would produce a paper now with that name may seem strange to some of you. On the surface you are right, but before we move on to the next phase, we must once again ensure that our own home affairs are fully in order.

Housekeeping, therefore, for us means covering our tracks and obliterating out trail. The public must never know our part in this project. Securing this will ensure and facilitate our nation's participation in the New World Order that is about to be created.

This is what we have to do:

First: Leave no paper trail. No documents, or any papers whatsoever, can be left around about this project. They should already all have been destroyed. If not, DO SO NOW!

Second: Secure our members and eradicate loose talk.

We must be sure that anyone who was part of, or who has helped in, or has any knowledge about, this project – is still secure and will not talk, or divulge any information whatsoever about it. Anyone, suspect in any way, shape or form, must be investigated and either cleared and made secure, or be eliminated.

In Ulster our task will be made easier on both these issues, because a similar secret, but official, exercise is to be carried out on our undercover war in the Province – and all those who took part in it. All links to any illegal activity will be removed, destroyed, and loose mouths closed. Our more selective housekeeping for our project can, and should, fit in with this – and appear to be a part of it.'

At the end of 'or be eliminated,' there was an asterisk, with an explanation below that said:

'Please note – this should be arranged through us, as we have recourse to a non-official – but secretly officially sanctioned – organisation, which can arrange lethal accidents silently, securely and in a way that leaves no trace or possibility of any subsequent investigation.'

As soon as I read the paper, I thrust it away. There were many things in it that I did not want to contemplate. This was worse than I'd thought – much worse! And Stone Eyes had just caught me with my hand in the till, so to speak.

'Arsehole!' 'Stupid cunt!' I started labelling myself with all the names in the book again.

I knew, though, that I had to stop panicking.

'Be careful,' I muttered to myself, 'just let it go, see what happens.'

And to tell the truth, not much happened. Over the next few months I did not get so much as a flicker of animosity from either the Major, or Stone Eyes. In fact, they were friendly – and proved very cooperative job wise.

Any fears I'd had started to dissipate, but were revived that day when I was in the office on my own, and I found out that the combination numbers on the safe had been changed.

'Was that to do with me being caught out by Stone Eyes?' I questioned. Rather than freaking out, though, I again decided to see how things would go. And once again things went well.

Then, towards the end of the year, the Major told me he'd some bad news for me. Seemingly, information had come in that suggested the micks were compiling a list of those in the security services who'd handled informers. And it was thought likely that my name would be on it.

'It'll only be a killing list, so, be careful – and keep your wits about you at all times,' the Major cautioned.

I felt touched by his concern and was glad that I seemed to be getting on like a house-on-fire with him and Stone Eyes. Another year was passing, peace was in the air and things – apart from the threat from the micks – appeared to be looking up.

CHAINS-LAND

A nation that oppresses another
forges its own chains.
Karl Marx (1818-1883)

When Ginge died, as the nurses consoled each other, Gwendolyn had put an arm around Elsie and given her a hug.

'I was so sure that he would recover,' Elsie said, blinking away a tear, 'and now I'd just like to forget about him.'

'We all get like that girl, now and again,' Gwendolyn reassured, 'but they're in here for a reason – some make it, and some don't.'

Elsie had worked in the hospital long enough to know that this was true. Deaths like his could be expected to happen from time to time. She therefore decided to banish Ginge from her mind – and that included the recorder and cassettes, which reminded her of him.

So, after Ginge's death, Elsie took the recording machine with the last cassette, and dumped them with the others at the back of her underwear drawer. Six months later, she packed them all into an old shoebox and placed that in the back of her wardrobe.

'Out of sight, out of mind,' she'd thought.

Her curiosity about the tapes had also died with Ginge. He had always been so anxious that neither she, nor anyone else, should listen to them. So, she felt that she was carrying out his last wishes by still concealing them.

The truth was, however, that she had listened to one of his tapes. It had happened a couple of months before he died, after the recorder had thrown a wobbly and she'd taken it back to the shop. The man there said that sometimes that model did go wrong – and usually it needed a little modification, which he undertook to fix as soon as possible.

'The repair will be free,' he said, 'as the machine is still under guarantee.'

True to his word, after a few days he called to say it was ready for use again – and Elsie collected it after her shift, on the way home. That evening she suddenly thought that it might be a good idea to test the machine, before smuggling it back in to Ginge. The only tapes she had, however, were his. So, she took his then last recording – the one he'd called: 'Log 9: Hush Puppy – autumn 1973,' and tentatively fitted it into the recorder and pressed play.

Elsie was dumbfounded by what she heard. She'd expected a bit of derring-do, but this was about torture and murder in Northern Ireland and other, far off, lands.

'No wonder Ginge is on edge,' she'd thought, 'if all that was going on.'

'But, if he knew, why did he remain a part of it?' she questioned.

'Perhaps all soldiers in conflicts get caught up in the situation,' she reasoned, 'a cog in the machine. Theirs to do, or die, and not to ask the reason why.'

After a while, the memory of Ginge dimmed and Elsie became reconciled to her feelings of loss. Now and again, however, recollections about the wounded soldier would come to her. Like how, once before when she'd been tending him, in a lighter moment and after a bit of teasing, Ginge had admitted that his favourite colour was blue.

From time to time the recall of this would pop-up in Elsie's mind. 'True blue,' she'd wonder, 'will that ever be reconciled with Ireland's green?'

In 2004, to commemorate the pit strike of twenty years ago, Amy and Eddie had produced their ten layout boards again. Elsie still met up with the couple on a regular basis and now, while viewing their exhibition for the second time, she chatted to them.

'See this about Pinochet, Thatcher, Northern Ireland, the Falklands and our pit strike,' Elsie said, pointing to the writing on the last board, 'was that really the way it happened?'

'Well, look at Chile,' Eddie said, 'a group of Milton Friedman's Chicago boys drafted a neoliberal economic programme, which they handed to Pinochet after his victory. It advocated using 'shock treatment' to force free-market policies on a reluctant population.'

'And all that was completed there in a couple of years – by murder and repression,' Amy added. 'But something similar is occuring here, only it's taken three decades, or so, and it happens by political intrigue, spin and distractions.'

'When we were writing that bit,' Eddie said, 'we were not so sure then. But we were just saying how lucky this neoliberal lot seemed to be – everything just seemed to go their way. In the background we had our TV on and it was showing a golf match. The commentator was interviewing a player and showing some of his wonder shots. 'Some say you are a very lucky golfer,' the interviewer said. 'You know, the more I practice the luckier I get,' was the golfer's reply.'

'That's when we looked at the things that were making the market-is-boss agenda a dominant force,' Amy cut in. 'And other things that helped – like Northern Ireland, the Falklands and the pit strike. We couldn't help thinking how lucky they were, but then we questioned if it were luck. 'What if it's all prepared, organised and then achieved?' We thought. 'Just like the golfer with his practice'?'

'It's a bit more obvious now, with the G-20 meetings and Bilderberg and all that,' Eddie added, 'but before, I admit we were flying a kite a bit – with that last board, anyroads. But they're not going to tell us how they did it, are they?'

'We are right, all the other bits fit in with it,' Amy said firmly. 'It's like a jigsaw, it wouldn't work otherwise.'

Elsie had missed the significance of the text on the last board the first time around, because she'd still been in shock over Ginge's death. Now it engrossed her. Especially the implications it had for what had happened to Bloodworth and the whole country.

She remembered bumping into Alec at the end of the nineties, a few years after Labour had returned to power under Tony Blair.

'We spent years and years working, hoping and praying to get rid of the Tories and get our Labour back,' he'd said, 'only to discover, that when we did, someone had stolen our party and put another in its place. These new bastards have been nobbled, they're bloody worse than the Tories.'

'He has a point,' Elsie had thought, as he'd moaned on about the state of politics and the country.

'How do the bastards keep getting away with this neoliberal shit? He'd continued, 'no one in their right mind would vote for it. But all the parties, although they try and hide it, are implementing it. So what choice does any voter really have?'

'Perhaps, that's the way they get away with it,' Elsie now thought, remembering the message on the last layout board. 'We've a state that has moved seamlessly from the Cold War to the War Against Terror. With this continuity of supposed deadly external enemies, our state therefore has to be strong. It can then remove any rules from the banks and the corporations – to make big bucks for the top people. But at the same time repress, subordinate and manipulate the ordinary population, under the cover of these global threats.'

It was now 2008, fourteen years since Ginge had died, and for the last four years Elsie had taken to visiting the grave of the bomb victim on the anniversary of his death. When making this annual pilgrimage, she'd taken a cloth to wipe his headstone and a hand brush to sweep the area clean. Also, as a token of remembrance, a little pot of intense blue forget-me-nots.

'This is the least I can do.' she felt, 'no one else seems to care.'

It had been seeing Eddie and Amy's layout boards again that had caused Elsie to remember Ginge again. And to wonder about his role in the political, social and military events that had dominated her life. Not to mention, creating the problems now affecting the country and most of the world.

Elsie knew the difficulties at the hospital had just rumbled on and on and got worse and worse – and there seemed to be no end. Outside, if anything, things were grimmer, as the place had become more and more of a wasteland. In Mugsfield, many of the old shops had closed, to be replaced with 'Charity' shops, 'Pound' shops, 'Buy Your Gold' shops, 'Pawn' shops and 'Loan' shops.

In Bloodworth, unemployment was sky-high and rising, with drug taking and dealing now prevalent. As economic conscription increasingly took hold, youngsters in army uniforms were leaving in rising numbers. Not for Northern Ireland and the Falklands as before, but now for Iraq and Afghanistan.

Some came back in boxes and were given, just like Ginge, a full military funeral. And, as the Union Jack was laid proudly over their coffins, local dignitaries would say solemnly that 'the heroes have fought for British honour and glory, their sacrifice has been worthwhile – has not been in vain'.

'It's funny them saying that,' Elsie's brother Sean had said after reading the account of one of the latest funerals, 'because I see precious few of the toffs' sons or daughters wearing the military khaki.'

'Agh, the great British Army,' her Dad muttered, 'nowadays, it's just a militia for the good old US of A – and the big corporations.'

'And now, to cap it all,' Elsie thought, 'many of the big banks, who we were told: 'Have been freed to forge a new era of prosperity for the whole world,' are now on the brink of bankruptcy and about to come crashing down. With the politicians, who'd released them from state regulation, using spin and weasel words to hide the banks dodgy dealings from public view.'

'Guess what?' Elsie remembered her Dad saying, when she'd returned home one evening, 'the politicians are now proposing that the failing banks should be propped up with taxpayers' money?'

In the fourteen years after Ginge's death, Elsie couldn't help feeling increasingly cynical. But there are good reasons, she told herself as she sought inner reassurance. A sense of outrage now set in and she sought to clarify her own views.

'While, how the neoliberal agenda has come to dominance is still open to question,' she felt, 'the fact that it has happened is clear.'

What she also knew for sure was what this had led to, because she encountered it daily at work and all around.

'The great and good have turned out to be vampires,' Elsie thought, 'sucking the life-blood out of the country and the ordinary people.'

Feeling her instincts were right, she arranged a meeting with Eddie and Amy. Elsie's inhibitions about Ginge's recordings were now gone – and her curiosity about them had fully returned.

'Perhaps, the tapes might shed some light on the issues outlined on the last layout board,' she thought.

When they met up, with a feeling of relief, Elsie blurted out to them the story of the recorder, cassettes and logs. She then described her part in the action and how she'd rescued the last tape after Ginge's death.

'My god – you've still got them?' Eddie burst out, after she finished.

'Aye,' Elsie replied, 'I've got them at home, in the back of my cupboard.'

'We must hear them,' Amy said excitedly, as if a pot of gold had just been discovered.

So they made plans to listen to the recordings in sequence, on various evenings over the next few weeks.

LOG 21: MUGSFIELD GENERAL – Oct. 1994

I think this will be the end of my story, although I still have a few things left to say. I'll start with this observation, which came to me the other day after Elsie was talking to me about Ulster.

'Who's really running the Troubles over there?' she'd asked.

'The PIRA,' I replied, without hesitation, 'and we and the prods respond to them.'

Later, I questioned if I believed that anymore, because, when I thought about it, I'd remembered the things I'd done, seen and heard. And I had to admit that it was us who were proactive; we'd been the ones in the driving seat. So, if Elsie were to ask me the same question again today, I'd have to say it was ourselves who ran the Troubles – and it was the micks and the prods that were responding to us.

There was one other thing I meant to mention earlier about the Major's papers. It's something I forgot, which was written on the back of the 'Towards a New Britain' text – the initiator one I discovered in 1985. It seemed to be a reaction to what was said in the documents and it's probably not very important.

It was in a scratchy scrawl, which I later recognised as the Major's handwriting – and this is what it said:

'Like with General Pinochet in Chile, a gangrene threatened our great land.

But we became praetorians again to make our stand for England – and now our enemies are falling and we will triumph.'

Once again I'd difficulty understanding this, because it seemed to me that it was another load of bollocks. That's probably why I forgot about it. But now, as I've remembered it again, I just thought perhaps I should mention it.

The ceasefire still seems to be on; it's shaky if you ask me, but perhaps the peace will hold. I felt before, that I couldn't wait to get back to Belfast and sort out the micks who'd fucked me up. But now I'm having second thoughts about that too.

Like Geordie, I'm starting to think that maybe I've had enough – peace or no peace. I've had one extension to my service anyway, but that's nearly up now and I don't feel like signing on again. Maybe I'll just see out my time and go back to my cottage and gaze out on the Druid Stone – and, perhaps, face the friends in Bloodworth I betrayed during the strike ten years ago?

Talking of Geordie, I remember the last conversation I had with him on the phone. I told him about the last document that I'd discovered, and he said that the Major's stuff fitted in with some gen that SS, his ex-Int source, had let slip during some of their drinking sessions. Seemingly, SS had boasted that his lot's friends abroad had been responsible 'for chopping that pinko cunt Palme in Sweden and fucking-up Whitlam in Kangaroo land'.

He'd also whispered to Geordie that there was some shadowy group of ex-military state players who'd do the murky work for the bigwigs in 'good old Blighty.'

'But that's all hush, hush,' SS had said, drawing a finger across his throat.

'Not the Increment, as they're aal serving,' Geordie said he'd suggested to the source, with a wink. 'Must be Group 13 then?'

He described how SS had looked horrified and hurriedly changed the subject.

From his tone I could tell Geordie was pleased with himself, and he told me he'd made it his business to find out about such things. All of this, though, including the names, meant fuck all to me. So, by way of changing the subject, I asked Geordie if he thought the peace process would stay on course.

He replied that he didn't know, himself, but his source had made the following prediction about it: 'Even if it goes up and down a bit, like a whore's nickers, in Ulster it will prevail. Because the top boys need it now – as across the world, they've bigger fish to fry.'

His source had also intimated that anyone in the know, who was not trusted – or the ones with loose mouths – would be shut up.

'So, we have a need ter look terwards our own safety,' Geordie muttered to me, 'in case they get their eyes on us too.'

'I don't think we need worry,' I replied, thinking the silly old fucker was getting a bit paranoid.

'Well, what about the Willy Wonka getting spattered aal over that hill in Jockland,' Geordie retorted. 'My RUC source said that the radio beacon had been moved, an' nearly aal the top brass of our undercover war were taken out in one go.'

I was flabbergasted at what he seemed to be implying, but at the time words failed me.

'Poor Geordie,' came to mind, but I kept that thought to myself.

'We should look out for ourselves and each other,' I said to placate him.

Thankfully, that seemed to work. But his car crash had come just a little bit later. And, after Geordie's funeral, I did wonder if the faces his missus had talked about had been pushing him over the edge?

I now come to what has happened so far this year and why it

has not been a good time for us. It started with that helicopter crash that Geordie mentioned, on the Mull of Kintyre. We lost a colonel, three lieutenant colonels and five majors. Five of MI5s finest also went out of the game, and the RUC lost their special branch chief and eight other heads of special units.

Then word of Geordie's death came in and I felt I just had to go to his funeral. Even if we were in turmoil after the Chinook prang in Jockland. But when I said this, the Major was furious and stated that I had to stay put and he'd arrange for some of our people in Blighty to represent us at the ceremony.

I dug my heels in, though, because I felt I owed so much to Geordie that I just had to go. The scene was set for a right fookin' ding-dong and, in the event, I was bracing myself for some serious aggro. But surprisingly, this seemed to take place between the Major and Stone Eyes, rather than with me.

They were facing each other outside, when I spied them through the office window. From their lips I could see the Major was talking about me – saying a house something, or other – while Stone Eyes appeared to be placating him.

'Don't worry. I'll see it still happens,' he was saying.

They then moved on and it was a bit later when Stone Eyes approached me.

'The boss's still fuck'n mad,' he said, 'he's saying you're bolloxed – and this is a black mark against you. But I've persuaded him to let you go to Geordie's funeral.'

Stone Eyes shrugged off my thanks.

'Look, the boss has a lot of guts,' he said, 'but to him, sympathy is just a word between shit and syphilis.'

I kept stum, but my sardonic consideration was: 'Who'd have thought it?' As I reckoned he was stating the bleedin' obvious by suggesting that there was a certain lack of empathy in the Major's attitude at times.

So, to recap, in 1994 we had a bad start to the year, losing a load of our top brass when the Willy Wonka went down. Geordie died just after that – and I got my own way about going to his funeral. Then, I was blown-up by the bastard micks and ended up in Mugsfield General, all fucked up.

No doubt any perceptive mind will have noticed that this is a very minimal account of what I must have witnessed. Army units have many officers and loads of other ranks within them; but, because I've worked on the 'need to know' principle, I've only mentioned a few – and no real names at all. So, at all times, when revealing these logs I've tried to remember our mantra, 'no names, no pack-drill'.

I think I've remained true to my story, while at the same time keeping faith with my oppos – by protecting them. On that positive note I'll end, as I think that's everything. Now, as I lie here in Mugsfield General, my mind is – and I do hope in the future some others might be too – going over my story and trying to make sense of it.

So, that's all folks – the end.

• • •

I've come back because something strange is happening. This morning, a bit after Elsie finished with me, I had lunch and settled down for a snooze. I've just wakened and found the Major and Stone Eyes staring at me from the open doorway.

The Major had visited me previously a couple of times, but I've not seen Stone Eyes since Belfast. Now, they've just gone off to get some goodies and that's given me a chance to mention it. Luckily, the recorder is still in place under my pillow, waiting to be collected by Elsie later on.

I'll have to stop when they get back, though. Agh! I can hear them coming now. I'll have to switch the tape off and continue after they've gone.

* * *

They've gone now – and I've only got a short time to mention what's happened. They came in full of cheer and loaded with coffee and Mars bars, and closed the door behind them. Soon, we were drinking, chomping away and reminiscing about old times.

'You'd better be well the next time we come, 'cause the boss's gonna be promoted to Lieutenant Colonel,' Stone Eyes said. 'A crown and a star, you'll have to stand to attention then!'

I laughed with them and offered my congratulations.

Then I rapidly felt very tired, and it suddenly occurred to me that this felt just like the time when they killed my man SB.

'Fuck! Have the bastards drugged me again?' I thought.

The Major stared at me keenly.

'I expect you're wondering what's happening?' he asked, before angrily adding, 'you're a bolshie chappie and we've kept you in this hospital to stop you infecting other soldiers with your subversions.'

The Major jerked his thumb towards Stone Eyes.

'He persuaded me to give you another chance, after 13 messed it up the first time. Because of the balance of doubt I did so, but now that has shifted.'

Stone Eyes then jumped up, and I could see his manner had changed as he stood over me.

'Simple Simon met a pie man going to the fair,' he hissed, 'said Simple Simon to the pie man what have you got there?'

'Pies you stupid cunt!' he snarled loudly, before thrusting his face close to mine, 'and that's what you are, a stupid fuck'n cunt! I told you before, to sort yourself out. Now it's too late. We've just found the copies of the boss's papers you stole. 'Psy-ops Crap' – you cunt! Hidden under the stairs? Well now, your going out the fuck'n game!'

He moved to the bottom of my bed and undid the blanket and sheets that Elsie had tucked in before she left. He uncovered my lower limbs and jerked my left foot back. I could feel nothing, but my knee was now raised directly above my foot.

Stone Eyes then took a small container and a bottle from his pocket. I only got a quick dekko, but I'm sure the label said Potassium Chloride. Extracting a syringe from the case he plunged the needle through the bottle cap and sucked up the fluid. Lifting my left foot he peered at it intently for a few seconds – before plunging in the needle and injecting in the liquid.

My mind was full of horror. Suddenly, though, it changed for an instant – because I'd felt the needle entering my foot.

'Hooray, the feeling's come back,' I thought, as my mind went from dismay to joy and then back to fear again.

I suppose I should have offered some resistance with my hands, or shouted out. But I felt totally paralysed by the drug in the coffee and overwhelmed by what was happening and being said.

Stone Eyes scratched at the injection area on my foot and undid a plaster, which he then stuck on.

'Don't worry,' the Major whispered to him, 'I'll see to it that our chaps do the examination, anyway.'

My leg was laid flat and the blanket and sheet were quickly pulled back over my feet and tucked in again. The Major produced a black plastic bag from his briefcase and they tided away all the plastic coffee cups and Mars wrappers. When all traces of their visit had been removed, they made towards the door.

As Stone Eyes opened it, the Major turned to one side and murmured something to him.

'It's just a bit of housekeeping, well done,' I managed to lip-read, before he closed the door behind them.

I need to say this quickly, because I'm struggling to keep awake. I'm sure I'll die soon of a heart attack, because I know what potassium chloride can do. Geordie told me about it; in the past he sometimes used it to kill off troublesome prisoners.

And now, it's being used on me! Argh, my mouth feels dry, but I'm sweating my cods off and I'm being hit with pains across my chest. I feel totally shagged out and the ache is spreading to my neck and jaw.

My god, with what the Major said it's suddenly come to me. It weren't the micks who planted that bomb in my car – that was just a previous attempt by the Major and Stone Eyes and their mates, Group 13, or something. It's not the micks who have me on a killing list, it's them bastards and they've been trying to get rid of me for some time.

And what about Geordie's accident, was he on their list too? If they thought I was a threat, they might have considered him one as well? The dirty cunts, they've become paranoid about their poxy little secrets.

Awk, I feel like spewing and the pains are now coming in waves. It's like my chest is caught in a giant vice that some bastard is tightening. I have to concentrate though, I must get this said.

That thing I mentioned earlier – the Major's handwritten note about a gangrene threatening the land and them becoming praetorians again. Well, I'm beginning to see a lot clearer now and that's exactly what he and his mates have done. But it's them fuckers who are the gangrene – they're the ones destroying the country and all our lives.

They've certainly kicked mine into touch. Fuck! All I ever wanted to do was to tell my story, so people might understand....

Acknowledgements

The author would like to thank Veronica Quilligan, Ben Griffin, Phil Clarke and Roberto Valente for their assistance. And Tony Zurbrugg, Adrian Howe and the rest of the team at The Merlin Press, who were generous with their aid and expertise.

Particularly helpful and unstinting with their time and hospitality were John Lloyd and Peter and Dorothy Berresford Ellis. (Dorothy's passing dismayed all who knew her – she is greatly missed).

I would especially like to thank Elsie McKeegan for her help, encouragement and support.